The Seventh Seed

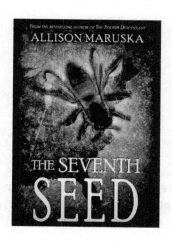

by Allison Maruska

Edited by Dan Alatorre – danalatorre.com

Cover design by Perry Elisabeth Kirkpatrick
http://perryelisabethdesign.blogspot.com

Advanced Praise for The Seventh Seed

This standalone sequel to the bestselling novel The Fourth Descendant is absolutely gripping from the opening words. Fast paced and intense, it is an amazing story ripped from today's headlines by way of the brilliant imagination of Allison Maruska. If you liked The Fourth Descendant, you will love The Seventh Seed.

- Dan Alatorre, author of *An Angel On Her Shoulder*

Beautifully crafted and anxiety producing, The Seventh Seed is an intelligently crafted look at what happens with big brother and big pharma have a love child and use it to rule the world.

- T.A. Henry, author of *Scripting the Truth*

From the first page to the last, The Seventh Seed does not slow down. Set in the near future, the characters never catch a break. Being on the run makes it difficult for them to develop a cure for the virus that is killing many, and just when they're making progress, the tyrannical time turns their cause to ending the controlling government's rule. This story made me worry it wouldn't take much for our current way of life to become similar to the one in this story. I highly recommend.

- Dana Griffin, author of *Blamed*

Action packed and fast paced from the first page, reading The Seventh Seed feels like watching an exciting movie. The story jumps right off the pages. If you like smart, action-packed conspiracy novels, grab a copy of The Seventh Seed!

- Jenifer Ruff, author of *Only Wrong Once*

Just check out the first scene of Allison Maruska's The Seventh Seed, and you'll see how her skill as an author makes her books come alive. You'll be dropped smack dab into the action, as if you were right there with the characters. Keep reading, and you'll notice her carefully crafted storytelling with its satisfying plot twists and perfect pacing. You'll be impressed by her excellent character development and attention to setting detail. Finish the book, and its unobtrusive theme will stay with you.

But hey, you know what? You might not notice any of those things. You may just notice that The Seventh Seed took you on a great ride, and who the heck cares about the internals, it's a fun book.

Recommended!

- Al Macy, Author of *Yesterday's Thief*

DEDICATION

This book is dedicated to the fans of The Fourth Descendant. Your love of that story made this story possible.

Chapter One

Javier grabbed the headrest in front of him as the car peeled around another curve. Hale groaned, cranking the wheel and keeping them from flying over the mountainside. Craning his neck, Javier strained to see the dash between the two men's shoulders. The speedometer was near sixty.

He squeezed the edge of the seat. If these guys planned to get him to Missouri alive, this was no way to do it.

"Shit." Hale steadied the wheel with both hands and pressed himself into the seat as he mashed the brake.

The car didn't slow.

Oh God. Javier held his breath.

In the passenger seat, Sanderson fumbled for the seat belt. "What are you doing? Slow down!"

"I can't!" Hale grabbed the parking brake between the seats.

Jaw clenched, Javier checked the speedometer again—almost seventy-five. *This old car won't do well in a crash.*

The car swerved into the oncoming lane.

A straight stretch of road appeared, and Hale gripped the brake. "Hold on!"

He yanked on the lever.

The car lurched forward. Javier's seat belt smashed into his sternum. A bang and a jolt slammed him into his seat as the car resumed its race down the inclined road.

"Son of a—" Hale downshifted and when that only revved the engine, he squeezed the wheel as the car veered around another turn, heading straight for a van coming the opposite way. "Shit!"

Javier grabbed the headrest again. His heart pounded in his ears.

The van's horn blared and Hale yanked the wheel, sending the car over the edge. Javier's stomach jumped to his throat for the few seconds they were airborne.

It landed with a jarring crash then bounced over rocks and scraped trees, filling the cabin with a horrible cacophony of bangs, scratches, and yells.

Javier's head smashed against the window. He cried out in pain. Black spots flashed in his vision.

Sunlight glinted off the new cracks in the tinted glass.

Javier stared out the windshield. When would they reach the bottom?

The trunk of a massive pine loomed ahead.

"Shit shit shit!" Sanderson thrust his arms in front of his face.

Hale jerked the wheel to the right.

Javier squeezed his eyes closed.

The groan of twisting metal and shattering glass covered the men's screams. Javier's head lurched forward and his seat belt dug into his chest. Then nothing but a hissing sound.

Opening his eyes, Javier ran his fingers over the stabbing pain in his forehead and the sticky trail coating his cheek and neck, ending at the wet patch on his collar.

The tree's thick trunk rested against the dashboard on the driver's side, having shoved the engine into Hale's lap and crushing him into an impossibly small space. Sanderson was gone. Bloody glass shards surrounding the hole in the windshield told how he'd left the vehicle.

Javier shook his head, sending a jolt of pain down the back of his neck and a wave of nausea through his stomach. Fatigue threatened to take him, but he couldn't stay here. Another pair of men in another old sedan could show up at any moment to finish the job these two guys started.

Pulling on the handle did nothing, so he slammed the door with his shoulder, sending a new shock of pain through his head. No good. Leaning across the seat, he kicked the cracked window until most of it broke free and fell to the ground. As he crawled through the opening, a remaining shard sliced his forearm. "Dammit!"

He tumbled over the glass and onto dry pine needles blanketing the ground. The gash on his arm oozed blood. *Good. I'll live.* He trudged a few steps to the front of the car and froze.

Sanderson had saturated the forest floor with blood from a gaping neck wound. His bulging, dead eyes glared, relaying the horror they'd seen.

Javier's stomach lurched. He fell to his knees and threw up.

In the days since the men had taken him from California, Javier had hoped to convince Sanderson to release him. Hale had been a hard ass. But Sanderson seemed conflicted about their task, as any reasonable human would when told to kidnap a young prodigy and drive him across the country. Javier had suspected Hale would kill him before reaching "the facility in Missouri," as they had called it. Maybe this wreck was his attempt gone terribly wrong.

Javier rolled back onto his butt and squeezed his eyes closed while panting the chilled autumn air.

Then, a memory plowed into him: *My case!* He snapped around, sending another jolt of pain down his neck.

Rubbing his temple, he hobbled to the back of the car and pulled against the trunk lid. Locked, of course. He moved to the shattered driver's side window. The key—and the entire steering column, for that matter—were indiscernible. *Crap.* Returning to his broken window, he eased back inside and examined the seat. These old cars sometimes had a way to access the trunk from here.

Gritty bits of glass moved under Javier's fingertips as he examined the space between the seat and the rear window. If there was a release, it would be in this area. Reaching around the back of the headrest, his fingers found a rectangular piece of plastic. He pulled at the edges until it gave way with a snap. The seat pushed against him.

Javier moved to the floor and lowered the seat back, revealing an opening to the dark trunk and more importantly, his stainless-steel case, glinting just enough in the feeble light.

With shaking hands, he wiggled it through the gap and lowered it out the window to the ground. Careful to avoid the glass, he slid outside and reached for the key in his pocket.

He glanced up the mountain—it wouldn't be long before more agents arrived. Better to wait until he was in a safe place to make sure everything had survived the wreck. Suppressing the compulsion to check, he pressed the key deep into his pocket, as if that would keep it from getting lost.

Grabbing the handle, he stumbled away from the car.

Head throbbing, he headed to a river at the bottom of the incline and walked alongside it, hoping it flowed into a town. Maybe he would reach a friendly stranger before he passed out.

****

Liz leaned towards the easel and squinted. With her stained fingertip, she smeared the colors of the acrylic paint, blurring the lines between land and sky.

She stepped back and scrutinized her work. Not a professional artist by any means, she got by well enough to instruct the shelter's residents on Saturday mornings. This painting seemed easy enough for them to handle.

After washing the palette and brushes in the bathroom connected to her office, she clicked on the lamp on top of her bookshelf. The last rays of sunshine settled on the unkempt courtyard of the former high school.

At the wall-sized window, she lifted her glasses to the top of her head, making a mental note to ask for volunteers to clean the property before winter arrived. Tall grass crowded the area in the middle of a circle of benches, a place meant for friends to gather. The shelter's residents rarely used the space, and it seemed to ache with loneliness.

A shadow to the right of the circle caught her attention.

A man, hunched over and carrying a case, trudged through the courtyard. Liz couldn't discern his details in the dim light. He was probably looking for the way in, as so many wanderers did. "Go around the other side," she said to the window. "Through the door marked 'entrance.'"

He took a few more staggering steps and collapsed. When he didn't get up, she bolted into the hall.

Liz burst through the exterior door and raced over the dead grass, reaching him in seconds. His eyes were closed, but he was breathing.

Her heart pounded. She'd trained for first aid emergencies but hadn't had to use her skills. She patted his cheek. "Are you okay?" Stupid question. A gash stretched across half his forehead, paired with another cut on his arm. "Sir?"

Moaning, he opened his eyes halfway. "Water," he said in a raspy whisper.

She added dehydration to her mental list of his ailments. "I have some inside. Can you walk?"

He nodded. He was young and skinny, so Liz guessed she could help him get to his feet. She crouched, pulling his uninjured arm around her shoulder. He dropped the case, and it hit the ground with a heavy thud.

She stepped towards the door.

"No." He twisted around. "I need that."

"Let's get you inside first. I'll come back for it."

"It's important." He pushed away from her then stumbled back and fell.

Scowling, she snatched the case and helped him up again. What would he have that was so important he couldn't leave it for a few minutes to get a much-needed drink? "I've got it, okay? Let's get inside."

He leaned against her as they entered the building, and Liz considered where to take him. The common area might not be smart. In his condition, the tougher guys could see him as easy prey. When she connected with his eyes, a familiar face flashed in her memory—Travis.

No. The common area wouldn't do.

After leading him to her office, she put the case by the wall and sat him in her desk chair. She entered the bathroom and returned holding a plastic cup filled with water, which he grasped with both hands and downed in one long gulp. He exhaled and looked at the cup.

"More?" she asked.

He nodded and held the cup out to her.

She took it to the bathroom and repeated the process.

After swallowing the last drops, he scanned the room. "Where am I?"

"This is a shelter for homeless folks. What happened to you?"

He stared at the cup.

"Where you from?" She leaned against the edge of her desk.

His eyelids drooped.

"Hey." She reached for his chin and lifted his head. "Stay with me, okay?"

"I have a headache."

"I bet." She opened a drawer and grabbed a bottle of ibuprofen. "Here."

He swallowed a couple of pills, but they wouldn't do much. His fatigue, confusion, and cut on his head suggested concussion, and since the crappy hospital would make things worse for him, it wasn't an option. She'd have to ask the night nurse to keep an eye on him.

That would mean leaving him alone, though, which felt wrong. But why? This kid appeared to be Travis's age, and he had dark eyes like her son's, but the similarities ended there. The guy before her looked like a migrant. But he understood English, and migrants usually showed up in better shape and without shiny personal belongings.

"What's your name?" she asked.

"H . . . Hector."

"I'm Liz. I'm a program director here. You want to clean up? Then I'll take you to get something to eat."

He nodded and pushed himself up from the chair. Swaying, he put his hand on the desk.

She stood and grabbed his arm. "Maybe sit down a little longer."

"No. I just need a minute."

He definitely wasn't a migrant. He didn't have even a hint of an accent.

After steadying himself, he walked into the bathroom and leaned his tall, thin frame over the counter. He touched the cut on his forehead as he looked into the mirror. "Do you have a towel?"

"Oh, yeah." She pulled a hand towel from a small drawer under the sink and handed it to him, then retrieved some bandages from the cabinet over the toilet.

He wet the towel and kept his eyes on his reflection as he wiped away the blood.

"How old are you?"

"Nineteen." Wincing, he cleaned the skin near the wound. *Just a little younger.* "You homeless?"

He stopped wiping and looked at her reflection. "You can say that." He rinsed the towel.

"Where'd you come from?"

He tilted his head and wiped his neck. "It's better if you don't know much about me, okay?"

She stared at him. "Sure, *Hector.*"

As he cleaned up, her initial impression about him changed. He was rather well put together for a guy who had collapsed in the courtyard of a homeless shelter. His black hair was cut short, he was clean shaven, and his clothes looked new and unstained, aside from the surface dirt and bloody collar. "Anything in that case I should know about?"

"Nothing dangerous, if that's what you're asking."

She considered pressing the issue, but he'd have to leave it if he wanted to eat. His reaction would tell her everything she needed to know.

When he finished cleaning up and bandaging his wounds, he grabbed his case, and she walked him towards the cafeteria, stopping him at the door. "We'll set you up in a bunk tonight. I can leave that on your bed." She gestured to the case.

He shook his head. "I need to keep it with me."

"You're not allowed to bring it into the cafeteria. It's a safety issue. Residents can't bring personal items in here."

He glanced into the room. Dozens of the shelter's residents proceeded down a food line, filling their plates. He shifted on his feet and swallowed. "Then I won't eat. Can you show me where I'll sleep?"

Liz groaned to herself. Procedure said she should search his case. His possessiveness of it meant it likely held drugs or dangerous materials. But experience told her the residents never clutched such things so tightly, because doing so would guarantee a search. Either there was nothing dangerous in the case, or this kid had no idea what he was doing.

"Wait here." She left him in the hall and entered the cafeteria, prepared a plate of food, and rejoined him. "Let's go back to my office."

****

Javier picked at the gooey, congealed mass on his plate and took occasional small bites. Liz had said it was stroganoff. The noodles must have been boiled into oblivion. He forced it down in the hopes that eating some carbs would help his headache.

Liz leaned on the desk and crossed her arms, seeming to pick him apart with her eyes. Javier guessed she was the same age as his mother, but she looked tougher. She was fit and kept her glasses on her spiky, salt-and-pepper hair. Her button-down shirt tucked into black jeans matched clothes his uncle wore.

Javier took a bite of the stale dinner roll. He wanted to start a conversation but kept quiet, fearing any little thing he said could put him and everyone here in danger.

"So where're you from, anyway?" Liz asked after several silent minutes.

Javier allowed the glop to slide down his throat and sipped his water. "I told you. It's better if you don't know much about me."

"Look, kid. I'm doin' you a huge favor here. You're not like the others we get. I want to know why, and I think you oughta tell me. We toss the guys who are uncooperative."

Javier glanced at the case by his feet. If Liz kicked him out, he'd be wandering around God knows where with this conspicuous, silver thing in hand. Plus, his headache was threatening to rip open his skull. If he had a concussion, he'd be better off among an organized group, like this one. The homeless on the street would be more likely to relieve him of his earthly possessions, including the case.

"I'm from California."

"You're gonna have to do better than that. How'd you end up in Colorado?"

"Some guys drove me here."

"Some guys?"

Javier nodded.

"Like . . . government guys?"

Javier suppressed a smile. Liz seemed wise enough to think around the nightly propaganda. "Sort of. I think."

"Well, if that ain't the most wishy-washy answer I ever heard." She stood. "All right, Hector. Tell you what I'm gonna do. You can stay here. In my office. You're too soft to last long out in the main hall. Most guys are decent, but we get the occasional assholes who stay just enough inside the lines to keep us from booting them. I wasn't planning on staying over tonight, but I will."

"Why? You don't know me."

"Not sure. But it'd help to know what you're carting around there."

"I can't tell you. You'll be in danger if I do." That should keep her from pressing the issue. Plus, it was true.

"In danger? Seems like I really should know now."

"The contents aren't dangerous. What they mean is dangerous. You're better off if you can play dumb about it."

She raised her eyebrows. "Back to the government guys?"
He nodded.

"Fair enough." She walked to a bookshelf and pulled a mat from under it. "I sleep here when I stay over, but you can have it. I'll get blankets from the laundry."

"Where will you sleep?"

"Don't worry about me."

****

Liz sat in her office chair, watching over Hector as he slept. She'd done the same thing with Travis when he was little, and repeating the practice now gave her an odd comfort.

Travis had been an average boy—smart enough to get by, handsome enough to stay attached, naïve enough for others to take advantage of him. Hector was different. He seemed detached somehow, like he knew more about the world than someone his age should. And that case had something to do with it.

He'd placed it next to him, between the mat and the bookcase.

She rocked with her elbows on the arms of the chair, tapping her thumbs together.

Quietly, she pushed the chair from the desk. She walked to the mat, grabbed the case, and lifted it over Hector.

He stirred, and she froze.

He rolled over and mumbled in his sleep.

She released her breath and carried the case to the bathroom, setting it on the counter.

It was heavy and solid, like one a photographer might use to store expensive equipment. Unlike Hector, the condition of the case was perfect. She analyzed the top, looking for the release.

The lock kept her from opening it.

She huffed but didn't give up hope. She'd picked more than her fair share of locked items in her years here, mostly from transients who'd abandoned their belongings. The luggage usually contained nothing more valuable than a pair of dirty socks. She sensed this one was different.

After retrieving a small screwdriver from her desk, she went to work on the lock.

Breaking into someone's property could get her fired, but she'd become less worried about her job over the years. There weren't many others who would spend so much time among the homeless. Her coworkers often thanked her for her extra hours; a few even called her selfless. She didn't tell them her devotion came from the need for an effective mental distraction. If she stayed home, she'd have nothing to do except think about everything she'd lost.

"What are you doing?"

Liz jumped, dropping the screwdriver into the sink. She looked in the mirror. Hector stood in the doorway, squinting in the light and unconcerned that he wore only boxers and a T-shirt.

"I . . . I need to know what's in here."

"So you're helping yourself?"

"If it's something dangerous, I need to know. I have a responsibility. If you won't tell me, then you need to leave."

He glanced towards the office door, then back to her. She expected him to take the case and go, possibly forgetting his pants in the process.

Instead, he went to the mat, retrieved something from his pocket, and returned to the bathroom. "Fine. I'll show you, but you have to keep it quiet. I wasn't kidding about it being a danger."

He laid the case on its side, put a key into the lock, and two metal flaps popped open. Pressing those toward the handle, he lifted the top.

The padded interior held dozens of transparent plastic cubes, each one labeled and containing . . . a bug? "What are these?" She resisted the urge to pick up one of the cubes.

Hector grabbed one and held it in front of her. A small, dead bee was inside.

"Apis mellifera." He rotated the cube in the light. The bee rolled along with it. "It's a honey bee. These all are. I collected them from different regions." He put the cube back in its spot and closed the case. "Are you happy now? I don't think I'll be killing anyone with dead bees."

"What's so dangerous about dead bees?"

"It's complicated."

"Complicated?"

He nodded.

"You're nineteen. How complicated can it be?"

"I study them. It's my job."

"Isn't your job to date girls and get into trouble?"

He laughed and shook his head. "I finished grad school last year. I have a doctorate in entomology."

"At nineteen?" She didn't try to hide her skepticism.

He ran his hand over his hair. "I can tell you I'm twenty-five, if that's easier to believe."

"I'd rather know your real name. And why I found you in the courtyard."

He grabbed the case and carried it back into the office, returning it to its spot next to the bookcase. "Let's say it has to do with those government guys." He settled into the blankets. "And my name is Javier."

Chapter Two

Charlie stopped reading case updates when the alert on his holo-dock pinged. A four-inch-tall image of his teenage nephew appeared on the desktop, though the display cut off the top of his hair, which he'd styled into the poofiest fro Charlie had seen outside of a textbook.

"Hey, Uncle Chuck!" Mattson beamed, apparently dying to see Charlie's reaction.

"Wow." Charlie stepped back, scrutinizing Mattson's appearance. "Did you do something different with your hair?"

"You like it?" He patted the edge of the poof. "It's for 70s day at school."

"I never thought I'd say this, but the braids were better." Charlie recalled that argument—while Mattson resembled him more as he grew up, Charlie always preferred the shorter styles that required little maintenance. That is, until he went bald and was left with a zero-maintenance, shiny brown dome.

"I think I'll keep it." Mattson held up a hand mirror, admiring his work.

A second call came in. Sylvia's name appeared over Mattson's face.

Charlie pressed *hold*, showing his nephew again. "Like your mother would allow that. I gotta go. One of my agents is calling."

"Later, Uncle Chuck."

"Don't call me that."

Charlie switched to Sylvia's call, and she appeared on his desktop. "Can you take me off the dock?"

"Why?"

"You probably don't want anyone who walks by hearing this."

Charlie pulled his phone from the dock and put it to his ear. "Okay. What's up?"

"Mendez is missing."

"What?" Charlie bolted to his feet and paced behind his desk "What do you mean he's missing?"

"Just that. He's somewhere in Colorado. That's all we know."

"What about the agents? Didn't they go after him?"

"They're dead, sir."

Charlie froze. The plan had worked well enough in the past—a little mechanical sabotage, and they didn't have to worry about the nosy scientist any longer. "What happened?"

"Hale hit a tree and the airbags failed. Sanderson flew right out the windshield. He might've lived if he'd worn his seat belt. Why were they driving such an old car, anyway? We have plenty of new squad cars that drive themselves."

Because they couldn't look like Homeland Security agents. Charlie swallowed. Sanderson had been his friend since the academy. Why hadn't the bastard put on his seat belt? Maybe he wasn't used to riding in antiques that didn't automatically secure you, but he had to have remembered using seat belts as a kid.

Charlie rubbed his hand. "Colorado, huh?"

"Yeah. We don't think the kid could've gotten far. There was blood in the back seat . . ."

Thinking the call was dropped, Charlie checked the screen then returned the phone to his ear. "What aren't you telling me?"

"The case is gone. He must have taken it."

Charlie squeezed his phone. "We need to find that kid. Put out a press release. Describe him as armed and dangerous. If that doesn't get us any leads, we'll offer a reward. Someone will squeal."

****

On her way through the common room, a news report caught Liz's attention. Javier's face was on the screen, though the eyebrows were wrong, as if someone had altered the photo to make him look menacing.

"Federal authorities are searching for nineteen-year-old Javier Mendez, who was awaiting trial for killing a five-year-old girl in a hit-and-run last month in Los Angeles," the reporter said.

A photograph of a cute little girl holding a puppy appeared next to Javier's picture, and Liz's stomach knotted. *Did I let a killer in here?*

"When police caught up to him, he was intoxicated, and an unregistered handgun was found in his car. Mendez escaped custody while being transferred between holding facilities yesterday. He has family in southwest Colorado and may head there. He is considered armed and dangerous. If you see Mendez or know where he might be, contact your local authorities."

With the new information nagging her, Liz continued the walk to her office. Javier had spent most of the last three days there, working on the computer and writing in a notebook. He'd said his research was related to the bees, but that was the extent of her knowledge. Whatever it was, it looked complicated. The only reason she allowed him access to her computer was the government seemed to be against what he was doing—meaning it must be something noble.

Javier was young and intelligent, and he seemed compassionate. Not the type to drive drunk and run over a child with his car. She'd trusted him enough to let him use her unrestricted internet access.

The words from the news report echoed in her mind. The ten years since the war had shown her how the media fabricated whatever information would serve the interests of anyone supporting them, but still, doubt invaded.

She hurried down the hall, as if Javier would completely change now that she'd seen the report. Fumbling with her lanyard, she struggled to locate the key to her office. She clicked the lock and threw the door open.

He sat at the computer with his back to her, just as he'd been doing for most of the past three days.

Sighing, she shut the door. "Cops are looking for you."

"Sounds about right."

"They said you hit a girl with your car."

"Was that the best they could do?" He kept his eyes on the screen, which displayed thick blocks of text in a tiny font. "I was hoping they'd call me a terrorist or a drug lord. Something like that."

Staring at him, she eased her way around to the front of the desk. *Could this be part of an act?* "It's not true, right?"

He looked up with raised eyebrows. "Of course not. You know the news is bullshit."

"So why are they after you?"

His focus returned to the screen. "I know why."

"Care to enlighten me?"

"It's better if I don't."

"Sticking with that, huh?" She analyzed his face. If he had any guilt, he hid it well. "Anyway, they know you're in Colorado. The report said you have family here. So folks will be on the lookout."

"Did the photo look like me?"

"An angry you."

He scowled.

She laughed. "Yeah, something like that."

"Think anyone here will connect me to that?"

"Maybe. Better not give them another chance. You either need to stay in the office or leave the shelter for good."

He pursed his lips and glanced back at the screen. "I'd like to stay."

"All right. I'll get to the kitchen before lunch and get some food for you." As she headed out, she peeked at him through the cracked door. He didn't stop reading from the screen and taking notes. She would ask to see his notebook when she got back. If it looked suspicious at all, she would tell him to leave.

The thought made her uneasy. If he was up to something criminal, what did the bees have to do with it?

****

Two days after Liz saw the report, Javier read through his notes one last time. He'd reached the end of what he could do with the computer and needed to get to a lab and a virologist.

He cleared his search history and scratched his jaw. The beard he was allowing to grow would eventually offer a disguise. At the moment, he looked like a bum—ironic, considering where he was. His hygiene had been reduced to sponge baths in the connected bathroom, which didn't leave him feeling much cleaner than when he'd started. He'd give anything to stand under running, hot water and use more soap than he needed. Being a wanted fugitive and fastidious at the same time didn't work.

He walked to the window and separated the blinds. The day was sunny, and it looked warm. A few residents mingled in the courtyard.

Anxiety collected in Javier's stomach. The longer he was stuck in that office, the smaller it felt. He couldn't save anyone while under house arrest.

The doorknob rattled and Liz entered, rushing to the desk chair and typing on the computer. "We have another problem."

Great, what now? Javier stood behind her. A video appeared on the screen.

"Crap, it's making us watch an ad." She clicked a few places on the page. "I can't skip it."

We at LifeFarm know the health of your family is your top priority...

"Can't you just tell me?" Javier grimaced. Nothing was worth watching this garbage.

...new practices in agriculture resulting in a twenty-five percent increase in crop yields in 2040 alone...

"This won't take long to get through. I want you to see for yourself."

...future of mankind.

Liz maximized the window. "Okay, it's starting now."

A blonde, middle-aged woman sat at a news desk, and the photograph of Javier was displayed above her left shoulder. "New developments this morning in the search for fugitive Javier Mendez. Police say he's suspected of operating a drug trafficking operation in Los Angeles and may have moved business to Colorado. This is in addition to the hit-and-run and weapons charges. Police are now offering a fifty-thousand-dollar reward for tips leading to Mendez's arrest." The report went to a full-screen shot of his face, and a phone number covered the bottom fourth of it.

Fifty thousand dollars! Javier dug his nails into his palm. He wouldn't last long with that kind of bounty on his head.

Liz spun her chair around, facing him. "You need to tell me what's going on. My boss asked who I'm hiding in here. I told her you were my son and you've hit a rough patch. Now the cops are offering big money to find you. I don't know what you did to piss them off. But give me a reason to keep lying for you."

Javier swallowed. Liz was right. If he expected her to protect him, she deserved an explanation.

He leaned against the edge of the desk. "Before I tell you, you need to know that what I have to say could put you on their radar as well."

"I figured."

He took a long breath. "I discovered something LifeFarm doesn't want me—or anyone—to know about."

"LifeFarm? I thought you said those guys were government."

"They are. You think LifeFarm and the government aren't connected? They run pretty much everything."

She shrugged. "Okay, sure. I just hadn't thought LifeFarm was connected to your guys."

"I didn't either, until they started driving me away from California."

"So what'd you find?"

Javier glanced at the closed door, then shook his head at his paranoia. No one was listening. "Last year, I was hired by an independent firm to research the incidents of bee deaths around the country. Die-offs have been intermittently occurring for the past forty years, but certain regions have experienced an increase in hive demise."

"Well, that's no big surprise, with all the crap LifeFarm uses on the crops."

"Exactly. That was my prediction too, but I thought, 'Hey, if this company wants to pay me to point out the obvious, let them.' So I got to work collecting samples and running tests. The bees were indeed being killed by the stronger insecticides, but that's not the whole story."

"What's the rest of the story?"

"I found bees and other insects that weren't dying."

Liz scowled. "Why is that important?"

"Because they should have died. Chemical insecticide use on crops is an old practice, but since LifeFarm forced all organic and home farms out of existence, it's exploded. Nature fights back, though, as the bugs showed me. They've adapted to the poison over time. LifeFarm has had to use stronger and stronger pesticides."

"I still don't get why this makes you a threat. Everyone knows our food is sprayed with that stuff."

"Right, but what everyone doesn't know is the adaptations have created new breeds of insects—superbugs. They haven't responded to even the strongest poisons, and LifeFarm can't use a stronger one at this point, not without endangering human health and further damaging the soil and water supplies."

"It's already damaging our health. Why do you think hospitals are such a mess?" Liz crossed her arms.

"Yeah, but that's not the problem. The problem is, not only are these superbugs not dying, they're carrying a virus." Javier stood, his pulse racing. Saying out loud what he'd discovered scared him.

"A virus? What kind of virus?"

"It's like dengue fever, but it's new. The bees are carrying it, but they can't transmit it to humans. The mosquitos are a different story. I haven't figured out how both species became carriers." He paced and talked with his hands. "The best I can figure is there was a common host somewhere."

"The pesticides caused a virus? I haven't heard of anyone getting sick."

"The chemicals didn't cause the virus. The superbugs and the virus appearing at the same time is a coincidence. And of course you haven't heard of anyone getting sick. You think LifeFarm would let that get out? This virus is basically their fault—if the carrier insects could be eradicated, there would be no problem." He sat on the edge of the desk. "There have been outbreaks in several cities and towns in the Midwest, where farming is concentrated. A few dozen people have died, last time I checked. When I presented my findings to my employer, they contacted the CDC. The next day, the suits showed up. They said they wanted to celebrate my achievement."

"How's that?"

"I was to present my findings at an industry luncheon. They said I was the first to discover what was causing the illnesses. The next day, I loaded up my case with the specimens and got into their car." Javier looked at the floor and shook his head, lamenting how easily he'd let flattery get to him.

"So instead of taking you to a banquet, they drove you to Colorado. Why?"

"This wasn't supposed to be the final destination. Somewhere in Utah, the passenger said they had to keep my discovery hidden, and they were taking me to a holding facility in Missouri. After a gas stop around here, the driver lost control of the car and hit a tree. They both died, and I ended up here."

****

Liz tried to piece together everything Javier was telling her. LifeFarm was a dirty company, but she hadn't suspected such close ties to the government, and she certainly hadn't predicted they would hide the existence of a virus that was killing people. Looking back, she should have. All agriculture-related legislation worked in their favor. But could they have the government illegally detain and kill anyone who learned the truth?

She'd figured LifeFarm controlled the hospitals, or they wouldn't be able to influence hospital policy. Most hospitals were privately owned, so LifeFarm used the courts to keep doctors from connecting agricultural practices to health, unless it benefited them. A couple of cases went to the Supreme Court, and the rulings always worked in LifeFarm's favor—or that's what the media reported, at least. It was like they had a cheat code that allowed them to use the government as a tool in controlling everything. It could be money, but was it that simple?

"So LifeFarm wants to keep the virus under wraps, and that means keeping you quiet. Is that about right?" she asked.

"Basically."

"But they can blame the virus on anything."

"Doesn't matter. They can't kill the virus-carrying insects. Releasing information about the superbugs could turn the people against them—it's the same reason they haven't developed a vaccine. They'd have to admit fault to have known about the virus so early."

"So, what's your plan?"

"I need to go somewhere to lay low and find a sympathetic virologist to help me." He gestured to the notebook on the table. "That's part of what I've been researching. I was thinking about a small town in Iowa called Hayes. It's scientifically advanced. There's a pharmaceutical lab, and the population is young. There's a university in a neighboring city. I think I can blend."

Liz leaned towards him. "And how do you plan to get there?"

Javier pursed his lips. "I was hoping you could help me with that."

She sat back. Of course he needed her help. It wasn't like he could walk to Iowa with his shiny briefcase and no other belongings, and with his face plastered all over the news, taking a bus was out of the question.

His story was unbelievable—or it would be to most people. Liz had seen enough of the government's and LifeFarm's dirty underbellies to know what he said was true. "When do you want to leave?"

"Now would be great."

Liz laughed. "Best I can do is tomorrow morning."

****

Charlie stared at the photograph of Mendez with LifeFarm's tip line displayed underneath it. Why hadn't anyone turned the guy in? Fifty thousand dollars was a lot of money.

Maybe Mendez was dead in a ditch somewhere near the crash site. That would make Charlie's job much easier—assuming he still had his job by the end of the week. He'd assured the Captain he'd have Mendez back in custody within three days. That was two days ago.

Charlie took a swig from his water bottle and went back to monitoring the various news reports.

"We found him!" Sylvia's voice came from the doorway. She held a few papers and a big smile.

"Where?"

"Gunnison, Colorado. Been hiding out in a homeless shelter." She approached the desk and held out the papers. "Here. A resident called it in half an hour ago."

Charlie smiled. "Get a team organized. We'll get him after dark."

Chapter Three

The sound of shattering glass yanked Liz from her dream. Lifting herself onto one elbow, she listened through the closed door. A man yelled. A woman screamed. Gunfire.

Her heart rate skyrocketed. She wrestled out of her blanket and stood on the mat she'd placed behind her desk. Javier stood frozen next to the bookcase, his wide eyes asking the same question she had: *what the hell is going on?*

Javier grabbed his pants from the floor, yanked them on, and stuffed the rest of his belongings into the backpack Liz had given him for the trip.

More gunfire, closer this time. Then a woman's yell. "You killed him!"

"Where is this kid?" The demand came from a man with a deep, gritty voice.

Liz swallowed. Who had been gunned down? Fighting the urge to find out, she grabbed her own bag and slung it around her torso. "We can't go out that way."

"No kidding." Javier put on the backpack, threw on his baseball cap, and grabbed his case. At the window he yanked open the blinds, examining the edges of the pane. "Does this open?"

"It will in a second." Liz's eyes darted around the room. What would quickly break glass? She grabbed a souvenir baseball—her son's—from the shelf and hurled it at the window. It cracked the glass and bounced back, landing near her feet.

The doorknob jostled.

No time to try again. She grabbed Javier's arm and pulled him into the bathroom, locking the door behind them.

A loud crash came from the office door.

From the cabinet under the sink, Liz removed the small fire extinguisher and held it in front of her. Javier yanked the ceramic lid from the back of the toilet and held it up on the opposite side of the door frame.

Liz's heart pounded in her ears.

The knob rattled. The door was designed to swing out, so the intruder couldn't kick it open easily. It wouldn't take long to figure out how to break in, though.

Holding her breath, she repositioned her feet and tightened her grip on the extinguisher.

Bullets exploded through the door around the knob, sending splinters of wood into the air. The intruder yanked it open. He stood before them wearing a dark uniform, complete with a helmet and assault weapon.

Javier leapt into the office and smashed the lid over the gunman's head, shattering it over his helmet. The guy stumbled back and fired aimlessly, peppering the ceiling with bullets. He reoriented himself and aimed the gun at Javier.

Liz pulled the extinguisher's pin and squeezed the handle.

White foam covered the gun-toting bastard. His arms flailed as he tried to wipe it away, but Liz kept spraying.

Javier ran behind her and grabbed her arm. "Come on!"

She dropped the extinguisher. It clanged on the floor as Javier dragged her away.

****

Javier peered into the corridor. A body lay on the floor, and an officer stood with his back to them. Others ran down the hall, yelling and firing weapons. SWAT wouldn't fire recklessly like that. *Who are these guys?*

Making sure Liz followed, Javier hurried across the hall and into the reception area. They ducked under the desk, where the night nurse had taken cover. She was crying and shaking.

Liz took her hands. "Are you hurt?"

The nurse shook her head. "They killed Stephen."

Liz pulled her into her arms.

Ignoring his stomach tightening, Javier set the case next to the nurse and crawled away from them. There was only one way to stop this.

"Wait, what are you doing?" Liz asked. "Get back under here!"

He made eye contact. "I can end this right now. They're after me. They won't kill anyone else if I surrender."

"But more people will die from the virus if you do that. You think these guys will let you live?"

Javier gritted his teeth. Not only would these guys kill him, Liz knew enough for them to kill her too. But what she knew might not matter. They'd killed a resident who knew nothing. "We need to go. The one you blasted won't be long." He crawled to the corridor and peeked out.

An officer faced Javier, but he was looking to the side. His foam-coated colleague joined him a moment later, and the two split up, one heading right for them.

Javier pulled back under the desk, joining the women. He held his breath until footsteps on the tiles passed them. Javier pointed and mouthed, "Back to the office."

Liz put her hand on her friend's shoulder. "Stay here until they leave. They'll probably follow us."

The nurse nodded and scooted farther under the desk.

They ran back to the office and pulled the desk in front of the door. Liz snatched the extinguisher from the floor and returned to the cracked window, using the heavy canister to whack at the weakened glass. After four quick hits, a small hole formed. Two more made it big enough to escape.

She stuck one leg through the hole and eased her body through.

The desk scooted across the floor. "In here," a man yelled.

"Hurry!" Liz held out her hand. "Give me the case."

Javier handed it over and climbed through the hole, careful not to touch the glass. Crouching, Liz led him through the darkness along the wall, stopping at the corner. She looked left and right before running along the next wall. "My car's in the lot over here."

The crack of gunshots echoed around them, and something zinged past Javier's ear. A sharp pain hit his calf. He screamed through clenched teeth and looked back. The shooter hid in the darkness.

Liz grabbed Javier's arm and ran. He limped along, ignoring the fire in his leg and keeping up with her pace.

****

Liz fished her keys from her bag as another bullet whizzed by them. Twenty feet from her car, she pointed the fob at it. The doors unlocked and the engine started.

She opened the back door, and Javier lunged inside, lying across the seat. He'd screamed before she grabbed him, but she didn't know where the bullet had hit. The shot must have come from a small pistol, or he'd be in much worse shape.

After slamming his door shut and falling into the driver's seat, Liz sped towards the lot's exit. Two parked sedans blocked it. She held her breath and veered to the side, mowing down a section of the short fence surrounding the property. A clank came from the back of the car—a bullet had hit the trunk.

Squeezing the wheel, she mashed the accelerator to the floor, keeping her headlights off until she was farther down the road. "Where'd it get you?"

"My leg."

She stole a quick glance behind her. Javier had sat up and held his calf.

"Did it go through?"

"I don't think so." A zipper sounded when he opened the backpack.

She twisted around for another peek, looking back in time to run a red light. Fortunately, no one else was out at this hour. He'd rolled up his pant leg and was tying a shirt around the injury, groaning when he tightened the makeshift bandage.

It wasn't ideal first aid, but it would have to do.

****

Javier leaned against the door and propped his leg up on the backpack. Liz sped along the winding road, frequently looking in the rearview mirror at him.

"Are they following us?" he asked.

"No. I turned onto a back-mountain road. It'll take us to the highway eventually. I doubt those guys will think to come this way. How's the leg?"

Pain surged through his calf, but he didn't want her to worry. "It'll be all right. The bandage is helping." He hoped that was true. "Who was Stephen?"

"A resident. Would come and go, stay for a few months, then disappear for a while. Did that for years. Sweet man." Her voice wavered. "His mind didn't fare well in the Debacle."

Javier sat up a little straighter. "You call it that?" Since the Eurasia War ended ten years earlier, only those most critical of the government called it the Debacle.

"Course I do. It took my husband."

Javier settled back against the door, unsure of what to say. Though the media had reported a U.S. victory in the war, suspicions surrounding its cause, money spent, and outcome lingered among the population. How could peaceful countries, ones that used to be allies, suddenly pose a military risk? And only agricultural areas were targeted—at least that's what the conspiracy sites said. The rumor was LifeFarm had tried to take over farming practices worldwide, and it failed miserably. Thousands of soldiers and countless more civilians were lost for no apparent gain.

After several silent minutes, Liz cleared her throat. "Kyle was stationed in Eastern Europe, near the end of it. Was his third deployment in as many years . . . this was after his retirement, mind you. He knew by then things weren't on the up and up."

"What did he see?"

"It was more about what he didn't see. No signs of aggression, only defensive action. Our guys were torching fields of supposed enemies to get the leaders to cooperate. The army says he died in an air raid in the Czech Republic. Wasn't anything left of him to send home."

Javier touched the bandage. It hadn't bled through yet. "What do you think happened?"

Liz drove in silence, tightly gripping the wheel.

"I'm sorry, I just–"

"I don't know what happened. I do know that the guys who tried to speak up tended to disappear or end up dead. He told me that after the second deployment." She clicked on the radio. Static came through the speakers, and she turned it off. "It'd probably do you good to get some sleep."

****

"Okay, Chief Rice. We go live in one minute." The producer took his place behind the camera.

"Yeah, I know. I've done this before." Charlie made one last adjustment of his jacket, making sure everything was flat and neat. He stood across from the reporter, a tiny blonde thing who looked like she'd blow away in a strong wind. Next to her, Charlie felt like a linebacker. They stood in front of a bright green screen. During the interview, an image of the shelter where they'd found Mendez would be projected.

Charlie ran his hand over his bald head. The lights made him sweat, and his brown skin did little to hide the perspiration. The best he could hope for was a short interview.

The anchorman appeared on the screen before them, though he was physically just twenty feet beyond that. He looked at the camera and started speaking. "Good morning. We have a breaking story, which you'll only see here on KRN. A fugitive by the name of Javier Mendez, wanted on vehicular homicide, drug, and weapons charges, escaped capture by an elite force of Homeland Security agents overnight. We have the man in charge of that team, Chief Charles Rice, to offer more information about Mendez and what's being done to apprehend him. He's standing by with KRN's Molly George in Gunnison, Colorado. Molly?"

The little blonde looked into the camera and spoke into her mic. "Thanks, Connor. I'm here with Chief Rice, who's graciously agreed to give us an update on the dangerous fugitive." She turned to Charlie. "Chief, what additional information can you give us?"

She held the mic up, but Charlie still had to bend over to speak into it. "He's considered extremely dangerous. He shot at our agents, killing a homeless man. He escaped with the aid of a shelter employee, a woman named Elizabeth Carson, and he's believed to be injured." A photograph—the one on file at the shelter—of the woman appeared on the screen where Charlie's had been.

"Why is this woman helping him?"

"We're unsure at this time. For now, she should also be considered armed and dangerous and is wanted for aiding a fugitive. She's driving a silver 2030 Honda Civic and may be headed northeast, possibly through Denver." A photograph of the car appeared on the screen. "If anyone sees the car or either of the suspects, contact your local authorities immediately."

"Thank you, Chief Rice. Connor, back to you."

The lights on Charlie went out, and he wiped his head again. Hopefully, someone would see the car and call it in. If this kid got away, not only could sensitive information about the virus get out and cause a panic, but Charlie's job could be in jeopardy—even with a security team at his disposal, he'd failed to neutralize the threat twice. He couldn't let it happen a third time.

****

Liz put her elbow on the restaurant's table and hid her face in her hand. "Crap."

"What?" Javier's back was to the TV. Liz pointed to it.

He looked behind him in time to see a photograph of her, followed by one of a car like hers. He faced her again. "They want you now?"

"And they know what car I drive. We need to leave right now." She put two twenties on the table, and they left half of their breakfast combos uneaten. Didn't matter. Her nerves crowded out her appetite.

Javier limped behind her. She almost told him to smooth out his gait so he wouldn't appear injured.

She opened the back door. "Lie down in the back seat."

"Why?" He climbed in.

"They're looking for us together. It'll take longer to make the connection if I'm alone." She closed the door behind him and walked around to the driver's side as casually as she could.

The TV had been muted, but text had scrolled across the bottom of the screen. They knew she was heading for Denver. "We need to change course a bit. It'll add time. You good? How's the leg?"

"Do what you need to do."

"Any idea how they knew which way we're going?" She started the engine.

"No. I cleared the browsing history on your computer after I decided to go to Iowa." He groaned when he shifted in the seat. "I'm guessing it's because the virus is there."

"All right. Well, we can't go through Denver now." Liz picked a route of mountain roads leading to Cheyenne and entered the course into her GPS. Through the mountains was the safest way out of Colorado.

Chapter Four

Charlie pulled the key out of the lock and opened the door to his sister's house. Her place was on the way to work from the news studio, and his stomach was reminding him of the importance of breakfast. Annie either enjoyed his company enough to feed him a few times a week, or she took pity on her divorced brother. Charlie didn't care which it was. In addition to home-cooked food, Annie's hospitality got him away from the apartment he'd shared with Mikayla for five years, until she'd decided he loved his job more than her, divorced him, and moved to Seattle.

The empty apartment seemed to taunt him after that. He guessed Annie knew that and offered him an escape.

Finding the kitchen unoccupied, he obeyed his growling stomach and searched the fridge for leftovers.

"Hey, Uncle Chuck," Mattson said from behind him.

Charlie peeked around the fridge door. His nephew wore a ridiculous getup: saggy jeans, an oversized flannel shirt, and a baseball hat worn sideways. At least the fro was gone. "Damn, what happened to you? And don't call me Chuck."

Mattson flashed his movie-screen-sized smile. "Sorry, Chuck. It's '90s day at school. We get extra credit if we dress up for these. Why are you here so early?"

"I was on the early news broadcast. Are you sure people in the '90s dressed like that? You look like a damn punk."

"This is what they looked like in our textbooks." Mattson retrieved a box of cereal from the pantry. "What were you on the news for?"

"Oh, you know. Homeland Security Chief stuff." After pulling a container of leftover home fries and three eggs from the fridge, he set a small pan on the stove and cranked the burner up to high.

"Protecting LifeFarm from the dangerous independent thinkers again?"

Charlie stifled a groan. If this kid didn't get over his skepticism, he'd have real problems later. All it would take was evidence of him speaking against LifeFarm or the government, and he could kiss college goodbye. "You need to watch your mouth."

Mattson rolled his eyes as he poured milk onto his cereal. "Yeah, whatever. You know people are starving on the other side of the world, right?"

"You also need to quit reading that garbage online. Nothing good can come from it."

"How did you get back from Colorado so quickly?" Annie's question interrupted the argument, thankfully. She came down the stairs and joined them in the kitchen.

Charlie gave her a hug. "The wonders of modern technology." He returned to the counter and cracked an egg over the hot pan, sending a satisfying sizzle into the room. "Thanks for breakfast."

She laughed. "Anytime. So, are you worried about that kid?"

"He looks like a punk. You sure you want him going to school like that?" Charlie winked at Mattson.

Annie laughed. "Yeah, but I meant the one from the news."

Charlie put the container of hash browns in the microwave and started it. "He's pretty dangerous. But we'll get him eventually."

"Kid? How old is he?" Mattson asked through a mouthful of cereal.

"Nineteen." The word made Charlie pause; Mendez was just two years older than his nephew. Charlie reminded himself that the lies he and LifeFarm used to catch the kid were necessary for the good of the world—how else would they be able to continue producing more food than the population needed? Everyone was better off, despite what Mattson thought. Mendez had knowledge that could irreparably damage LifeFarm, and by default, those who would starve if the truth about the virus got out and supplies suffered.

"Nineteen? And you guys can't catch him? Must be pretty smart." Mattson shoved another oversized spoonful of cereal into his mouth.

"He is. But he's out-resourced. It's just a matter of time before he—" Charlie's phone rang, and he checked the screen. "Before he slips up." He answered while turning off the burner. "Yeah."

"The woman's phone pinged off a cell tower in northeast Colorado, outside the national park," Sylvia said. "I'm sending some guys to intercept."

"Fantastic. Keep me posted. I'll get to the office in an hour."

****

Liz turned onto Highway 125 after deciding to edge the west side of Rocky Mountain National Park. She kept her phone in the holder on her dash, using her GPS to guide her. The mountain roads offered anonymity simply because they weren't as well used as the interstates, but the likelihood of getting lost was greater.

She'd ducked into a drugstore in the last town to pick up ointment, gauze, and antibiotics for Javier to treat his leg. He worked on wrapping the wound while lying across the backseat.

"How's it look?" She glanced in the rearview mirror as she calculated how much bribing the pharmacist for the pills had set her back. A black SUV, the only other vehicle on the road, followed several car lengths behind. She dismissed the thought that someone was following her so soon after the report aired.

"It's not bleeding anymore. It's smaller and more jagged than I expected." He wrapped the gauze around his lower leg. "No exit wound."

"Might have been a fragment. Maybe the bullet ricocheted off the building first."

"It felt like the whole thing. At least I can say I have part of a bullet in my leg for the rest of my life. Women dig scars, right?"

Liz laughed. "Sure, as long as—"

A bang sounded and her car jolted forward. The SUV's engine screamed as it shoved into her rear bumper. "What the hell?"

"What was that?"

"Don't sit up." Adrenaline racing through her body, Liz clenched the wheel and mashed the accelerator. The force let up a little, but her car had nothing on the SUV's horsepower. Now traveling twenty miles per hour over the speed limit on the winding road, they crossed the center line on the tighter curves. Her tires squealed as she corrected.

The SUV backed off but rammed her again. The wheel ripped free from her hands. She grasped for control as her car crossed the oncoming traffic lane and rolled down an embankment, bouncing over rocks and between trees. A river loomed ahead.

Liz thrust her arms in front of her face. A deluge of white covered the windshield. The car came to rest, sticking out of the river at a sharp angle like the sinking Titanic. Water rushed through the base of the front doors, and Liz curled her legs up.

After taking a second to catch her breath, she looked into the back seat. "You okay?"

"Yeah." Javier crawled off the floor and onto the seat. "Can I sit up yet?"

"Hold on." She eyed the mirror. The front of the SUV was visible through the trees, but no one was heading their way. "He might be waiting for us to leave the car. Just stay back there and play dead."

****

Javier couldn't get his heart to stop racing, yet Liz seemed so calm. This was the second time in twelve hours someone had tried to kill him—and her, by association—and she acted like nothing unusual was happening.

Wincing, he adjusted his injured leg. "How did they find us?"

"No idea. Maybe someone saw the car and called it in."

"Is the other car still there?"

"Yeah." She didn't move. "Crap. Where's my phone?"

Javier tried to sit up enough to see where she'd had it on the dash, but he couldn't without being seen through the back window. "It's not where you left it?"

"Nope." After a minute of silence, she said, "I see it. Not gonna be good for much now."

"Where is it?"

"On the floor, under a foot of water. I hope they get bored and leave soon. I'm getting a cramp curled up like this."

The realization hit Javier almost as hard as the car had hit the river. "I know how they found us."

"How?"

"Your phone."

"But I wasn't talking on it."

"The GPS tracking was on. All you had to do was drive by a tower after they had your info."

"Well in that case, I'm glad it's toast. Wait, they're heading for us. Play extra dead."

Extra dead?

Liz gasped. "Geez, this water's cold!"

This was the plan? Pretend the not-so-bad wreck had killed them both? "This isn't going to work."

"Shut up."

A few moments later, the door next to Javier's head opened. "Hey, look who's here!" a male voice said.

Crap. Was this guy going to drag him out of the car? Javier held his breath, as someone extra dead might do.

Footsteps crunched on leaves, then a female voice said, "Looks like you were right."

"Chief's gonna love this. I'm not sure I can get to her." His footsteps moved towards the front, he grunted, and Liz's door opened. "She doesn't look hurt, but she's out."

Something poked Javier's cheek, like a fingertip. A tickling sensation followed, moving up and down his jaw. It felt like a fingernail. He focused on holding his breath—one slip and she'd have him.

"Hey, what're you doing?" the man asked.

"Just seeing something." Javier felt her move away from him. "He doesn't have a pulse."

"Are you sure? The wreck wasn't that bad."

"I know how to take a pulse."

She didn't check his pulse, and he obviously had one. Why would she say that?

"Well, she has one," the man said. "What if the kid is just stunned or something?" A sliding sound followed, like a gun leaving a holster.

Javier's burning lungs begged for oxygen, but he held his breath. His chest tightened.

"Come on, Jake. He's dead," the woman said. "She will be by morning after the cold gets her. Save your ammo. No sense in making a bigger mess."

"But they're right here. This could be our only chance—"

"To do what? Shoot corpses?" She huffed. "Let's go. You're being ridiculous. We'll come back in the morning. Then we can report it as an accident without raising eyebrows. Do you need another questionable shooting on your record?"

Silence followed. What was the man doing? Aiming at Javier's head?

"Fine. You win."

Footsteps moved away from the car, and Javier took a long breath.

****

Liz waited until the SUV drove off before she lifted her numb legs out of the water. "Well, if I wasn't gonna die of hypothermia before, I will now." She climbed between the front seats and fell into the spot next to Javier. "Why did she say you were dead?"

"I guess I'm a good actor." Sitting up, he rested his feet in a couple inches of water.

"Got any bright ideas?"

"We need to find somewhere to build a fire and get you dried out." He grabbed his case and backpack and climbed out the still-open door.

Liz snatched her bag from the front seat before leaving. There was still plenty of daylight left, but they would need all of it to figure out how to survive the night. Her thin jacket wasn't guarding her against the cool mountain air, and the temperature would drop upon nightfall. Her feet already hurt from being so cold.

****

"Dead? Are you sure?" Charlie leaned into his desk, giving every ounce of attention to the man on the other end of the phone.

"They will be by morning."

"What does that mean?"

"The kid didn't have a pulse, and the woman was unconscious. The cold night will finish the job. The woman was halfway in the river."

"Did you collect the kid? We need him back, dead or alive."

"No, sir, those weren't our orders."

Charlie tightened his fist. "Those *were* your orders, officer. Go back and get him."

"Sir, with all due respect, the sun has set here. We won't be able to find the car–"

"Get a flood light!" Charlie stood and paced. "I don't care how hard it is. Do your job. Within the hour, I want this phone ringing with confirmation that you have his dead body in custody."

Chapter Five

Javier set sticks in a pyramid formation over the pile of dead leaves and smaller sticks. He glanced at the sun's rays disappearing behind a mountain and clenched his jaw. They should have stopped sooner. The temperature would drop quickly now.

Groaning as he stood, he balanced on his injured leg, hobbling around the trees and brushing away the carpet of pine needles with his foot. There had to be stones that would work to create a spark. The forested area where they'd settled would keep outsiders from seeing them, but the mess the trees dropped made his rock-finding mission impossible.

"Here. Use this." Liz tossed an antique Zippo lighter at him and closed her purse.

Javier scowled. "How long were you planning to keep this a secret?"

"Just long enough to make you nervous." Liz's teeth chattered, and she scooted closer to the makeshift fire pit, as if the flames were already blazing.

Javier struck the lighter until a flame appeared. "Why do you carry a lighter? You don't smoke."

"It was my husband's. His father gave it to him. It's come in handy a few times, so I keep it fueled."

The leaves ignited but the flames disappeared in seconds. He lit the ends of the sticks and added more dead leaves around them. As he worked, the smoke came and went, becoming inexplicably thick at times, given the lack of fire. Hopefully, the darkness would keep anyone from seeing their billowing signals over the trees.

By the time he had a decent fire going, the sun had set, and Liz had curled into a ball. She shivered while staring at the orange flames.

"Are your shoes still wet?" he asked.

She nodded and reached for her shoe. With violently shaking hands, she untied it, and after struggling to get it off her foot she flung it, almost hitting the fire.

Javier walked around the pit. "Here. Let me help you." He removed her other sneaker and her socks then laid her footwear on the rocks surrounding the fire. He rubbed her feet; they felt as cold as the night air.

She focused on the fire, her arms clutching her torso.

Guilt filled Javier's gut. She might not survive the night, even with the fire. And he was the reason she was here.

He cupped her foot in his hands and hoped he could at least offer a distraction from her misery. "Can I ask you a question?"

"Sure."

"Why are you helping me?"

She looked up at him, as if weighing an appropriate response. "You remind me of my son."

Surprised, Javier arched back. "I do?"

She nodded. "He was taken from me."

He waited a few moments for her to elaborate. "What do you mean?"

"He's a little older than you. First year he went to college, LifeFarm recruited him. Said they would pay for whatever he needed if he promised to work for them after graduation. You can imagine how that went over. We argued. I told him the company killed his daddy, but he doesn't believe that's what happened. I couldn't talk him out of it, and then he quit talking to me."

She said everything robotically and without looking away from the fire, as if she'd disconnected herself from what happened. Unsure how to respond, Javier focused on warming Liz's feet.

"So you get it now?" She looked at him again. "LifeFarm took my family from me. They took . . . ." Her voice caught, and she cleared her throat. "If you have a way to bring them down, I'm gonna do my damndest to help you."

Javier glanced at his case sitting next to a tree. It looked innocuous enough, but she was right: its contents could bring down the company hell-bent on taking over the world. All he had to do was prove the virus existed and that LifeFarm was responsible.

****

Liz lay as close as she could to the fire, but the cold reached all the way to her bones. She'd stopped shivering—a bad sign. She could be in the grips of hypothermia.

Javier poked the flames with a long stick, making them grow. Though the heat reached her, it wasn't enough to stave off the cold. He must have sensed the same and added another log.

What if nothing he did was enough?

She pushed the thought away, having seen more than a few homeless veterans die after giving up. This was one night. She could survive that.

But what would they do in the morning? They had no water, no food, no car, and they were supposed to be dead.

Her heavy eyes begged for sleep.

"Liz, stay awake."

Blinking, she forced her eyelids to stay open.

"Here." Javier took off his jacket and draped it over her.

"No, you'll freeze."

"I'll be all right." Wearing only a T-shirt, jeans, and his cap, he settled next to the fire. The flames reflected in his eyes, and when they looked over her, his jaw dropped.

The sound of a cocking gun came from behind her, followed by a gruff male voice. "What the hell do you think you're doin'?"

Javier stood with his hands by his face, in a posture of surrender. "I'm sorry. We were in an accident. We're just trying to stay warm."

Was it an agent? Liz struggled to twist around and get a look at the man, but her stiff neck prevented it. She resigned to listening.

"What's wrong with her?" the man asked.

"She's cold. I think she's hypothermic."

"You related?"

If she weren't freezing to death, she might have laughed. She and Javier looked nothing alike.

"She's my aunt."

"Well, you all better come back to the house. Can't have you freezing on my property. Come on."

She put her hands on the ground and lifted herself, but her elbows buckled. She fell back to the dirt.

"Sir, can you help her? I'm injured."

"All right. Here." The man passed his rifle over her to Javier.

He was quick to trust strangers. Maybe the hypothermia made them look anything but threatening. That, or he was tricking them into a more dangerous situation. Her lethargy overshadowed her ability to care.

The man wiggled his arms under her, and he grunted as he lifted her. As he walked away from the fire, her body pressed against his stocky form and his uneven gait jostled her with each step. He coughed, cleared his throat, and panted like he had trouble breathing when he exerted himself. His clothes smelled of a mix of smoke, dirt, and sweat.

Eventually, he reached a small house and carried her inside. A dim light came from somewhere behind her. It must have been warmer here, but she didn't feel it.

"Hey kid, get that switch by the door, will ya?" the man asked.

Overhead lights came on, and he lowered Liz onto a couch. She rolled onto her side. A wood burning stove sat a few feet away. The man opened it and threw a log inside. Without another chair in the room, a shivering Javier sat on the floor and leaned against the couch near her head.

The man put a blanket over Javier's shoulders and draped Liz with a comforter. "I'm Duane."

Javier looked up. "I'm Hector. She's Marie."

Marie. She'd have to remember her new name. Though if this guy kept up with the news at all, fake names wouldn't matter. The bounty was still on Javier's head, and Duane would need a compelling reason not to collect it. Most people she knew had gone without too long.

A painful shiver raced through her body. She gasped while arching her back.

"Good, she's recoverin," Duane said. "I'm not sure she would've made it through the night."

Javier slumped, wrapping the blanket tighter around himself.

"Your aunt, huh?" Duane looked from Javier to Liz, then back to Javier. "You don't look alike."

"I was adopted." Javier's eyes met Liz's.

Don't worry, I'll remember.

The shivering increased, and she pulled the comforter to her chin, wishing she could lapse into unconsciousness.

****

A gurgling coffee pot woke Javier. Sitting up in the chair where he'd passed out, he curled his arm over his head and pulled until his neck cracked. Daylight spilled through the windows. How long had he been asleep?

He inhaled the coffee's aroma, and his stomach rumbled.

Liz slept on the couch. Her color looked better than it had the night before.

His guilt made him restless. If Duane hadn't found them, she wouldn't have survived the night, and the only reason she was in that situation was he'd stumbled into the shelter's courtyard. It would have been better for her if he'd died in the wreck or from the gunshot.

But then LifeFarm would continue killing people and denying culpability.

He had to move to relieve his anxiety. Upon lifting himself from the chair, his leg wound reminded him of its painful presence. Limping around loosened it enough to make it little more than a nuisance.

A final gurgle came from the coffee pot, but Duane wasn't around. Javier peered down a short hallway before going in search of a mug.

The first cabinet was full of jars of canned food: peaches, beets, and apple butter, according to the labels. Other foods filled the remaining two shelves. The next cabinet held dried meat in vacuum-sealed plastic.

This guy was prepared to live on his own for some time.

Javier opened the next cabinet and found plates and bowls.

"Can I help you find something?" Duane asked from behind him. The front door slammed closed a moment later.

Javier turned. "Mugs?"

Duane set a large ax near the door and carried logs to a pile near the wood burning stove. In the kitchen, he opened a cabinet next to the fridge and handed Javier a faded Disneyland mug. He grabbed a second mug and filled it with coffee, then held the pot out to Javier.

With full cups, the men sat at Duane's small kitchen table.

"Do you live here alone?" Javier asked. He hadn't heard anyone else in the house, and Duane seemed remarkably unconcerned about his appearance. His jeans were stained, his flannel shirt torn, and his gray hair needed a trim. A few days' worth of beard growth covered his rough face.

Duane nodded as he took a sip. "Yep. Live off the grid. I hunt or grow all my food. Power is solar, water comes from a well."

"Why?" Javier sipped from his mug, suppressing a wince at the lack of sugar and cream.

Duane cleared his throat. "Now, I don't go around asking others to explain how they live. I'd like the same courtesy. I could have asked you how you ended up in the forest with no supplies or means of survival."

"I told you. We were in a wreck."

"People in wrecks call for help."

Javier stared at the table and took a sip. How could he keep Duane from figuring out the truth?

"It's all right. Everyone's got something to hide." Duane stuck his foot out and lifted his pant leg, revealing an artificial limb that looked like a metal representation of the bones that had once been there. "Got this as a souvenir in the Iraq war after 9/11. Before your time. They wanted to pull me into Eurasia."

Javier did the math. "Weren't you a little . . . advanced for that one?"

"Yeah, but you remember how it was." He paused. "Or maybe you don't. You were probably a baby. Anyway, the government fired up the draft again. I was still serving in a desk job. But I could walk well enough, so they signed me up for combat and promoted me, as if that would help." He laughed and took another sip. "I had a funny feeling about that operation. Didn't want any part of it. So I took off."

Javier surveyed the interior of the cabin. This man had lived here under the government's radar for the past eighteen years, and he was spilling his guts about it to a stranger. "Aren't you worried I'll tell someone where you are?"

He shook his head. "Don't think I need to be, Hector. Or should I call you Javier?"

Javier gasped. He glanced at the door, figuring he could wake Liz and run out in less than a minute. But how would they get past Duane? And where was the gun?

"Relax, boy. I heard on the radio this morning. Cops are looking for a kid who looks like you traveling with a lady who looks like her." He gestured to the couch. "Thought I'd throw the name at you and see how you react. What I've seen and what the report said don't match. I know the media is full of shit. So I decided to trust you. Stay here as long as you need to." He held his hand across the table. "I'll keep your secret if you keep mine. Deal?"

Javier paused then reached out, shaking Duane's hand. "Deal."

"You hungry?" Duane stood and walked to the fridge. "Toast?" He held up a loaf of bread at the same moment something broke through the window over the sink.

He collapsed, blood streaming from the back of his head.

A second shot hit the freezer.

Oh, God. Javier fell to the floor and crawled to the front door.

Liz crawled up next to him. "What the hell happened?"

"They found us." Javier stood up on his knees and gripped the ax in both hands, listening. The shooter would arrive any second. He swallowed despite his dry mouth. "Hide behind the couch."

"Like hell." Hunched over, she hustled down the short hall.

The front door burst open. A man with a chiseled face and butch haircut pointed a pistol at Javier's head.

Before he could think, Javier thrust the ax onto the man's foot. Butch screamed and lurched back, leaving half of his foot behind and spreading a blood trail across the porch.

A second man hurried to the door and trained his weapon on Javier.

Two shots fired. The gunman hollered and fell backwards. Blood ran from large holes in his chest.

Javier twisted around. Frozen, Liz pointed a rifle towards the open door.

Butch continued groaning. Sitting up, he wrapped his hands— one still holding a gun—around the remainder of his foot.

Javier rushed over and freed the gun from his grasp. Butch's eyes widened, as if he'd forgotten the gun was there.

Liz raced to Javier, and they both pointed their weapons at Butch, who was now sweating.

"Are there any others?" Liz asked while surveying the woods. The gun shook slightly in her hands.

Butch stared at her, the crease between his brows deepening.

Focusing, she closed the distance between the rifle and Butch's eyes.

He held his bloody hands near his face. "Okay! No, just us. Don't shoot."

She glanced at his foot. "You're bleeding a lot. I don't think you're getting out of here."

What is she thinking? Javier's hands were sweating. Shooting this guy would be killing an unarmed man—one who'd killed Duane. Unless the other guy did that. The only thing Javier was sure of was these men hadn't come to arrest them. They'd been searching for a more permanent solution.

The man's hands shook. "Please, don't. I was following orders."

"You always murder because it brings a paycheck?" Liz took a step towards him.

Standing, Javier looked into her eyes and tried to keep his voice steady. "Liz."

She didn't lower the weapon.

"Liz!" He tilted his head.

When her eyes met his, realization appeared to hit her. She lowered the gun.

Sighing, Javier weighed his options. How could he and Liz get away without Butch seeing them do it? "Give me your phone and I'll bandage your foot. You might live."

His hand violently shaking, Butch reached into his coat pocket and pulled out a black phone.

"Okay, here's what's gonna happen." Javier pocketed the phone. "We're gonna tie you up and blindfold you, and after we're far from here, I'll call for help." Leaving Liz to stand guard, he went inside to gather anything he could find to tie Butch up and bandage his wound, pausing to look at Duane's body. The old man had been murdered just for helping them.

The guilt returned to his gut. Anyone associated with Javier was at risk. Maybe he should figure out a way to ditch Liz before they killed her too.

****

"Sylvia, what's our status?" Charlie had the phone on speaker and put his face in both hands. Since learning Mendez and the woman weren't in the car, he hadn't stopped sweating and called every five minutes to find out if his guys had found them.

"Someone made an anonymous call to emergency services, directing an ambulance to a cabin."

He raised his eyebrows. "Okay. So?"

"Our guys were there. One was shot dead. The other was tied up, blindfolded, and had half of his foot cut off."

Charlie bolted to his feet. "He got away again?"

Sylvia didn't answer for a few seconds. "We're tracking him. We think he took the old man's vehicle. There were fresh tire tracks."

"What kind of vehicle?"

"We don't know."

"What about the phone?"

"Mendez ditched it."

Charlie sat again and rubbed his forehead, trying to calm himself. "Okay, so let's think this through. He has the bees. He knows about the virus. They went to northern Colorado. Why?"

"He'll need to go somewhere to develop a vaccine. A lab."

"Okay, so where?" Charlie tapped his finger on the desk. "The virus is in the Midwest. Mendez knows that. They were driving that way."

"So he'd look for a lab in the Midwest. I'm on it."

"Let me know when you figure it out. I'm going there myself this time. And lay off the news coverage. We want them to get comfortable. It'll be easier to catch them if they stop running."

****

Liz slammed the old passenger van into third gear, jerking the vehicle. She winced. "Sorry. Haven't driven a stick in ages." She tried to steady her hands on the wheel, but in the half hour since she found Duane's keys and they left in his van, she'd had time to process what she'd done.

Her husband had trained her to use a gun. He'd insisted on it before his third deployment, saying she might need the skills someday. He'd even bought her a small handgun, which she kept in a box in her closet. She hadn't wanted to consider the possibility of having to use it to protect herself.

But at Duane's house, after the agents killed the man who'd saved her, she didn't hesitate. She hadn't seen Duane's gun in the living room. His bedroom seemed the next most likely place for him to keep his rifle.

She'd raised the weapon, aimed, and fired. The man had looked at her in shock as she took his life, even as he fell back and blood drained from him.

If she hadn't, she and Javier would both be dead.

That didn't make the images any less vivid. Nausea took hold in her stomach.

"Are you okay?" Javier's voice brought her mind back to the van.

"Oh. Yeah." She moved her hands from eleven and one to nine and three.

"You did the right thing back there."

She clicked on the radio, in case anyone was reporting on Javier. Country music played through the speakers. She scrunched her nose and turned the dial.

"You don't have to stay with me if you don't want to. I mean . . . you've already saved my life a few times. I don't want to keep putting you in danger."

"They tried to kill us—both of us—back at the shelter. I'm not a coward, and I'm not quitting." She messed with the radio, glancing at the mostly empty road and stopping when she found a news broadcast. "Besides, now they'll be after us for killing that agent. It's a little late for me to back out."

Javier stared out his window. "I never thought going into science would be so dangerous."

"Science is seeking the truth, how the world works. You just stumbled onto the wrong truth."

Chapter Six

Javier drove the van into Hayes after midnight. The main street had three traffic signals and about a dozen street lights. The side roads were dark, save for the occasional porch light and regularly spaced bug zappers.

Liz leaned forward, peering out the windshield. "This is it?"

"Yeah. I told you it was small."

Finally arriving lifted the lingering fatigue he'd fought since they were halfway across Nebraska, when he'd offered to take over driving. The combination of evading whoever was trying to kill him, last night's rough sleep, and the boring drive did little to keep his head clear. He only felt awake when he saw black SUVs along the route, sending his adrenaline into overdrive.

But now that they were here, he wanted nothing more than to get settled and find someone to help with the vaccine. From his internet research, he knew what the lab looked like, but he wouldn't be able to check it out in the middle of the night. There were no apparent places to stay. He pulled the van to the side of the road in front of a darkened grocery store. "Where should we go?"

Liz scanned the street. "The next town is bigger. Let's head there. We'll look for a shelter."

"A shelter? Like . . . a homeless shelter?"

She nodded. "We'll go in separately. I doubt anyone will pay us much mind. We can get a shower and a place to sleep."

It wasn't a bad idea. The bits of news they'd caught on the radio talked about them but didn't say anything about the van or the dead agent. People this far away from the scene might not know their story.

Javier pulled the van onto the road and drove out of Hayes. He and Liz rode in silence until the city lights came into view, when Liz asked a question she must have had for a while.

"So . . . you've haven't talked about your family at all. Don't they wonder where you are? Will they try to track you—"

"No."

She stared at him.

Javier tightened his grip on the steering wheel. "I don't have one."

"Don't have one? Who put you through college at sixteen or whatever?"

"The school did. Scholarships. Letting me in was good publicity for them." Javier took a long breath. "My parents adopted me when I was four. They weren't able to have their own children, and they met me at an orphanage in Puerto Rico. They were older than most parents just starting a family. My dad died four years later, and my mom . . . she never recovered. She always talked about how smart I was and how my dad saw it right away. I don't think she believed she could raise me on her own. Or maybe I reminded her of my dad somehow." He cleared his throat, keeping his eyes on the road. "Anyway, the morning after I turned sixteen, I woke up and discovered she'd left."

In the three years since it happened, Javier had tried not to think about that day. His mother had been kind to him, but distant. Still, she was the only mother he knew.

A few silent minutes passed before Liz asked, "Where is she now?"

Javier shrugged. "Arizona, I think. My grandparents—her parents—lived there. I got a note from her a few weeks after she took off. She asked me not to look for her."

"And you didn't?" Liz sat up straighter and faced him. "Why didn't you fight?"

"I couldn't fight!" A lump formed in Javier's throat. "If I called the cops, they'd put me in foster care. I was going to college in a couple months, so I waited it out." His eyes burned. "I didn't want to be abandoned. But I couldn't do anything about it."

Liz stayed silent for the remainder of the trip, likely unsure of what else to say. That was fine. Javier didn't enjoy dwelling on his family problems.

When Javier drove down the city's main street, Liz pointed to the right. "Up there. That's a shelter."

"How can you tell?"

"That tree symbol. See it? Right under the porch light."

Javier pulled up closer to the small, brick building. A picture of a cartoonish tree hung to the left of the door, lit by the orange bulb overhead. The tree was wilted, like it was dying. "What does it mean?"

"The veterans recognize it. We have it on our place too. Only veterans and people helping them are likely to know what it means. The folks at the VA tell the soldiers soon as they get home. That tree means refuge. It's on soup kitchens and food banks too, but a building like this is a shelter. Let me see if we can get in."

Before Javier could ask what "a building like this" meant, Liz hopped out of the van, tried the door, and returned after finding it locked.

"Better find a place to park." She slammed the van's heavy metal door shut. "We won't be able to get in there 'til tomorrow."

Javier parked the van behind a supermarket, and Liz stretched across the back seat. In minutes, she was asleep. He tried to sleep sitting up in the driver's seat, but he couldn't get his mind to stop racing.

Before tonight, Javier had been portrayed as a drunk driver, weapons smuggler, and drug trafficker. Now, authorities could legitimately connect him to the killing of one federal agent and the wounding of another, and the media was quiet. It didn't make sense. Logic suggested his face would be plastered across the media even more than it was before.

About the time the sun peeked over the horizon, Javier grew tired of his own thoughts and decided to go for a walk. He hopped out of the van and winced as he stretched his injured leg, put on his cap and jacket, and walked to a street lined with stores and restaurants.

Only a coffee shop was open, and the aroma of the morning brew enticed him to enter. As he read the menu, a young woman rushed in and headed straight to the counter.

"Hey, Sam," the guy behind the counter said. "The usual?"

"You got it." She lifted her sunglasses to the top of her head. "Throw in a lemon Danish, too."

While she paid for her food, Javier fixated on her. She had smooth, black hair pulled into a ponytail, and her tan skin and face shape suggested a Latin descent. Only one feature threw off his guess: the freckles covering the bridge of her nose and the tops of her cheeks.

She looked away from the counter and made eye contact with Javier. "Hi."

Javier shook off his trance as heat rushed to his cheeks. "Hi." He stared at the floor.

She walked up to him and tilted her head. "I'm Samantha. I don't think I've seen you around here before."

He offered a nervous smile. "Hector." Suddenly aware of how long it had been since he showered, Javier took a step back. He waved a finger in front of his nose. "I was just noticing your freckles. I hope that's okay."

She laughed. "Yeah, you're not the first. They show more when I've been in the sun. I volunteered at a pancake breakfast outside the shelter on Saturday."

"You work at the shelter?" Javier already had an unwanted connection. He didn't need anyone from his temporary residence recognizing him later.

"No. I work at the college, as a T.A. The school is partnered with the shelter. It's horrible how our country has treated our veterans, so we do what we can."

"Here you go, Sam." The barista set her coffee and pastry on the high counter behind her.

She twisted around. "Thanks, Brad." She retrieved her order and returned to Javier. "So what brings you to town?"

"Oh, I..." He adjusted his cap. "It's a long story. I'm actually headed to Hayes."

"No kidding! My dad owns a restaurant in Hayes. It's up that road." She pointed then studied Javier. "How about we meet up there this evening? I'm off work at four. I can give you some tips about the area. Let's meet at six." She set her things on the counter, grabbed a napkin, and wrote something on it. "Here's the name."

Javier took the napkin as his mouth became as dry as the California desert. He hadn't interacted with a girl who was so direct before. "Sam's? Did he name the place after you?"

She laughed and picked up her food again. "Sort of. Also a long story. I'll see you tonight." She winked and left the shop, leaving him staring at the door.

Why was Sam so forward? She couldn't have known who he was. Maybe she was just friendly. She was obviously smart—an employee of the college, even. Perhaps she could get him in the door with a virologist.

The fact that she captured his attention so effectively didn't hurt either.

When Javier walked to the counter to order, Brad was grinning like an idiot. "You're lucky. I could never get her number."

Another burst of heat rushed to Javier's face, and he laughed awkwardly. "Don't spit in my coffee, okay?"

****

Bright sunlight shining on Liz pulled her out of her sleep. Sitting up, she fought her heavy eyelids and looked over the front seat—Javier wasn't there. Where had he gone?

A moment of worry passed through her before she decided that if something had happened to him while in the van, it would have happened to her too. He'd likely gone in search of a restroom.

She slung her bag over her shoulder and climbed out, surveying the area before deciding to wander to the shelter. Javier would figure that's where she went when he came back.

A long desk filled most of a front lobby. Unlike the shelter in Gunnison, no safety glass separated the employees from anyone who entered. The sight encouraged her. She'd pressured her own shelter's owners to remove that glass. It damaged the sense of trust they'd wanted to instill in the people who needed them most.

As she approached the counter, a young man with dirty blond hair and a rough complexion looked up. "Can I help you?"

"Yes. I saw the tree out there." She pointed towards the door. "I need a place to crash for a while."

He nodded. "Fill out this form," he slid a clipboard across the counter, "and we'll get you a bunk. Do you have any money?"

"A little."

"We ask those who can manage to pay five dollars a night."

"I can do that for a little while." She took the clipboard and sat in a line of chairs set against the window.

A television hung over the desk, tuned to a news station. Liz glanced at it, ready to run or hide her face if a story about her and Javier appeared. The reporters covered last night's football game.

Since they'd taken Duane's van yesterday, she hadn't heard a single report about the shooting or any of the other stories the media had conjured. The lack of coverage was especially strange now that she'd killed someone she assumed was a cop. The authorities had a legitimate reason to search for them.

Shaking her head, she returned her attention to the form. The media silence should have provided relief, but her gut told her it was only a matter of time before her picture was all over the national news again.

The form completed, Liz headed to the counter, where a short, young woman with a dark brown complexion took it. The woman unlocked a door adjacent to the desk and led Liz through it. Aside from a janitor, no other people occupied the space.

The woman glanced at the clipboard as she walked. "Hi, Marie. I'm Shana. Usually, residents are required to leave during the day to look for work and go to the soup kitchen for meals. Since you just arrived, you're allowed to stay today to shower and do laundry. But you'll have to follow the schedule after that." She entered a large room filled with bunk beds.

"I understand." Liz had better get used to being called Marie. She'd hoped using the name Javier assigned her at Duane's house would prevent any slip-ups later.

"Can you manage a top bunk?" Shana asked.

"Yeah."

"Okay." She weaved between beds, stopping at one in the back corner. The bottom bunk was neatly made, and a backpack rested at the foot of it. The top bunk held a set of folded sheets and a blanket. "This'll be your space. It's the women's wing. No men are allowed here. Report any that try to sneak over. That's a zero-tolerance rule." She stared at Liz for a few moments. "You're not from around here, are you?"

Liz leaned back but recovered, hopefully before Shana noticed. "No. Does that matter?"

Shana shook her head. "No. It's fine." She pointed down a hall to her right. "Showers are down there. You need some clean clothes?"

Liz nodded while staring at the floor, imitating the look of shame she'd seen on a few residents at her own shelter. While employees weren't supposed to practice favoritism, those residents usually received extra leniency when it came to the rules. If Shana had worked here a while, she would think Liz had escaped an abusive situation.

"Okay. Tell me your size and head to the shower. I'll leave some of our donated clothes in the bathroom for you." Shana put her hand on Liz's arm. "Marie, as long as you don't tell anyone where you are, you're safe here."

Liz offered a polite smile, wondering how long Shana's statement would be true.

****

After finding the van empty, Javier headed to the shelter. Liz had said she wanted to enter separately, so she wouldn't have had a reason to wait for him.

He checked in, and a young guy wearing a Captain America shirt led him to an area full of bunk beds, stopping at one in the middle of the room. "All right, Hector. You sleep here." He pointed to a bottom bunk. "You stay on this wing. Go on the girl's side, and you're out. No warnings. Got it?"

Javier nodded.

Captain America pointed down a hall. "Men's showers are down there. Remember, this is only for today. Tomorrow, you gotta get out of here by 9:00. Anyone staying here needs to be out trying to make money. I'll get you some clothes." He left Javier alone among the beds.

Javier made his way to the showers. The bathroom housed five small stalls, and there was no apparent place to put personal belongings. Reaching into his pocket, he ran his fingers along the napkin Sam had given him, and his stomach filled with anticipation. The longer he thought of their meeting that morning, the more he looked forward to seeing her again that night.

The name of the place—and her name—were simple enough to remember. She hadn't needed to write it down. But that didn't mean he wanted the note to get ruined in this dingy bathroom. He went to his bunk and placed the napkin between the folded sheets.

"What are you waiting for, a guided tour?" Captain America stood behind him, holding an armful of unfolded clothes.

Javier tried to keep his wince hidden. "No. I'm going." He took the bundle and returned to the bathroom.

He shook out the clothes—a pair of jeans that looked too big and a golf shirt. Hopefully, they were nice enough to convince someone at the lab to let him use some of their space. On the other hand, he had the bees and knowledge of the virus—as did the people of the town, judging by the abundance of bug zappers lining the street.

There had to be a way to use their knowledge to his advantage.

Chapter Seven

As Liz drove the van through Hayes, Javier pointed to a building on the right side of the road. "It's that brick one, up there."

"You sure?" Liz stopped in front of it, eyeing the small, one-story structure. "This looks like an old daycare center."

"Could have been." He grabbed his case and hopped out. "Come back in an hour. I should know by then if they'll let me work here." He slammed the door and walked limp-free up the path to the building. Hiding his injury must have been painful, but he managed it well. He didn't act as if he was nervous about the task ahead.

Driving down the quiet street, she wondered what to do with her free time. A few people strolled in front of the shops and restaurants. Liz spotted the diner Javier had told her about—Sam's. He was supposed to meet a girl there in a few hours, an idea that at first seemed foolish but understandable—a kid Javier's age would naturally be attracted to same-aged women. Liz asked to tag along, though, to be on the safe side.

The diner's white exterior and neon signs in the window—one advertising milkshakes—gave it a nostalgic feel. After parking the van, she headed to Sam's. Couldn't hurt to check it out. Plus, the milkshake sign made her want one.

A bell over the door jangled as she entered. The interior was bright, and folksy guitar music played over the speakers, contrasting with the old diner appearance. A young man eating a hamburger sat at a table, and a grungy guy stepped out from behind the counter, wiping his hands on a towel as he approached her. "Hi there. Welcome to Sam's. Table for one?"

He looked about thirty and sported light brown dreadlocks, two of which he'd used to tie back the others. The parts of his shirt unobscured by the apron appeared discolored, as if it was an old favorite. For some reason, she hadn't expected an Iowan—or a restaurant worker—to look like him. "Oh, no thanks. I'll sit at the bar. I'm just getting a drink."

"Fair enough." He held his arm out to the stools as he reclaimed his place behind the counter. "Take your pick. What can I get you?"

"Vanilla milkshake."

"Vanilla? We can do something more interesting than that. Mint chip, cookies and cream, we can even make it adult and throw some Kahlua in there if you want." He winked.

She laughed. "Nah, vanilla's fine. I don't usually order milkshakes, but your sign is persuasive."

"Well, that's encouraging, because it was expensive." He gathered ingredients from a fridge under the counter. "Where are you visiting from?"

"Is it that obvious?" She hadn't thought she looked out of place. But if this guy was the owner—and he must have been, or he wouldn't have known the sign was expensive—he probably knew all the locals.

He shrugged as he poured half and half into a tall metal cup. "People around here have a certain look. So it's pretty easy to spot the travelers."

"What's the look?" And could being without it put her at a disadvantage, or worse—make her stick out?

He paused in the middle of scooping ice cream. "It's hard to explain without being rude." He set the cup on the shake machine and switched it on.

"You can explain. I won't take it personally."

"Don't worry about it." He poured the shake into a tall glass, added a bendy straw and a long spoon, and set it in front of her. He held out a hand. "I'm Jonah. I own this place."

She shook it, feeling thick calluses on his fingertips. "Marie. And you're right. I'm visiting. My nephew's looking for work. I tagged along."

"Where at?"

"A lab down the road. He's a scientist."

"Hmm. That might not work out." He put the metal cup into the sink. "That lab is pretty specific in what they do."

"What do they do?"

Jonah glanced towards the ceiling, as if he was thinking. "Nutritional stuff. But I guess it depends on what your nephew is into." He returned to her. "Why don't you guys come by tonight? We'll have live music."

She sipped the shake. "We were gonna do that anyway. He's meeting someone. A girl he met in the next town."

"Oh, really?" He chuckled. "Probably my daughter. She loves to steer people over here. Your nephew must be a good-looking kid."

"Your daughter?" She stared at him. "I'm sorry. You don't seem old enough to have a daughter that age."

Jonah busied himself straightening the already-neat settings of salt shakers and napkin holders. "Good genes, I guess."

He wiped the counter while moving away from her. Apparently, their conversation was over.

****

Javier entered an empty front room, separated from the rest of the building by a closed door. He tried the handle: locked. A thumbprint scanner was to the left of the jamb. Above that was a small screen with an adjacent dime-sized lens and a call button. He pushed the button, sounding an irritating buzz, and stared at the black screen. *This is a lot of security for a small lab.*

Just when he was about to give up and try getting attention another way, a man wearing thick-rimmed glasses appeared on the screen. Whatever camera he looked into to project his image made his forehead look disproportionally huge. "Yes?"

Javier looked into the lens on his side, now self-conscious about the size of his own forehead. "Uh, hi. I need to talk to someone in charge."

"I'm in charge. What do you want?"

Javier felt a tinge of relief; he thought he'd have to negotiate through a few steps to reach the boss. "This is a lab, right?"

"In a manner of speaking. Look, I'm busy. If you're selling something, move on. We're not interested." The screen went black.

Javier pressed the button again.

The screen stayed black.

He banged on the door.

A few moments later, the door cracked open and Boss stuck his head into the gap. "I told you to move on."

"I'm not selling anything."

"So what's with the case?"

Javier glanced at the case in his hand. This guy wasn't likely associated with LifeFarm—he'd made that determination upon seeing how basic the facility was. But that didn't mean he'd eagerly let Javier in. Maybe direct was the way to go. "I know about your bees dying. And about the virus."

Boss grabbed Javier's arm, shoving him through the outer door and onto the path. "We're not doing anything against the rules here. Go tell your bosses we make vitamins using LifeFarm-produced ingredients. You have no evidence to the contrary and no reason to investigate us." He slammed the door, and the sound of a dead bolt locking followed.

"Crap." Javier paced in front of the building.

LifeFarm must have been sending scouts—spies—into these towns, probably to make sure the virus stayed a secret. Or maybe it was to enforce the use of their products. That would make sense, considering what Boss said. How could Javier convince these people he didn't work for LifeFarm—and that he could potentially save them from the virus?

He sat on the step. Maybe if he didn't leave, Boss would realize Javier was one of the good guys. The real spies likely didn't stick around.

****

Frowning, Javier climbed into the van and put his case behind the passenger seat. Not trying to hide his frustration, he slammed the door shut, rattling the windows.

"Uh oh." Liz raised her eyebrows. "What happened?"

"The boss threw me out. Wouldn't even talk to me."

"Did you tell them about the bees?" Liz pulled the van onto the road.

"I tried. I barely got five words in."

"So, now what? Should we head to the university?"

"I haven't figured that out yet." Javier surveyed the town. "Where are we going?"

"You're not meeting that girl until six, right? We have a couple of hours. Wanna go early?"

He shrugged, then remembered something. "Sam works at the university."

"Can that help you?"

"Maybe she knows someone who works in virology."

"Did she say what area she worked in?"

"No, but people usually know their coworkers." The thread of hope he held was thin, but it was all he had to go on. Plus, the subject would give him an obvious topic of conversation when he saw Sam. Avoiding awkward silences wasn't one of his specialties, especially if he was with someone who made him inexplicably nervous.

A few minutes later, Liz led Javier towards the diner bearing the girl's name. "I came in earlier. The owner's interesting."

"You mean her dad?" Heat rushed to his face.

She laughed. "Yeah. Don't worry. He's not intimidating."

Inside, a skinny, blond man was waving a black wand over the walls, tables, benches, and chairs. On the other side of the dining room, a man with long, light-brown dreadlocks opened a case and pulled out an acoustic guitar. He sat on a stool behind a microphone and plucked one string at a time, listening and twisting the pegs between each tone. Javier couldn't see a tuner—the guy must have been doing it by ear.

Liz crossed her arms. "The owner is the live entertainment?"

"He's the owner?" Javier looked away when the man made eye contact, pretending to be interested in the vintage movie posters hanging over each table.

"Come on." Liz stepped towards the guitarist.

"What? Wait…"

Before Javier could protest further, she was halfway there. The owner looked at her and smiled. "Hey, again. Marie, right?"

"Right." She gestured to Javier. "This is my nephew, Hector."

The guy held out a hand. "I'm Jonah. I hear someone invited you. Girl with long black hair?"

Javier shook Jonah's hand, doing his best to keep his nerves at bay. "Yeah."

He laughed. "She loves bringing people here. Been doing it since she was little."

"So this is your place?" Despite what Liz had said, Javier had trouble connecting Jonah to the girl he'd met at the coffee shop. Sam, with her jet-black hair and tan skin, didn't resemble this man at all. Maybe she'd been adopted, or her mother was Hispanic and had all the dominant genes.

Jonah nodded and gestured to a photograph on the wall that showed a man with short brown hair and a wide smile. "I named the place after him. He was my brother. Samuel. Named my daughter after him too." He plucked the last string and strummed the guitar. "Why don't you two grab a booth? This place fills up on live music night. Me and a couple other acts perform." Jonah played through a chord progression.

Javier and Liz settled at a booth. Before long, the wand-waving guy reached their table.

"What are you doing?" Javier asked.

He held up a finger, then ran the wand over their table and benches. "Sweeping for bugs."

Liz leaned towards the guy. "Bugs? Like . . . microphones?"

"Yeah. We find them sometimes. Actually…" He ran the wand over Javier and Liz. "Okay, you're clean."

Liz laughed. "Who would want to listen to what happens in a diner?"

He answered without looking away from the wand. "Some around here like to have really big ears." He stepped towards the next table.

Javier stood and followed. "Some who?" Leaning close, he whispered, "LifeFarm?"

Wand guy scanned the room and nodded, keeping his own voice low. "It's like a game. They plant, we remove. We sweep whenever newcomers arrive." He looked away, like he was embarrassed.

"You're worried we left something?" Javier asked.

Wand guy shook his head. "I know you didn't. Jonah said your aunt was legit. We rarely find a bug. It's procedure, though."

"Don't they get upset about you removing the bugs? They could shut you down. Or worse."

"We know that. They tried, actually. But we all have secrets." He moved to the next table.

Javier returned to the booth. It seemed the people in this community had problems with bugs of every variety—those that listen and those that could infect. And what secrets would a diner have to use against LifeFarm?

As the sun set and the crowd grew, a bright bug zapper came on outside the window, sending a purple glow into the restaurant. Jonah strummed the guitar and sang an acoustic version of an old pop song into the microphone. Javier glanced at his watch. Sam would be here soon—maybe she would be early, expecting him to be on time. How would it appear if she saw him already seated? Would it make him look desperate?

"Have you noticed something about the people who live here?" Liz asked, interrupting his thoughts.

"Like what?"

"Look around."

He didn't notice anything unusual. "What am I supposed to be seeing?"

"Point out someone my age."

Javier analyzed the place again. "There isn't anyone."

"Right. They're all young."

"Okay. So?"

"Don't you think that's weird?"

"I don't know. The university is in the next town. Maybe there are just more young people around here. Or maybe the older people are afraid to go out at night." He laughed.

"Yeah, because 5:30 is really late." She sipped her soda and bobbed her head to the music. "He's good."

Javier focused on the music, remembering the tune from his elementary school years. Near the end, he glanced towards the bar. With a soda in hand, Sam approached the table, grinning when she made eye contact.

Javier couldn't stop his smile.

"Hi, Hector. Glad you got here early. I forgot it was music night." She held out a hand to Liz. "I'm Sam."

Liz shook it. "Marie."

Sam set her drink on the table. "I'll be right back. I need to say 'hi' to someone." She sauntered across the restaurant towards Jonah, who was in the middle of a chorus. She wrapped her arms around his shoulders and kissed him on the cheek, causing him to hit wrong notes and sing off key.

Laughter moved through the crowd. A few greeted Sam by name.

She took a bow, eliciting more laughter. Javier was enraptured—he could never dream of stealing the show like that.

"They're obviously close." Liz stood. "I'll let you two sit together. There's an empty stool at the bar." She picked up her drink and left before Javier could argue—if he'd wanted to argue.

Sam took Liz's place in the opposite seat. "Glad you could make it." She hooked a thumb at Liz. "I didn't mean to chase her off."

"Oh. It's okay. I think she's giving us space." To keep the awkwardness to a minimum, he added, "She's my aunt. My mom has been pestering her to leave me alone."

Jonah finished the song, and applause followed. Sam cheered. "So, he's your dad?"

She nodded.

"He looks young."

She shrugged. "I guess. Haven't really thought about it. Some people just look young for their age."

"Does your mom look young too?" He suppressed a wince, wishing he could pull the words back as soon as they were out of his mouth. This girl he just met wouldn't want to talk about how her mom looks.

Sam stirred her drink with her straw and pursed her lips. "My mom died when I was fifteen."

Oh God. "I'm sorry." His stomach sank.

"Don't worry about it." She took a sip, eyeing her dad. "She had cancer. It was less than a year after Dad opened this place. I thought he'd shut it down after . . ." She cleared her throat and focused on Javier. "Anyway, this ended up being a good way for him to keep busy. And he wanted to be present for me and my brother." After another sip, she leaned into the table. "So what brings you to Hayes?"

Javier stopped tearing his straw wrapper into nanometer sized pieces and set what remained of it on the table. "I was trying to get a job at the lab down the road. But it didn't work out."

"Really? You're a scientist?"

"Yeah. An entomologist."

"That's bugs, right?"

He nodded.

"They don't do anything like that. What made you look there?"

Javier scanned the crowd; the other patrons focused on the music or on their own conversations. He leaned towards her. "It was a shot in the dark. Have you heard anything about a virus going around?"

"Yeah." She pulled on her sleeve. "It's getting colder now so the mosquitoes aren't as busy, but we think it's coming from them."

"You're right." Javier weighed how much to say. The locals didn't know who to trust, and after being tossed from the lab, he wasn't sure what magic words might get him tossed from here.

"Okay. And . . . you can do something about it?"

"Well…" He glanced at the crowd again. What other options did he have? Sam was his only hope to get connected to the university. "I have what I need to create a vaccine. But there are people out there who don't want me to have it or to tell anyone I have it. I also need to find someone who knows something about virology. That's not my area."

She sat with her mouth agape for a few seconds. "Seriously? That's huge." She stared at the band but didn't seem to be listening. "I might know someone who can help you. I work in the biology department. Brenda teaches virology."

"Really?" Javier's pulse quickened.

She nodded. "We don't get along, but she's definitely not associated with LifeFarm. I'll try to talk to her tomorrow."

"Why don't you get along?"

"She's . . . pretty weird. Nerdy and private. She doesn't get along with anyone, from what I can tell."

That worked for Javier. He'd probably be able to relate to this mystery girl. "If she can help, it's worth a shot."

Chapter Eight

With his case in hand, Javier walked beside Sam towards the four-story building. The sun reflecting off the glass front, which was flanked by brick wings, reminded him of the science building at his own university. He paused to appreciate the nostalgia. He'd spent so much time in the science building that his roommate joked the school could save on Javier's board if they just let him live in the lab.

Inside, the morning light spilled through the high windows. Bleary-eyed students wandered the halls, sipping from travel mugs and oblivious to the presence of a stranger.

Sam walked to a stairwell, holding the door open for Javier. "The elevator has been broken forever. I don't think they'll ever fix it." Following him, she let the door slam behind her. "Brenda's office is on the third floor. She's like a mouse. She skitters around the halls and avoids everyone she doesn't have to talk to—I think she's a little paranoid. My brother worked with her a little his junior year. I was a freshman then."

"Isn't your brother working in pharmacology?" Javier pulled the information from what Sam had offered at the diner the night before.

She rounded the switchback and exhaled. "He worked on his pharmaceutical degree here. Studying virology was a graduation requirement. He's in Arizona now, working on his doctorate. His mentor is there."

Sam opened the third-floor door and turned left. A skinny woman with short, blonde pigtails darted out of a room, scurried down the hall, and entered the last office on the right. As she closed the door behind her, a bang echoed through the empty corridor.

Another woman, this one younger and with long, brown hair, left the same room the skinny woman had left but headed straight for Javier and Sam. She eyed Javier as she walked by.

Sam slowed enough for Javier to catch up then leaned towards him and whispered, "She's LifeFarm."

Javier stole a glance back. "How can you tell?"

"By what she says and teaches. It's obvious. I'm pretty sure she's getting kickbacks from them."

Javier squeezed the handle of his case. If LifeFarm existed under this roof, how could he and the virologist create the vaccine without being discovered?

Sam continued down the hall, stopping at the office the skinny woman had entered. She knocked.

After a few seconds of silence, she spoke to the closed door. "Brenda, it's Samantha Ward. I need to talk to you."

Aside from the nameplate next to the door—Dr. Hagen—there was no indication the office was occupied. Brenda didn't even keep a schedule of office hours, as the professors at Javier's school had.

Sam knocked again.

A moment later, Brenda poked her head out the cracked-open door. She handed Sam an earpiece. As soon as Sam had it hooked around her ear, Brenda, who wore an earpiece of her own, said something Javier didn't understand. It sounded Swedish.

Sam replied in English, gesturing to Javier. "This is my friend, Hector. He knows about the virus and can help us. But he needs a virologist to help him."

The earpieces were translators. Javier had read about them but hadn't seen them in use. He wanted to snatch Sam's off her and try it.

Brenda responded in her own language while pointing at Javier.

"He's an entomologist. You should see what he has. And we shouldn't stay out here in the hall," Sam said.

Scowling at Javier, Brenda opened the door enough for him and Sam to enter. She handed Javier another earpiece from a box full of them then took off her jacket, revealing a short-sleeved shirt featuring an anime character and arms covered with tattoos, mostly of flowers.

Brenda plopped into the leather chair behind the desk, and Javier and Sam sat in the metal folding chairs on the opposite side. Brenda leaned over, studying Javier, but turned her attention to Sam. She spoke, and a second later a soothing female voice speaking English came through Javier's earpiece. "What makes you so sure you can trust this stranger?" Brenda's harsh tone didn't match the translator's at all.

Javier laughed to himself.

"He figured out LifeFarm is responsible for the virus and wants to develop a vaccine," Sam said. "Isn't that why you haven't started developing one from the patients? Because the sick could tell LifeFarm what you're doing if persuaded?" Her words came through the earpiece, but in her own voice, as if she'd spoken into a microphone. "This way, you can keep vaccine development a secret because anyone involved already knows about it."

Brenda shifted in her seat. "He could be here to set a trap. To see what side we're on. And I didn't start a vaccine on my own because it isn't certain the spreading illness is from a single virus." Her eyes went to the ceiling. "Plus . . ." She sat back. "I would be easily discovered here."

Javier straightened up. "What do you mean you don't think the illness is from a single virus? It obviously is. The symptoms are the same—first the patient thinks they have the flu, then it attacks the platelets, causing blood to clot. Unless the virus is successfully treated, clotted blood causes organ failure and death. I tracked patterns around the country. The fatalities are concentrated in the Midwest, in agricultural centers." He looked at Sam. "How could a virologist in the *same region* as the virus not know these details?" He glanced at the door—maybe they should find somebody else.

Brenda slumped and crossed her arms, telling him she already knew everything he'd said. "Have you considered that in working for LifeFarm, you had more resources at hand to figure out such a thing?"

"So you're waiting for them to solve it? That won't happen. And I wasn't working for LifeFarm."

"Of course you were. Otherwise you wouldn't have had access to such extensive data."

Javier clenched his jaw. "My job was to find a way to combat hive demise. Finding the virus was an accident. I used what I found in the bugs and aligned it with patterns of illness in the communities. After I was sure the virus wasn't airborne, I interviewed patients and doctors about symptoms to track patterns further. The numbers weren't supplied to me. I thought I'd made a breakthrough—until they tried to kill me." He fell back into his chair.

Sam pursed her lips. "Brenda, Hector's legit. We talked for hours last night. If he were LifeFarm, he'd have more than enough to turn me in." She glanced at Javier, connecting with his eyes. "I can just tell. I don't know how to explain it."

As he gazed into her dark eyes, he recalled their conversation that lasted until Jonah kicked them out so he could close the diner. They'd talked about family, childhood memories, pets, school . . . anything to keep the night going. His fear of awkward silences had quickly melted away—talking to Sam was shockingly easy. When she used his fake name, his stomach twisted. Even after learning so much about each other, she still didn't know his real name.

The translator's voice interrupted his trance. "Well, he doesn't look like LifeFarm. Those bastards all look the same." She held out her hand. "Let's see."

He lifted the case onto her desk and opened it.

Brenda picked up a cube with each hand and rotated them. "Developing a vaccine is usually a long process. There is a new methodology we can use as long as we don't tell anyone. It hasn't been approved but the vaccine is produced in a fraction of the time." She put the cubes back and scratched a plumeria tattoo on her wrist. "We can't do it here. There are LifeFarm sympathizers. I just finished fighting with one."

"We know; we saw her. I've been dodging her too," Sam said. "Do you have an idea where else we can go?"

Brenda nodded. "There's a lab in Hayes."

"The same one that threw me out yesterday?" Javier asked.

"Did they?" She stood and walked to the door. "Let me call. Come back this afternoon. I have to work now." She opened the door.

Sam took off her translator and gave it to Brenda. Javier picked up his case and followed her example.

On their way down the hall, Brenda's voice stopped them. "Lämna portfölj."

He turned around and pointed to his ear. "I don't understand."

She huffed, stomped to him, and gave him back the translator. "Leave the case."

Javier leaned away from her. "I can't do that. If something happens to it—"

"You came here for help, no? I can get started in here."

Javier glanced at Sam, who shrugged. "It's probably okay."

He couldn't stomach the thought of leaving it. "If it stays, I stay."

Brenda huffed again and grabbed the set off Javier's head, scratching his ear, then stormed back to her office. "Dumhuvud." She slammed the door.

"What did she say?" he asked.

Sam started back towards the stairs. "I don't know, but it didn't sound nice."

****

Charlie set the full plate of food on the placemat in front of him, ready to dig in to the gravy-covered pot roast, potatoes, and carrots. His mouth had been watering since he arrived at Annie's aroma-filled house an hour earlier.

He took his first bite at the same time Mattson entered the kitchen. "Hey, Chuck." Mattson grabbed a plate from the cabinet and piled food onto it from the slow cooker.

"I told you to quit calling me that."

Mattson laughed, apparently pleased with himself that he'd found one of Charlie's goats. He settled in the seat across the table.

"How's school going?" Charlie asked.

"Not bad. When they don't lie to us." Mattson stabbed a chunk of meat with his fork and shoved it into his mouth. "They're giving us all sorts of garbage about LifeFarm feeding the poor in Africa." He rolled his eyes.

"How can you be so sure that's not true?"

"Because it's not. I follow a couple bloggers who've taken video of starving kids in Kenya." After a bite of potatoes, he shook his fork at Charlie. "Think about it: the company has complete control of the media, and they want to make sure they look good to everyone. What better way to do that than to claim to feed the world?"

Charlie shook his head. "Those conspiracy types just want the attention. It's entirely possible that a company like LifeFarm could produce enough food to feed the world's population. It's easy, actually."

"Ha."

"Can you two please stop?" Annie joined them from the family room and filled a plate. "This argument isn't helping anything. It's just noise."

Mattson sipped his soda. "It's not just noise. We're lied to every day. And no one gives a crap."

Charlie slammed his fork on the table. "All that talk will get you is blacklisted. You think any college will want your brilliant mind then, smart guy? You'll be lucky if you can get a job at Taco Bell."

"I do like burritos." He smirked as he chewed.

"Mattson, stop it." Annie looked from her son to Charlie. "Be the adult here, okay?"

They spent the next few minutes eating in silence, until Charlie's phone rang from his pocket. He checked the ID. "It's Sylvia. I have to take this." He left the table, glancing at Annie's holo-dock on her desk, and answered the old-fashioned way when he reached the living room. The fewer eavesdroppers, the better. "Yeah."

"One of our bugs picked up something in Hayes, Iowa. It was in the lobby of a homeless shelter. A couple employees were making jokes about the young Latino guy hanging out with an older lady."

"Seems a little thin. Could be a kid and his grandma. Is there anything else?" After three weeks of silence, this news was better than nothing, but barely.

"No. I thought it seemed promising. Want me to send some guys?"

Charlie stared at the wall, playing out scenarios in his head. After the attempt to nab Mendez at the shelter in Colorado and again at the old man's farm, he couldn't risk another failure—especially based on a theory as thin as this. It only meant more embarrassment for his department. Better to keep those in the know at a minimum. "No. I'll head there myself in the morning. What was the town again? Hayes?"

"Yeah, Hayes. I'll text you the name of the shelter."

Chapter Nine

Javier stared at the black screen, waiting for Boss and his giant forehead to appear. Brenda stood behind him, but it was Javier's job to speak. Brenda didn't like to speak English, after all, and she couldn't hand Boss a translator through the screen.

Javier twisted around. "Can't you just do this? He's gonna toss me out again."

She shook her head and pointed to the screen. Boss was glaring at them.

Brenda had tried to call the lab yesterday after Javier and Sam left her office, but she hadn't been able to talk to anyone. She'd suggested appearing in person, saying the boss knew her and would probably let them in because of that.

Javier shifted his feet. "Uh, hi again. I still need to talk to you, and I brought someone to back me up."

"I see that. Good morning, Dr. Hagen."

"*God morgon.*"

Javier had to consciously not roll his eyes. *Just speak English.*

"I'll be there in a minute." The screen went black.

Javier faced Brenda. "How do you know this guy?"

She held up a finger and fished earpieces from her bag. When Boss arrived, she handed them out and put one on herself.

"Funny to see you here," Boss said to Brenda. "I'm surprised your enormous ego could fit through the door." He pressed his thumb on a small panel and opened the interior door, leading Javier and Brenda into the lab. "We'll talk in here."

As they entered the space filled with work stations and half a dozen employees toiling away with various instruments, unease settled on Javier. Boss and Brenda obviously had a contentious history between them, and neither of them seemed to like Javier. How would they get anything done?

"Are you sure there are no bugs?" Brenda asked.

Boss glared at her. "I don't let anyone in here. If there are bugs, they're in the front room." He addressed Javier. "I'm Trent, by the way. You were right to think she could get you in here, but she's difficult to work with."

Javier wanted to agree but offered an awkward grin instead. *Crap.*

Brenda pointed to Javier. "He has specimens. He wouldn't let me start anything yesterday, so I couldn't verify if they all have the same virus—"

"They do. I wouldn't have brought them all if they didn't." Javier scowled.

She scolded him with her eyes. "We need to determine the type of vaccine to develop and create a prototype." She looked at Trent. "That's simple enough for your lab to handle, right?"

Trent pointed at her. "Look, Hagen. I don't have to allow you in here."

"Yes, you do." Javier stepped between them. "How many around here have died? In Iowa?"

They were silent, so Javier answered for them. "Forty-four, last time I checked. And that's *just* in Iowa. Multiply that by the number of states in the Midwest, add a few more for the other states, then increase it exponentially in the spring when mosquitoes become more prolific, and *maybe* you'll have some grasp of the problem." He looked from Brenda to Trent, then back to Brenda. "Do you think we can stop acting like children for five minutes and do something about it?"

Brenda huffed, grabbed the case from Javier, and stomped towards an empty workbench on the side of the lab. The lab workers had frozen in place, still holding their various instruments, jars, and trays, watching the argument unfold. The only sound came from a cracked iPhone connected to an antique Bluetooth speaker cranking a Justin Timberlake song that was older than Javier.

Trent waved a hand at them. "Show's over, guys. Get back to it." He leaned towards Javier and lowered his voice. "I don't appreciate being scolded in front of my staff. But you're right. Dr. Hagen is a pain in the ass, but she's the best at what she does, and she's majorly anti-corporation. She looks for LifeFarm everywhere. We worked together at the university before I came here. Probably why she thought this would be a good place to operate." He glanced at the place Brenda had claimed. She had opened the case and was removing bees from their cubes. "Our positions on LifeFarm are the only thing we agree on."

Javier hurried to her. No one had touched the bees since he put them into the cubes, and seeing them out sent his pulse through the roof.

They'd have to come out eventually if he and Brenda were to develop a vaccine. Maybe he was confusing anxiety with the excitement that came from finally getting started.

Brenda pulled some equipment from her bag and gathered other supplies from the lab, helping herself to whatever she could find in the cabinets and drawers.

"What do you need me to do?" Javier asked. "And how long do you think this will take?"

"Do nothing right now. Hopefully it won't take too long. I need to work." She took off her ear piece and put it into her bag.

Great. How was he supposed to work with someone who refused to talk to him?

****

After activating his car's self-driving mode, Charlie shifted in his seat, trying to ease the pain in his lower back. He hadn't had to sit still for so long in ages, but driving from California to Iowa— even though the car was doing most of the driving—was a necessary burden if he wanted to get Mendez himself. He was only in Utah and wished he had sprung for a plane ticket despite air travel having become a mostly inaccessible luxury, a side-effect of air traffic control being privatized when he was in high school. The government wouldn't even cover their own employees' airfare unless they had to go over an ocean. Charlie hadn't stepped foot on a plane since he was fourteen.

Charlie imagined arresting Mendez—or shooting him, if the need arose—and he smiled. It would be extra sweet after his security team had failed to get the job done.

His phone rang, and he pushed a button on his stereo receiver, bringing the holo-dock on his dash to life. "Yeah."

A small, projected version of Annie appeared above the steering wheel, complete with her tear-streaked face. "Did you talk to Mattson before you left?"

"A little. Why? What's wrong?"

"I can't find him. He went to a friend's house last night and I haven't been able to reach him."

"Does he normally take off?"

"No. If he's gone for a while, he checks in. His friend said he left early this morning." New tears filled her eyes. "I'm freaking out here, Charlie. Should I call the cops?"

"Not yet. They won't do anything for twenty-four hours after he disappeared." Charlie racked his mind for any clues Mattson might have left. Last night, his nephew had left the table by the time Charlie had finished talking to Sylvia. Where had he been during the call?

"Annie, Mattson might have heard my phone call last night."

"So?"

Charlie pursed his lips, regretting his decision to not take the last night's call outside. "Well, if he was listening, he knows about Mendez and that I'm going to Iowa. I'm not sure why he'd care, though." He shook his head—she needed to hear something more reassuring. "He probably just went for a joy ride, being a dumb kid. We were there once. Remember when you spent a whole school day at the beach? Dad wanted to kill you."

She wiped her face with her sleeve, apparently unaffected by his attempt at nostalgia. "He's been talking funny. You know that. Stuff about the government suppressing infor–"

"Stop talking. We can address that later." If his phone was monitored—and he had no reason to doubt it was—just her saying those words could endanger Mattson. And possibly herself. "Call the cops in the morning if he doesn't turn up. Keep me posted."

****

Liz looked up when the bells on the diner's door jangled, then went back to filling the napkin holders. "Hi there. Welcome to Sam's."

Jonah had given her the job the day before, after she dropped off Javier at the lab for the umpteenth time. With no way to fill the hours and her money running out, she'd gone back to the diner and off-handedly asked Jonah if he was looking for any part-time help. He must have sensed she needed cash, because he said she would "unofficially" work for him and he'd pay her under the table.

"Hey." The lanky teen parked on a stool at the bar and took off his cap. He ran his hand over his short, black hair. "Can I get a burger?"

"Sure thing. Fries?"

He nodded. "A Coke too."

She hollered the order into the kitchen window, a bit of old-diner charm Jonah had insisted on, then returned to her customer. "Haven't seen you around here. You passing through?" Her whole three weeks in town weren't much, but she'd started to recognize the regulars.

"Kind of. I've been driving since last night. I'm meeting my uncle."

The bells on the door jangled again, and Jonah walked in. "Hey, Marie." He joined Liz behind the bar. After putting on an apron, he approached the teen and held out a hand. "Hi. I'm Jonah."

The kid leaned back at first but shook Jonah's hand. "Mattson."

"Cool name. Have you ordered?"

"Yeah."

"Good deal." Jonah patted Liz on the shoulder and walked into the kitchen.

"He's friendly," Mattson said.

"Yeah. Makes him good at what he does." She resumed refilling napkin holders. "The university is in the next town, if that's what you're looking for."

"It's not." He leaned over the counter and lowered his voice. "You're a local, right?"

"Sort of."

75

"You know anything about a virus going around? Something the news won't talk about?"

Liz stepped back, surprised both by his question and by his forwardness. He had no idea who she was or what side she was on. Plus, someone could have planted a bug in the place at any time, which Liz had learned was the reason Jonah introduced himself and chatted up anyone who came into the diner. A stranger was a potential bug planter.

She looked from side to side, as if checking the place, then put a finger to her lips. She nodded.

Mattson smiled and sat back. "I knew it."

****

Charlie rolled into Hayes after sunset. A few businesses were open, including a small grocery and a diner. He tried to focus on the task at hand, but worry about his nephew consumed his mind. Annie had called the police that morning. All they determined was Mattson and his car were missing. They'd discovered no new leads.

Part of him hoped Mattson had come to Iowa after hearing the call, but it seemed silly. Why would a seventeen-year-old kid want to get involved with this? Mattson only knew the authorities were looking for Mendez. He didn't know why. So why would he care?

Of course, all those sites Mattson looked at might have sent him on a crazy mission.

Charlie told himself there was nothing he could do about his nephew at the moment, so he'd need to find Mendez quickly. The shelter was in the next town. If Charlie's theory worked out, Mendez would spend the night in the shelter and work in a lab during the day. All he had to do was figure out which lab—one in town or at the university—and time it out.

His stomach rumbled, and he winced at the memory of the gas station hot dog he'd had for lunch. Not knowing where Mendez would be in the evening hours, he decided he could take time for supper. The diner looked inviting. He parked and headed inside.

A few patrons sat at the bar and a family sat in a booth. A government-planted bug might be here as well, so he'd have to watch his mouth.

One of the customers sitting at the bar with his back to the door caught his attention.

Mattson?

He shook his head and headed towards the bar.

Mattson was shoving fries into his mouth, oblivious to his surroundings.

"You'd better call your mom. She's worried sick."

Mattson jerked up.

Charlie put his hand on the bar. "What the hell are you doing here?"

Mattson glanced at the lady behind the bar, then to Charlie. "I heard you on the phone. I decided to check it out."

"You're a fool. Things could get ugly."

"Yeah? Well, maybe I want to see for myself."

Charlie sat on the neighboring stool.

"Can I get you anything?" the lady asked. With a shaking hand, she placed a napkin and a set of silverware in front of him.

Charlie nodded without looking up. "In a minute." He leaned towards Mattson. "You need to go home. Your mom called the cops."

Mattson wiped his fingers on a napkin. "I will. Later."

"You have no idea what you're getting into."

"Exactly. Maybe I want to learn. And now that you know where I am, don't you want to make sure I'm safe?" Mattson leaned over and whispered into Charlie's ear. "Besides, what's going on that's so bad the government would have to bug public places?" He sat back and raised his eyebrows before shoving half a dozen fries into his mouth.

Charlie clenched his fist. Where did Mattson get his information? Odds were even if he got Mattson to agree to go home eventually, he'd stay in Iowa for a little while to see what happened. "All right. You can stick around for a day. Got it? One. Day. You're heading home after that."

"I'll be done when you are."

"Dammit." Charlie stood and ran his hand over his head. Then a thought hit him: if Mattson stayed, Charlie could redirect the kid's thinking, discrediting whatever nonsense Mattson read online, with proof. He might not have a chance like this again. The way Mattson was going, he'd be the next Mendez.

Charlie reclaimed his seat. "All right. You win. You can stay. But if I find what I'm looking for, you have to wait in the car."

Mattson gave Charlie a thumbs-up and popped more fries into his mouth.

Charlie looked towards the waitress, analyzing her face for the first time. She made eye contact but broke it a moment later, giving all her attention to wiping the counter.

It couldn't be her. Why would Mendez's accomplice be working in a diner in Iowa?

"Ma'am?"

She looked up, and he gestured to Mattson. "I'll have what he's having."

The woman nodded and yelled the order through a window, all the while avoiding eye contact with Charlie.

****

Get ahold of yourself.

Liz took a long breath to control her panic. She recognized the man from the news the second he walked in the door, and she was failing miserably in her attempt to play it cool. If he hadn't recognized her, her behavior could tip him off.

She avoided looking at him, in case he remembered her from the photograph he'd used in the report. If this guy realized who she was, he would arrest her and possibly force her to tell him where Javier was.

"Ma'am?"

"Yeah." She kept her attention on wiping the already-clean counter.

"Can I ask you a question?"

"Sure." In an effort to act normal, she placed the rag near the sink and made eye contact.

"I'm a department head for Homeland Security. I'm looking for someone who might have come around here. If I show you a photograph, can you tell me if you've seen him?"

She nodded and approached, trying to keep her arms from visibly shaking.

The man pulled a photograph—the one of Javier he'd used in the report—from his pocket and held it out to her.

She studied it without taking it. "He doesn't look familiar."

"Are you sure?"

She squinted, pretending to think. "Yeah, I think I'd remember him."

He pocketed the photo while staring at her. "All right."

"I'll see if your food's almost ready." She retreated into the kitchen.

He hadn't seemed to recognize her. If he had, would he have shown her that picture?

She glanced at her watch. Javier would be done at the lab any minute, and he'd said he'd meet her at the diner. She had to find him before he could do that, or the cop's job would be really easy.

Jonah was working the grill, and she took off her apron as she approached him. "I'm not feeling well. Would you mind if I left a little early?"

He nodded. "That's fine. Take care of yourself."

"Thanks." She hustled out the back door and ran down the street towards the lab.

****

Charlie couldn't believe his luck. The woman had acted just as he'd expected she would when seeing the picture. She was definitely Mendez's partner. All he had to do was wait for her to finish here and follow her.

A few minutes after she'd gone into the kitchen, a guy with dreadlocks pushed the kitchen door open. He held a plate containing a burger and fries, which he placed in front of Charlie. Dreadlocks guy introduced himself.

"What happened to the lady?" Charlie asked after he shook Jonah's hand.

"She needed to head out. I've got you taken care of." He took Mattson's soda glass and refilled it.

Shit.

Charlie glanced towards the door, then to Mattson. "I forgot something in my car. I'll be right back."

Chapter Ten

Javier watched Brenda inject the guinea pig with the first prototype of the vaccine. When she removed the needle and let go of the animal, it darted to the corner of its cage.

Brenda stared at it while scratching her tattooed arm. Oblivious to the importance of this moment, Trent and the other lab techs worked on the same white powder they'd been manufacturing all day, every day, since apparently long before Javier arrived and in the three weeks since. It seemed to be the only reason the lab existed. Trent had said the powder was a nutritional supplement but insisted Javier not try taking it—an odd directive, as Javier hadn't considered ingesting the stuff. But now that Trent had said that, Javier wondered what would happen if he did take some. He'd decided to wait until after the vaccine was finished before risking it, in case there was more to it than Trent said and it hurt him somehow.

As Brenda kept her attention on the cage, Javier frowned. What was she waiting for? An immediate reaction? "Now what?" He adjusted the translator headset, thankful she'd let him keep it today.

"We wait and see." She dropped the syringe into a sharps container but kept her eyes on the guinea pig. "If there's an adverse effect, we'll know by morning. If nothing happens, either the vaccine is safe or it's not strong enough."

"Not strong enough? Are we guessing?"

"We're in a rush. If the animal survives, we'll distribute to a human population and see if they continue getting sick."

"That sounds kind of sloppy." *And dangerous.* Could people accidentally die from a problem with the vaccine? Voicing his concern might make her stop talking, so he kept his worry to himself.

She scowled. "Creating a new vaccine the traditional way usually takes years—up to a decade. We don't have that kind of time. Even the new protocol takes a few months, minimum. So I'm using that and cheating a little."

"Cheating."

She glared at him. "Do you want this quickly or not?"

"What if it hurts people?" To hell with his worry. If the antidote was as dangerous as the disease, he'd have to find another solution.

Brenda reached for the translator on his ear.

He cupped it in his hand and stepped away. "You need to tell me the truth. Is there any risk to people?"

She slumped and said an attitude-laced "No" in English. "Sit down."

After a moment of hesitation, he did so, though he leaned away.

"The risk is minimal. Any problems will be from patients with allergies to the components. Our bigger concern is if it's not strong enough. I'll inject myself first if you're worried." She loaded supplies into her bag, clearly not waiting for Javier to respond.

From the oldies station playing on the old stereo, a Fall Out Boy song started, and one of the techs pretended a flask containing a white substance was a guitar, making the other techs laugh. Trent scolded him with a reminder about the importance of their work.

If it was a nutritional supplement, why was Trent so serious about it? Maybe Brenda knew what it was. She wasn't from the town, but she'd worked with Trent in the past. She hadn't taken the translator, so it was worth a shot.

"Brenda, do you know what they make here?"

She glared at him, then focused on the bag she was loading. "Ask Trent."

"I did. He wouldn't tell me."

"Then I shouldn't tell you." Her eyes shifted to Trent.

"Just tell me. I know you don't care about protecting him. And you know I'm here to help."

She zipped the bag closed. "We'll check on the guinea pig tomorrow and plan from there." She held out her hand.

Javier brought his hand back to the ear piece. "Tell me first. Trent said it's like a vitamin. If that's true, then people ingest it, right? What if it affects the vaccine?"

"It won't affect the vaccine. I would know that." She reached for Javier's head.

Javier pulled back. "I helped you. If it weren't for me, you wouldn't have been able to create the vaccine."

"That doesn't obligate—"

"It proves you can trust me. You know I don't plan to hurt anyone." He raised his eyebrows.

She pursed her lips, moved her bag, and sat on the stool, leaning towards him. "It's our salvation."

Javier internally groaned. Plenty of "magic pill" companies had sprung up since LifeFarm took over everything. They promised to cure illnesses or even prolong life, but they always proved to be snake oil. But Brenda was smart—why would she fall for that? "I think you mean our salvation is there." He pointed at the guinea pig.

She shook her head. "Not from the virus. From LifeFarm. It's how we'll resist their power. Overtake them." She stopped speaking when the song on the stereo ended, and she drummed her fingers on her bag while she waited for the next one to start. After a quiet instrumental introduction played, she continued, still in a low voice. "It's how they came into power, and they think they control the entire supply. They don't know we have it."

"What are you talking about?"

Four loud bangs came from the door. After a few seconds, four more sounded.

Trent headed to the door, where he pressed the button for the intercom. "Can I help you?" His tone was sarcastic, likely in response to the disruptive hammering.

"I need to speak to Hector. It's an emergency." Liz's voice echoed from the speaker.

Javier glanced at the clock—he was a little late meeting Liz at the diner, but that certainly didn't warrant her tracking him down.

"Just a second." Trent eyed Javier, who took off the translator and made his way to the door.

Javier cracked it open and stuck his head out.

Liz yanked him into the front room. "Come on. They found us."

****

Liz pulled Javier onto the path, but he forced his arm away. "Wait. Who's 'they'?"

"That Homeland Security guy. From the news. He showed me a picture of you asking if I'd seen you." She eyed the front door. Where should they go? "Would it be safe to hide here?"

"No. We might have already said too much here." He continued down the path.

Liz followed him towards the dark street—it wasn't dark enough to hide their presence. "Let's go behind the buildings."

"The cop didn't recognize you. We have time to get to the van. This way is faster."

As they hurried away from the lab, a yell stopped them. "Hey!"

Holding her breath, Liz turned.

Trent stood on the porch, holding up the thermal bag Javier used to bring lunch to the lab. "You forgot this."

Javier dashed up the path while Liz kept her eyes on the diner. *We don't have time for this!*

Lunch bag in hand, Javier ran back to her. The lab's door slammed closed behind Trent. Liz winced and stole another glance at the diner.

****

Charlie stopped on the sidewalk, looking up and down the street. Which way would she have run? If Mendez was in a lab, she'd head there, but what does a lab in the middle of Iowa look like from the outside?

He picked a direction and as he passed the loud buzz of a bug zapper, a door slammed shut a few buildings down. A woman—the waitress—peered back at him then grabbed the arm of the bearded man standing with her. They took off, running along the dark side of the street.

Mendez.

Charlie yanked his pistol from its holster. "Freeze!"

The two kept running, ducking into an alley between a house and a convenience store. Charlie quickened his pace and caught up.

Mendez was standing atop a closed dumpster and pulling the woman up, apparently heading for the roof. "No, Liz! Put your foot over on that ledge. It's how I got up."

Charlie aimed his weapon. "I'd stop right there if I were you."

Mendez froze, holding Liz a foot off the ground by her arm.

She kicked and swayed. "Let me go. We're not gettin' up there now."

Mendez released her, and she dropped to the ground with a grunt. He stayed on the dumpster and glanced at the roof.

Would he leave her behind?

Charlie approached the dumpster. "Come on, young man. I can shoot you down from there and be a hero."

"So why don't you?" Mendez moved to the edge of the dumpster, the metal banging with each step. "What do you have to gain from keeping me alive?"

"Good point." Charlie centered the weapon on Mendez's torso and wrapped his finger over the trigger.

As he fired, someone yanked his arm. A bright flash and echoing boom filled the dark alley.

The bullet hit the dumpster with a ping, and Charlie glared. "Dammit, Mattson! What the hell do you think you're doing?" He yanked his arm away from his nephew's grip and resumed his stance.

Mendez darted for the other side of the dumpster.

Mattson grabbed Charlie's arm again. "You can't kill him, *Charlie*."

"Watch me. They're resisting arrest."

Mendez jumped to the ground and stood next to Liz, who struggled to her feet. Charlie kept the gun trained on Mendez's chest. He could get the kid and spare the woman, though it wouldn't be hard to concoct a story explaining why she was in the line of fire.

As Charlie brought his finger to the trigger, Mattson stepped in front of the gun. "Ask him why he's here."

Charlie's breath caught—half a second later and he would have shot his nephew. "You know why he's here. Move." Charlie shoved Mattson's shoulder, but Mattson didn't budge.

"No, I don't. Because I only know what the news says. He doesn't look like a child killer or drug pusher to me."

Charlie looked over Mattson's shoulder at the two fugitives. Liz eyed the street.

Mattson leaned into Charlie's line of sight. "Ask him!" He ran to Mendez and stood directly in front of him. "I'm not gonna let you shoot him if you don't. You'll have to shoot me first."

"Let me?" Charlie focused the weapon on the few inches of Mendez's face that was unprotected by Mattson's neck. The vile taste of rage sat in the back of his throat. He glared at his nephew, his hand shaking as he clenched the gun. He could end this in a second, eliminate the threat, and be a hero in the eyes of anyone who mattered.

Why was Mattson willing to die to protect this kid?

"Fine." With irritation knotting his stomach, Charlie lowered the weapon and made eye contact with Mendez. "Why are you here? Why Iowa? You could have run off to Mexico."

Mendez remained silent.

Charlie raised the weapon again. "I suggest you answer. I'm a good shot."

"Just tell him." Liz pulled away from Mendez's grasp.

Mendez gave Mattson a gentle push to the side and pointed to the street. "You saw the bug zappers."

"What does that have to do with anything?"

"Someone has to stop the virus. I'm close to a vaccine."

"The virus is a fabrication. Your bees proved nothing. Scientists and firms have been making that shit up for years to bring down LifeFarm."

"Did they tell you to say that?" Mendez stepped towards Charlie. "You know the truth. You have to."

"I know you want to damage the progress we've made. To irreparably harm LifeFarm's image. This virus is nothing. It will go away."

"It won't go away. It can't go away. LifeFarm made sure of that. How much are they paying you to protect them?"

"Boy, you better watch your mouth." Charlie tightened his grip.

****

"If you were gonna shoot me, you would have done it by now." Javier ignored the metallic taste in his mouth. "You can believe what LifeFarm tells you, or you can believe what the science says. If left unaddressed, the virus will wipe out thousands of people. And because of your bosses, we can't kill the carrier insects. They can't let that information get out. That leaves *us* to create a vaccine." He forced himself to take another step towards the man about to shoot him. Mattson was close by but wasn't acting as a shield any longer. "I don't know what LifeFarm has to gain from killing its customers, but that's exactly what's happening. The best I can figure is they're waiting for the virus to reach crisis level so they can charge exorbitant amounts for a cure. Isn't that why you have to stop me? They can't extort anyone if we also have the vaccine."

"See? What'd I tell you?" Mattson ran to Charlie and held his arm towards Javier. "The news says this guy's a killer, and he's trying to save everyone!" He grabbed for the weapon.

Charlie pulled it away. "Don't." He holstered the gun and stared at Javier, as if weighing his options. "I want you to show me."

"Show you . . . the vaccine?"

"You'd better be smarter than you sound or this vaccine will be worthless."

Javier's heart raced as hope invaded—maybe he could get this cop on their side. "Yeah. I'll take you right now." As he brainstormed how to get Trent to let them into the lab, the other possibility hit him—Charlie wanted access to destroy the vaccine. "Or in the morning." That would give him time to figure out a plan.

Charlie shook his head. "We'll go as soon as it's empty. The fewer people involved, the better."

"I don't have access if no one's there."

Charlie stomped to Javier and stuck a finger in his face. "You're gonna figure out how to get access, or we're back to the original plan." He opened his jacket enough to remind Javier the gun was readily available.

Javier drummed his fingers on his leg. What if he figured out an escape before morning? Brenda could finish and distribute the vaccine without him, and Charlie wouldn't have an in to the lab or even know where it was.

But if Charlie did know where it was, no one at the lab knew about him. Javier had to keep the lab protected, and fortunately, he had a way. "I can get us in if we wait until morning. The virologist gets there early, before anyone else. She'll let us in. She trusts me." No way she would let them in. All he had to do was drop the code word they'd created to warn each other in case LifeFarm became an immediate threat.

Charlie scowled and grabbed Javier's arm. "All right. We'll wait in my car."

****

With Mendez and Liz in the back seat and Mattson in the front, Charlie parked across the street from the building Mendez said was the lab. His car didn't have the protective barrier between the front and back seats that a patrol car would have, so he'd have to stay awake all night.

Charlie eyed Mendez in the rear-view mirror. "What time does the virologist get here?"

"Early. Around 5:30." Mendez stared out the window.

"Does she use the front door?"

"Of course she does."

Charlie twisted around and pointed. "I don't need you for this. You've given me enough. I can get to the lab and to the vaccine without you."

"So why keep me around?" Mendez scratched his beard.

"Mattson thinks there's more to this. I want to see if he's right. The first indication you're not doing what you say, I'll make sure this ends here." That should be enough to keep the kid in the car. "I need to make a phone call." Charlie opened the door and stepped out.

Shutting the door behind him, he accessed Sylvia's number and walked across the street, keeping his eyes on the car. "Hey. It's me. We need to pull something together, and we need to do it quickly."

Chapter Eleven

Javier bit the inside of his cheek as he watched Charlie pace outside, holding his phone against his ear. Who was he talking to? And if this was the guy who arranged the security team to come after him back in Colorado, why would he bother keeping Javier alive now? There could only be one reason.

Or maybe two reasons. Mattson seemed to be close to Charlie, maybe even family. Yet the kid saved Javier's life. He could provide enough pull for Javier and Liz to get out of this.

Javier glanced at her. She was staring out the window, likely at nothing in particular. If he hadn't gone down that damn alleyway, they might have been able to evade Charlie. She'd wanted to continue down the main street. And now they were prisoners with no idea how to escape.

Shaking off his regrets of the evening, Javier focused on what he could control: Charlie's access to the vaccine. Javier's ability to save it all came down to timing: Brenda would arrive at the lab half an hour before he'd said she would. Assuming Charlie fell asleep, that would get her comfortably inside instead of walking up the path, where he likely wanted to intercept her. Brenda would have the vaccine, the gun they kept hidden in a cabinet, and the upper hand, once Javier passed along the code word.

But if Charlie saw her arrive, he might jump early. Game over.

Charlie was still occupied with his phone, so Javier could risk getting a little more information. He leaned forward, addressing Mattson. "How do you know him?"

Mattson sat sideways in his seat. "Charlie's my uncle."

"Your uncle?" Javier glanced outside again. "I get why he's here. Why are you here?"

"To save you, apparently." He smiled, showing his perfectly straight, bright teeth. "I heard him talking on the phone to someone who tracked you down the day before he left California to come here. I guessed you were doing something noble, or the government wouldn't be trying to off you. So I left that night and beat him to it."

"Oh." Javier sat back. "Thanks."

Mattson laughed. "Anytime. Just so you know, I don't think Uncle Chuck plans to jump on board with you."

Liz laughed. "You don't, huh? Darn. Thought I made a new friend."

Charlie returned to the car, bringing the weight of the situation with him. "Let's get some sleep. I'm setting the alarm. If you leave, you'll wake up half the town."

****

Liz leaned against her arm on the window, wishing she had something soft to rest on and that she could turn off the street light invading their space. The shelter would have thrown away her belongings, since she hadn't come back before curfew. It didn't matter, though. Whatever happened in the morning would determine their next step, and it would likely involve running away again, assuming they figured out a way to escape. She'd have to figure out how to get her purse—her money—from the diner. She'd forgotten it in her rush to find Javier.

Discomfort took hold in her gut. She'd started to like this place. Jonah was one of the best bosses she'd had, and Sam and Javier seemed to grow closer every day. Leaving her wouldn't sit well with him—a budding new romance was especially difficult to leave. Though maybe it hadn't hit him yet. He was more concerned about the lab, or at least according to what he said.

As she leaned her other arm on the back of the seat and lowered her head to rest on it, her eyes caught Javier's.

He checked the car's other occupants. Mattson was asleep, mumbling a little. Charlie was reading something on his phone. Javier focused on Liz again and brought his finger to his lips. On the seat between them, he traced capital letters that faced her: W-E

After Liz nodded, he wrote out the rest of his message. W-I-L-L F-I-G-H-T

Liz took over and wrote her own message: H-O-W-?

Javier pursed his lips. T-R-U-S-T M-E

His message didn't help her predict what would happen, but the prospect of fighting gave her hope. She couldn't let LifeFarm keep her on the run.

****

A muffled pop followed by breaking glass yanked Javier awake. The noise came from the lab.

He sat up in horror—how could he have fallen asleep? He'd planned to stay awake and keep an eye on the building so he'd know when Brenda arrived. The clock on the car's dash read 4:23. Was Brenda early? The sun was starting to rise.

The time zone. Charlie had come from California. It was 5:23 here. Brenda would have arrived by now, but Charlie was still in the car, staring out the window at the lab.

"What was that?" Javier kept his eyes glued to the building.

"Shut up," Charlie said.

Three armed men dressed in dark clothing ran out and away from the road. They'd have to run between buildings that way— why do that?

Javier pulled on the handle of his locked door. "What the hell was that?"

"I said, shut up."

"Dammit!" Javier punched the back of the cop's seat. "I thought you wanted to see the vaccine. What did those guys do?" His stomach knotted. All of his work might be destroyed, and what if Brenda had arrived on time? He had to get in there and find out. He slammed the door with his shoulder. "Let me out of here!"

Charlie pointed his gun at Javier. "Settle down. That lab is dangerous. My men confirmed it. They're running to decontamination right now. You had no business being in there."

Javier's chest tightened.

Charlie's phone chimed, and he glanced at it. "We can go." He pushed a button on the key fob, disarming and unlocking all the doors.

Javier rushed out and ran towards the building so quickly he tripped. He reached the front door and flung it open, slamming it against the brick wall. The hydraulic arm was broken.

In the front room, bits of glass crunched under his shoes, the result of the screen being shattered. The thumbprint lock was smashed and the inner door open a crack.

Javier's braced himself for what he might find inside—the guinea pig dead or stolen, his bees gone, his research destroyed along with any hope of defeating the virus.

With Liz, Charlie, and Mattson following, Javier pulled open the door and entered the dark, silent lab. After flipping on the lights, his eyes went straight to his work station, then to the floor in front of it.

Brenda lay in a pool of blood coming from her head.

Javier fought the urge to vomit and rushed to her side. Her dead eyes stared at the ceiling, and blood obscured her blonde hair above her ear. Javier lifted her hair, discovering a golf-ball-sized hole. His stomach rolled again. Powering through the visceral reaction, he turned her head and found the entrance wound above her other ear.

His mind racing and his face hot, he jumped to his feet, spun around, and slammed himself into Charlie with a scream, smashing him into the wall.

With his arm pressed against Charlie's neck, Javier grabbed the gun. Twisting, he freed the weapon from Charlie's hand then stumbled backwards, training it on the cop's head. "You asshole! You killed her! Admit it or I'll blow off your damn head!"

Charlie held up his hands. "She resisted, or they wouldn't have killed her."

"Of course she did! She knew what was at stake!" Keeping the gun pointed at Charlie, Javier inched his way to the counter. The guinea pig's cage was smashed, as was the animal inside. The locked cabinet where he'd kept the bees and all of Brenda's supplies had been pried open and cleaned out.

But Javier's work wasn't the only target. Half of the cabinets in the lab were open, equipment was smashed, and white powder covered one counter and the floor beneath it.

Javier rushed to Charlie, stopping with the gun barrel against his bald head. "Sit on the floor."

"Is this how you want to go, boy? You're not fighting for anything here now." Charlie glared into Javier's eyes. "Threatening me is an automatic life sentence."

Hot tears burned Javier's eyes, but he refused to let them out. "It's either this or the virus. Your guys made sure of that." He pressed the weapon into Charlie's skin. "Besides, you've already tried to kill me a few times. A life sentence would be an upgrade. How many people have been murdered by your subordinates? Maybe I should make sure Brenda is the last."

"Whoa, ease up." Mattson moved from where he'd been frozen by the door, appearing next to Charlie with his palms out. "Let's step back a second."

"What for?" Javier tried to steady his shaking hands and ignore the sweat forming on his brow.

"Maybe Uncle Chuck can help us find the guys who did this. Maybe get your stuff back." Mattson stood face to face with Charlie and forced Javier to back off. "Right, Uncle Chuck? Don't you want to do the right thing?"

Charlie's eyes went from his nephew to the gun, then back. "I did the right thing."

Javier's pulse pounded harder. "You . . ." He shook out his shoulders, steadying his hands. "Killing Brenda was *not* the right thing."

"She shouldn't have been here. Shouldn't have helped you."

"So she deserved to die?" Fury coursed through Javier's body, and it took every ounce of resistance to keep from pulling the trigger. "Don't you see how insane that is?"

Mattson slowly reached for Javier, putting his hand on his shoulder. "There has to be another solution. Killing a federal agent will only make things worse."

Javier swallowed through the lump in his throat. Maybe there was another solution, but he couldn't think of it now. "Liz, go find help."

Liz had crouched next to Brenda's shoe, touching it. "Who? The authorities are the ones who did this."

"Just find . . . someone. I need to figure out how to reach Trent. He needs to know about this."

She stood and put her hands on her hips. "I have an idea."

****

Liz ran down the street towards the diner. It wouldn't open for an hour, but she had to get out of the lab and away from that murderer. The only way Brenda could have wound up dead was if Charlie had arranged it. Liz would wait at the diner until Jonah arrived. He was anti-LifeFarm. He'd have an idea for what to do.

She ran to the back of building, where Jonah's SUV was parked outside—maybe he arrived early to take care of paperwork or prep side dishes for the breakfast rush. She pounded on the back door, and after no one answered, she pounded again.

Jonah cracked open the door. "Marie. What are you doing here?"

"I need help. Can I come in?"

Jonah held the door for her and she entered the kitchen. One of the chefs stood at the grill, preparing potatoes. He saluted with his spatula. "Hey, Marie. I found your purse." He pointed to her bag sitting on the end of the counter.

She wrung her hands. "Oh. Thanks." After she retrieved it, she stepped close to Jonah. "I need to talk to you."

****

While Mattson kept watch at the door, Javier sat on a stool a few feet from where Charlie reclined against the wall. Keeping the gun pointed at the agent, he occasionally glanced at Brenda's body, forcing himself to keep his composure.

"What's the plan? Keep me here until . . . what?" Charlie bent one leg and rested his arm on his knee.

"That depends on who Liz finds." He swallowed. "You don't understand what you've done. More people will get sick and die because of this. We were close to a vaccine."

Charlie pointed. "The virus. Isn't. Real."

"You know it's real!" Javier jumped to his feet and knocked over the stool, sending it to the floor with a crash. He closed the distance between himself and the agent, staring into Charlie's eyes. "I don't know what kind of hold LifeFarm has on you, but it's real.

It's killed people. I have . . . had the proof. That's why they tried to kill me in the car accident, isn't it?"

Javier set the stool upright, sat on it, and dropped the weapon to his side as his grief for Brenda and his frustration at losing his research rushed to the surface. He strained to fight back the tears. "We can't kill it. We can only prevent it." He clenched his fists. "You have to help me understand. Why is LifeFarm okay with letting people—their customers—die? How do they make money if everyone's dead?"

Charlie stood and eyed the gun. "It's not like that."

Javier gestured to the room with the gun. "So, enlighten me."

Charlie slumped. "The virus has been overblown."

"No, it hasn't." Mattson left his post by the door and joined them. "You'll see. Sooner or later the truth will come out. He knows." He pointed to Javier. "He can stop it if you stop being an asshole for five minutes and let him."

The front door banged, and Jonah stormed across the room, eyeing Brenda's body and the white powder covering the counter. "Oh, God." He pulled his phone from his pocket, pressed a contact, and held the phone to his ear. "It's Jonah. The Seventh has been compromised. We're heading your way."

Chapter Twelve

Javier drummed his fingers on his knee as he sat on the porch, waiting for Sam to arrive. He was thankful for the brief respite from playing the bad guy. Or the good guy. Or whatever living on the opposite side of the government, the mega-corporation that ran the government, and the majority of the population made him.

On the sidewalk, Jonah paced with his hands on his hips or while talking to Trent on the phone, judging from the things he said. What would a diner owner have to do with this? And since he appeared to be an authority figure in whatever this was, how much did Sam know?

Standing, Javier peered through the lab's front door and propped-open interior door. He could only see Charlie sitting on the floor and leaning against the wall from that angle. Liz was doing a good job keeping him in check.

What would they do with Charlie after this? And with Mattson? Not only had they threatened a government official, but that official now had spent enough time with all of them to pursue them indefinitely, if he didn't arrest or kill them first.

On the other hand, the guy had ordered Brenda's murder in addition to the attempts he'd made to capture Javier. Those had all resulted in someone dying.

They couldn't simply let Charlie go.

An old, silver Volkswagen pulled up to the curb, and Trent rushed out without closing the door. He ran past Javier and to the lab, slamming the broken front door against the brick wall as he bolted inside.

Javier braced himself for Trent's reaction. A moment later, Trent's voice yelling, "Oh, God!" reached him. The memory of what Trent was now seeing flashed in Javier's mind.

No other sounds came from the lab, but Javier guessed decisions were being made. As he headed inside, another voice coming from the street stopped him. "Dad!"

Sam, loaded down with a large backpack, hugged Jonah. She hurried towards Javier, tears welling in her eyes.

An odd mix of joy at seeing Sam and despair from their situation took hold in Javier's gut. "You heard about Brenda?"

Nodding, Sam wiped her face with an open hand. "I can't believe it." She wrapped her arms around him. "How are you doing?"

In an effort to stay in control of his emotions, he'd tried not to think about the answer to that question. He closed his eyes, enjoying her warmth. "I'll live." *Maybe.*

Sam pulled back. "There is a bright side, though."

"Really? What?"

Pulling back, she looked into his eyes. "We've been waiting for this. We knew it would happen. We just didn't think it would be this soon."

"You knew what would happen?"

The door banged against the bricks again and Trent rushed out, followed by the others. Charlie's hands were secured behind him with a zip tie.

"Where's everyone going?" Javier asked.

"We're leaving." Liz slowed, allowing Charlie to pass her and motioning Javier and Sam to walk with her. "Trent said there's a plan."

"There is," Sam said. "I'll fill you in on the way."

"On the way where? And what about him?" Javier held a hand out to Charlie.

"He has to come with us," Liz said.

"What?" Javier shook his head. "No way. What about the guys who trashed the place? They might be looking for him."

"They didn't stick around. I doubt they're hanging out waiting for Charlie to make contact," Liz said. "Besides, what other options do we have? Do you want him chasing us himself?"

Javier scowled. "He's not exactly fighting us. Why would he go along willingly when he was supposed to arrest us?"

She shrugged. "Like I said, we don't have any other options." She hurried down the path to catch up, climbing into the back seat of Trent's car, next to Charlie.

Javier froze, watching everyone move around him. Sam grabbed his hand and pulled him. "Come on. We have to leave."

"What about Brenda?" Javier glanced back at the building.

"Dad will call the cops when we're half an hour away. We have to leave before they get here."

"Wait. Stop." Javier yanked his hand away from Sam. "What the hell is going on? Where are we going? And what does your dad have to do with this?"

She stepped towards him, whispering, "It's a long story. We have about twenty hours of driving ahead of us. The person we'll talk to when we get there will tell you everything."

"No. I need to know what this is about. Brenda is dead and the vaccine is destroyed and I need to know why."

"Hector . . ." She sighed. "You have to trust us. This is something we've been waiting for." She took his hand and led him towards the street.

He stopped her. "Wait. I have to tell you something."

She tilted her head. "What?"

"I'm not . . ." He shut his eyes. "My name isn't Hector."

She pulled her hand away. "What do you mean?"

"Hector was the name of my friend back in Puerto Rico. My name is Javier."

"Javier." Her eyes narrowed, and the corners of her mouth curled up. "I'm guessing the reason you lied is also a long story."

He chuckled. "Yeah. You can say that."

"Well," she tilted her head towards the street, where Jonah had plopped himself behind the wheel of her car, "we have plenty of time for long stories."

Javier followed Sam to her car but stopped short of climbing in—his bees were gone, but maybe not all hope of creating a

vaccine was lost. "Hold on. I need to grab something inside."
Without waiting for an argument, he jogged back up the path.

After creeping through the silent lab, Javier grabbed a paper
towel and reached into the guinea pig cage, wrapping his fingers
around the smashed animal. He made a mental note to pick up a
cooler and dry ice at their first stop.

He stared at Brenda's body one last time, his heart aching.
"I'm not sure how yet, but I think we did something significant.
And I'll make sure we finish this." He held up the guinea pig, as if
she could see it and understand. Part of him wanted to believe she
could. "They won't win, Brenda. I promise."

Without another look back, he rushed out the door.

****

Liz put Charlie's gun in the pocket behind Trent's seat but
kept her eye on the cop. Charlie sat perfectly straight, with his
hands bound behind him, though a few times since their journey
started hours ago, he nodded off. Mattson glanced at them from the
front seat periodically but stayed quiet, until he managed to scare
the crap out of her and everyone else in the car with a "Hey!"
shouted in Charlie's direction.

Charlie jerked awake, and as Liz's pulse settled back to
normal, he glared. "What the hell was that?"

Mattson smirked. "I just realized I was right and wanted to rub
it in."

"You were right?" Charlie shifted. "I'm only going along with
this so you can see what's really going on here."

"I'll tell you what's going on here." Trent's eyes darted from
the windshield to the rear-view mirror. "We have to rush the plan."
He rubbed the back of his neck.

"All right." Liz crossed her arms. "I'm tired of the 'saying
stuff but not saying anything' nonsense. Just say it. What plan?"

"Robert—the man in Arizona—will explain all that." Trent
twisted around, eyeing Liz directly for a moment. "I'll say this has
been in the works for twenty-five years, and we've been waiting
for the right time. It's not the right time but now we have to move
forward because of the Seventh." He shook his head. "Sorry.
Hayes. Because of Hayes."

Mattson sat back and nodded. "Yeah, that's what I'm talking about. I read about this stuff. Underground plans? Secret meetings, right?" He punched Trent on the arm and leaned forward. "Right?"

"Don't touch me!" Trent glared at Mattson while the car drifted into the oncoming lane. Another car was a ways off but closing the distance between them.

"Trent!" Liz held her breath.

From behind them, Jonah honked.

Trent's attention snapped back to the road, and he corrected his course.

Trent eyed Liz in the mirror again. "Does this kid have to stay with us?"

"Yes." She stared at Charlie. "We'd be dead if he hadn't shown up."

****

Charlie scratched the back of his hand the best he could with them bound behind him—was the chip working? He'd argued with his supervisor when the department released the things, but after a rash of officer kidnappings and ransom demands, he agreed to the implant. Now, being tracked didn't seem so bad. He'd missed his last scheduled check in. One more, and it would only be a matter of time before a team was dispatched. They'd be in Phoenix by then, and the woman's gun would be of little use. He could then alert the team to whatever was going on with this "Robert" guy and get Mattson back to his mother.

That is, if the chip was working. His hadn't been in the recalled batch, but he'd never had reason to test it.

Charlie arched his aching back, assuring himself that he'd have both relief from sitting and an answer in a few hours.

Chapter Thirteen

As Phoenix came into view, Javier shifted in his seat. Jonah had said they'd get answers there, but how could that be? All the work Javier and Brenda had done on the vaccine was stolen, and even if he had the bees and another virologist, they'd have to start all over—unless the guinea pig managed to survive its adventure in the miniature cooler.

Sam's brother had studied virology. Maybe he would know the best course of action, and Sam had said he would meet them when they arrived.

In a busy commercial area, Jonah parked in the lot of a large building with a large, marble sign that said *Desert Industry* standing in the grass. "Come on. We're a little late."

Trent parked in the neighboring spot, and everyone left the vehicles. A burst of heat hit Javier—Phoenix didn't get a reprieve from summer, apparently, even in November. With Jonah taking the lead and Liz with a now-unrestrained Charlie bringing up the rear, they entered the building. Liz likely kept the gun in her purse until they were in a less public place, though Charlie went along as a compliant prisoner.

A young man with tan skin and dark hair stood inside the front door. Sam rushed past the group, giving him a big hug. Javier scowled. *That guy had better be her brother.*

Jonah hugged the stranger next, then faced the group. "This is my son, Damien. He works here with Robert."

Damien offered a casual wave. "I'll take you to our lab. Follow me." He led them past the elevators and to a stairwell. "Our space is in the basement and not accessible by elevator."

When they reached the correct floor, Javier moved to the front of the group, walking next to Damien. "I was working on a vaccine for the virus. I was hoping you could help me start again on that."

They reached a door with white lab coats hanging outside it. "I'm afraid we have bigger fish to fry."

"Bigger than a pandemic?" Javier looked back to Sam and Jonah—had he been wrong to trust them? "People are dying."

"Yeah." Damien pressed his thumb onto a glass plate, and the door hissed open. "You'll see."

"No, stop. I'm beyond tired of no one explaining anything." Javier glared. "People are dying. I had a way to keep that from happening, and not only was it stolen from me, the virologist helping me was murdered. That tells me we were on the right track."

"I understand. Robert can explain better than I can. I will tell you that if we solve the bigger problem, the virus will sort itself out."

"How? I'm not going in there until you tell me."

"Javier . . ." Sam put her hand on his shoulder. "LifeFarm already has a vaccine."

From the back of the group, Charlie snickered, followed by an order from Liz to be quiet.

"What?" Javier stepped back. "How could you know that? And if it's true, why didn't you tell me before I wasted all that time, risked my life, and got Brenda killed?" His yell echoed through the hall.

Damien pursed his lips and stepped past Javier, addressing the others. "Please, step inside. Ma'am, you can leave your weapon with me. I'll secure it for you."

Javier snapped around; Liz had the gun trained on Charlie again. If it was because of the laugh, she wasn't putting up with any nonsense from him.

"That's not a good idea." Liz tilted her head towards Charlie. "Maybe I'll wait here with him. He probably shouldn't know everything anyway."

Damien looked from Liz to Javier then back to Liz. "All right. Everyone else, come inside. Robert is waiting for us." He held open the door.

Liz made Charlie sit on the floor, and the others filed into the lab. Javier stood in place.

"Come on." Sam took Javier's hand. "It'll be okay. I promise."

"Nothing about this feels okay." He glanced back at Liz guarding the cop. Would she be okay on her own?

Sam reached out and squeezed his hand, leading him into the lab.

The others had crowded around a workbench, where a tall, blond man stood with his hands clasped in front of him. He looked up and smiled when Sam and Javier entered. "Samantha! So good to see you again. Though I am surprised it is so soon."

"Hi, Robert. And I know." She hugged Robert then gestured to Javier. After an introduction, she said, "He's the one I told you about who was working on the vaccine."

"Oh, of course." Robert approached Javier. "I'm sorry we couldn't tell you the truth earlier. We thought if you and your virologist friend succeeded in creating the vaccine, it would create another front in our attack."

"Wait, what?" Javier held up his hand. "Sam was right? If that's true, why was Brenda killed? They wouldn't have cared if we created the vaccine when they already had it."

"If anyone else has the vaccine, they can't extort people who need it. LifeFarm, and the government, must maintain control, and they will do anything to do so, even if it means killing the opposition."

Javier huffed, remembering waking up in the back seat of the sedan back in Colorado and Brenda's body lying on the floor of the lab. "You have no idea."

Robert put a hand on Javier's shoulder, leading him towards the workbench. "Again, I apologize most sincerely. Your discovery would have been a great asset. I trust what I'm about to tell you all will satisfy your curiosity. Please." He tilted his head to an open space around the bench.

Sighing, Javier squeezed between Mattson and Trent. Instead of scientific equipment covering the counter, as Javier had expected, a paper map of the U.S. took up every inch of space and hung over a few inches on one side. The map was marked with circled numbers on various locations, including Hayes, Iowa, which was covered with a circled number seven in red marker. In the middle of the country was a red, hand-drawn star.

Robert took his place between Jonah and Damien. "It is time to execute the plan we've been forming for twenty-five years. The locations marked here have been activated, but before I explain, you need to know why these places exist. Trent, will you please describe what your job was in Hayes?"

"Sure." Crossing his arms, Trent focused on the map. "We were creating a longevity drug called Deinix." He looked up, connecting with Javier. "That white powder in the lab. Until you and Brenda worked on the vaccine, Deinix was the only purpose for the lab's existence."

"Longevity drug? What's that?" Javier asked.

"Exactly what it sounds like. It gives us longevity. Allows us to live longer than we could without it. Robert created it by accident 130 years ago. Twenty-five years ago, it fell into the wrong hands—"

"Wait a second. Robert," Javier pointed to the blond man, "*that* Robert, created something over a century ago?"

"Exactly." Trent held his hand out. "Robert is . . . what, 160 by now?"

Robert laughed. "Close enough."

"How is that possible?" Javier held up his hands and backed away. "He looks like he's in his forties. What's really going on here?"

"This is the truth, Hector . . . or Javier, I guess." Trent gestured down the line. "Jonah is forty-eight. I'm fifty. We all take the drug, and it slows our aging. A pharmaceutical company attained it several years ago, and they developed it. Rather than sell it or give it away to help people, they used it to protect their own interests in the government."

Javier connected the dots in his head. "They lobbied with it. Made sure legislation always worked in their favor."

"Precisely," Robert interjected. "And these . . ." He put his finger on each numbered circle, in order, "are Seed communities. My colleague and I planted them, if you will, back when the drug left our control. We trained young scientists, like Trent, in small towns to develop Deinix and quietly distribute it to prepare for what we now face—we would need a large number of young people who knew the truth to defend it and save the country from the oligarchs and corporate interests." He put his finger on the circled seven. "Hayes was the seventh, and the last, Seed. As you can see, no two communities are within a thousand miles of each other, and only the head scientist in each one—Trent, in this case—knows about the other communities."

Mattson looked up from the map. "Okay, but how will a bunch of random people fight the government like that?"

Trent put his finger on the red star, centered over St. Louis. "That's where this comes in. There's a facility near here—"

A siren wailed from the hallway, followed by white smoke spilling under the door.

****

Thick smoke poured from one of the grenades that had bounced down the hall, and Liz covered her face with her shirt collar. The gas from the other still managed to break through and burn her throat.

Coughing, Charlie jumped to his feet and squeezed her arm, grabbing the gun. She gripped with all her strength, but with a twist the cop had relieved her of the weapon.

He pointed it at her. "Up the stairs. Now." His eyes were watering but he ignored them.

Overhead sprinklers came to life, showering them with cold water.

"Shit." Charlie nudged her in the back with the barrel. "Hurry up. My people are out there."

"Your people? How did they—" She coughed. "How did they find us?"

"Just go!"

As water and smoke blurred her vision, she reached the stairwell. A man dressed in riot gear handed Charlie a gas mask.

Riot Gear man grabbed Liz's arm and pulled her up the stairs. As they reached the ground floor, the air cleared. He led her across the lobby and through the front door.

****

Removing the mask, Charlie examined the lot—five cars and a Homeland Security van. Overhead, a drone monitored the property. Perfect. They could capture everyone and leave without breaking a sweat.

He turned around, facing the door. Mattson and the others would appear any minute. That gas was pungent as hell.

"Chief." A middle-aged man wearing a suit shook Charlie's hand. "Glad to see you're okay. We responded as quickly as we could when your unit alerted us to your location. When we followed the signal downstairs and saw the woman holding you at gunpoint, we called for backup and moved in."

"Thank you. A group should be here any second." Where were they? Where was Mattson? "There probably isn't another exit from the basement."

"Captain!" A uniformed officer yelled from across the parking lot. "We've got runners!" She ran around the side of the building, followed by three other officers.

"Shit." Charlie ran after them. How the hell did they get out?

From the back of the building, a group that included Mattson ran into an alley. One of the officers pointed her sidearm at them, keeping the other cops from pursuing.

"No! My nephew is one of them!" Charlie ran ahead, into the line of fire.

"They held you hostage, sir. We have orders to shoot on sight."

"Give me a second!" Charlie rushed towards the group.

The officer's voice came from behind him, sounding like she spoke into her radio. "Are you sure? The Chief is going after them."

After a pause, a bang echoed off the neighboring buildings, followed by a whizzing sound.

Charlie spun around and froze. "What the hell are you doing?"

"I have orders, Chief. You might want to get out of the way." The officer held up her firearm.

"I'm getting my nephew! I'd rather not get shot doing it." Heart pounding, Charlie sped up.

Another bang. Another zing.

Mattson looked back as the group reached the street. He didn't slow. A blond man holding a large paper under his arm led the way. Overhead, the drone kept up with them. What was the range on that thing?

Another bang sounded. A sharp pain hit Charlie's hip. He yelled as his legs buckled. *She shot me!*

Mattson broke from the group. "Uncle Chuck!" He ran in Charlie's direction.

Another bullet whizzed by.

Mattson winced. "Let's get out of here." Grabbing Charlie's arm, he heaved the man up, and they stumbled behind the dumpster.

The officers ran after Mendez and the others.

****

Javier squeezed Sam's hand as they ran, following Robert down the street. With gunshots sounding from behind them, Robert took a sharp right onto a sidewalk that lined a busy street. and led the group into a thrift store.

"Where is he going? That drone will see us!" Javier looked back. The cops hadn't caught up yet.

They darted between racks of clothes, reaching the back of the store, where Robert pressed himself into the wall and squeezed behind a bookshelf.

What the hell?

One by one, the others followed. Was this the plan? Hide behind a bookshelf?

Javier and Sam were the last to reach the shelf. Behind it, a door-sized panel was open and everyone was gone. Sam squeezed herself behind the shelf and slipped through the open space. Javier followed close behind, entering a dark office.

Panting, Robert locked the door and flipped on the light. He unrolled the map on the desk. "My friend owns this store. We set up this room as a hideout. We can stay here for a while. The walls resist heat-detection instruments." He coughed.

"The cops will be looking for a while." Javier eyed the door. "If they show up here, why wouldn't employees tell them where we are?"

"They won't. This is a designated hideout. Some of the people here are already on LifeFarm's radar for various reasons, so they won't want to draw authorities. Now," Robert pointed to the red star on the map, "as Trent was saying, this location in St. Louis is a facility that, frankly, we know little about. But we know it's important to LifeFarm to keep it hidden. The next part of the plan is to stake it out—"

"What about Liz and Mattson? We just left them back there," Javier said.

Robert settled into the creaky chair behind the desk. "That is regrettable. Your friends will likely be arrested. We cannot risk breaking them out without being captured ourselves. The plan needs as many as possible."

Javier crossed his arms. "Mattson is Charlie's nephew. He won't be arrested. And I can't leave Liz behind. She saved my life—more than once."

"Javier . . ." Sam stroked his arm. "We need you with us."

"Why? I haven't agreed to anything." He scowled. "You weren't planning on me being part of this before."

Sam's face fell.

"He's right." Trent sat on the edge of the desk. "He deserves to know the whole deal before he comes along, even if only to understand the risk involved. Whether he joins us is up to him."

"So tell me. In any case, I'm going back for Liz."

Damien rose from where he'd been crouching against the wall. "All of the Seeds have been activated. That means anyone who knows about Deinix is mobilizing now, to St. Louis."

"Even the people in Hayes?" Javier asked.

Trent nodded. "I started the process before we left. By the time we get to the point of contact, the few hundred in and around Hayes will be joined by thousands from the other Seeds."

"So our force to take down . . . LifeFarm, or whoever, is composed of thousands of young-looking senior citizens?" Javier raised his eyebrows.

Robert laughed. "Most aren't so old, but chronological age matters little. They don't just *look* young—they *are* young. Trent has the strength and vitality of someone half his age. Deinix slows aging to about a tenth of normal, so while he's aged twenty years, his body 'thinks' it's aged two in that time."

"And not everyone in the Seeds takes the drug," Damien said. "It halts fertility, so only those who don't want children or prefer a natural lifespan take it. There will be more in the resistance than those taking Deinix."

Javier waved his hand. "Okay, I can buy that for a minute. What I'm still fuzzy about is why . . . what are you resisting?"

"You are too young to remember." Robert leaned back in the chair. "Before LifeFarm took control, people had freedoms to develop new ideas in science and industry. We weren't held at the mercy of the government if something they did made us sick. The government answered to the people, those who elected them. Now, they look out only for their own interests."

"You're using 'LifeFarm' and 'the government' interchangeably."

Robert nodded. "You figured it out back at the lab. LifeFarm uses Deinix to buy off government officials. They also control the pharmaceutical industry."

"So . . ." Javier rubbed his neck. "Basically, LifeFarm *is* the government and Big Pharma."

"Precisely. We aren't fighting separate entities. They're all connected."

"That's why they haven't released the vaccine." Sam took off her backpack and set it on the floor. "They'll wait until the outbreak reaches a panic level, then they'll charge ridiculous amounts for the cure. People will pay anything to protect their loved ones."

"And that's why they killed Brenda." An image of Brenda's body, and her pooled blood, flashed in Javier's mind.

Aside from Jonah clearing his throat, the office was silent.

"How can we possibly take down something as huge as LifeFarm?" Javier asked.

"It starts with computers." Jonah moved over to the desk. "With dark networks. We'll access their systems—security, mainly, and break them down from the inside."

"Then what?" Javier asked.

"Then . . ." The corners of Jonah's mouth curled up. "The real fun begins."

"Yeah, a few communities against the whole government sounds like lots of fun." Javier huffed. "I have to get Liz. Anyone want to help?"

Sam crossed her arms. "If you fail, you'll end up in prison."

"I know that. But I'm not leaving her there."

Chapter Fourteen

Liz peeked through the window of the small jail cell. The sun was setting, and the guards had offered little information about what would happen to her. Or to Charlie, who slept restlessly on the cell's only bed. Nice of them to cram all three of them into one cell. After the display of force back at the lab, she didn't buy their explanation that staffing problems meant fewer cells could be used and the setup was only temporary. They just wanted to be assholes.

"Those bastards better do something." Through the bullet-created hole in Charlie's pants, Mattson examined the bandage the paramedics had taped over the wound. "I think he's still bleeding."

"They don't care." Liz sat on the floor under the window. "As long as we're a perceived threat to law enforcement, they can hold us no matter what condition we're in."

"But he *is* law enforcement." Sitting at the foot of the bed, Mattson put his head in his hands.

"He got in the way when they were trying to arrest the others. That makes him the enemy."

"He got in the way to get me." Mattson looked over his dozing uncle.

"Yeah."

"They could have shot him in the back or the head if they wanted to take him out."

Liz shrugged. "They probably would have if he wasn't a federal agent." She closed her eyes, allowing her exhaustion to get the better of her.

As sleep pulled her away, Mattson brought her back. "Do you think Javier and the others will break us out?"

"They might have been captured." She opened her eyes. "Or worse." They weren't in these cells, so if the cops reached them, they obviously hadn't been arrested. Shaking her head, Liz forced her imagination to stop forming scenarios of what might have happened. She couldn't stomach the idea that Javier had been killed, especially after all they'd been through.

Charlie stirred and groaned, lifting himself onto his elbows. "Man, what did they give me?" He fell back onto the mattress with his hand on his forehead.

Probably a horse-sized painkiller. Liz glared at him. "How did the cops find us?" The question had been burning in her mind since the smoke bomb went off. She'd been sure no one followed them while they were driving to the lab.

Charlie held up his hand. "Tracker."

"Huh?"

He pointed to the back of his hand. "All law enforcement personnel have one."

Liz jumped to her feet. "That's why you came along so easily."

With a long sigh, Charlie closed his eyes and folded his hands on his belly.

Mattson stood and backed away. "You asshole."

"Hey." Charlie's eyes popped open. "I had a job to do."

"And they shot you for your trouble."

Charlie sat up on his elbows again. "I did that so they wouldn't shoot you!" He winced. "You should have gone home when I told you."

"No way." Mattson glanced through the plastic wall separating the cell from the corridor, then focused on Charlie. "I was right the whole time. I can't go home and pretend nothing happened. Your buddies killed that woman."

"And if he'd gone home when you found him," Liz added, "you would have shot Javier. And maybe me." The reality that she was trapped with someone who had probably wanted her dead two days ago struck her. "We shouldn't have brought you along. Either of you."

Dozing again, Charlie exhaled deeply. "I didn't know they would kill that woman."

Mattson stared into the corridor. "Yeah, right."

****

The side of Charlie's hip was a giant knot. The drugs the paramedics had injected into him had sent him into a stupor, but staying in a fog became more difficult as the hours passed.

After the sun set, Mattson took off his shirt and bunched it up under his head, using it as a pillow as he stretched out on the floor. Liz slept sitting up under the window—or maybe she had just closed her eyes.

The pain worsened with every minute. Charlie considered yelling for more drugs, but unless the guards at this jail were friendlier than the ones in his hometown, it would have no effect. As part of an authoritarian government, law enforcement ruled without question and any dissenters were locked up indefinitely with little cause. Sometimes, being a "perceived" threat was enough. It didn't matter what condition the prisoners were in. Enough died in custody for the public to notice, but the media only reported on the cases that demonstrated what would happen if someone dared to resist.

After getting in the way of an arrest or "threat neutralization," as the official manual called it, Charlie was now on the other side of the law. Cops and federal agents weren't allowed any more leeway—they were simply made into examples. That kept everyone in check and following orders.

They wouldn't care that he was in pain. All yelling would do was wake up Mattson and Liz.

He sat up on the bed. Moving it seemed to help. He suspected the bullet was lodged in the muscle or perhaps rested against the bone. The risk of a blood infection from a gunshot was slight—the greatest risk was blood loss, and he'd already lasted long enough for that not to be an issue. All that was left was dealing with the pain, which without treatment, would probably last for the rest of his life.

"Hey," Liz muttered.

Charlie connected with her eyes.

112

"How's the hip?" Her words were laced with animosity.

He looked away. "About how you'd expect."

"Nice way for them to show their appreciation for turning us in."

"It didn't exactly go as planned." Standing, he tried putting weight on his leg.

"No shit. If it had gone as planned, everyone would be locked up, not just me. Or maybe you wanted the cops to shoot us all while you and your nephew went home to celebrate. Is that it?"

Charlie swallowed. What could he say?

"So, what happens now?" she asked.

He'd been debating that for hours, and every conclusion he reached was a bad one. "Well . . . usually, when a law enforcement officer breaks protocol, they face a court martial-like hearing and indefinite imprisonment."

"Seems harsh for protecting a family member."

"Doesn't matter. They see Mattson as an enemy. And now so am I, for trying to save him." His words hit him in the stomach— law enforcement was his whole life. He'd sacrificed having a family so he could work the long hours promotion required. He never asked questions when suspicious directives came down the line, because he wanted to be someone the people looked up to. Someone his sister, nephew, and at one time, his wife, would respect.

And now it was gone. Even if he was excused from the charge and avoided prison, he would never work in law enforcement again.

The thought weighed heavy on his chest.

He sat back down on the bed, eyeing Mattson. His punishment would be worse. They'd get into his computer and find what he'd been reading and doing online. At best, any prospects of gainful employment would be ruined. At worst, he'd get a conviction of treason along with a life sentence, complete with full media coverage. Another dangerous criminal neutralized by the department Charlie once served.

The emotional weight grew heavier.

Annie's face flashed in his mind. Her son's life was ruined, all because he wanted to save the world. Charlie tried to bury the regret boiling beneath the surface. He should have made the kid go home and saved him from this fate.

****

In the cover of night's darkness, Javier and Jonah sat in Damien's car, watching the small police station from the lot of the drug store across the street. Robert had said Liz would have been brought here until authorities brought her to trial and imprisoned her. They would likely transfer her tomorrow, so Javier only had one chance to break her out.

Patrol cars came and went periodically, but the place looked quiet. No other suspects were brought in.

"Can you see an AC unit?" Javier narrowed his eyes as he peered through the windshield.

Jonah scanned the building with binoculars. "I think so. It looks promising. As long as it's running, it should pull in enough smoke." He handed over his phone. "Go ahead and call in the order. I'll get set up."

"Wait . . . what if the guards don't take prisoners with them?"

Jonah opened the door. "We'll just have to hope they do."

As Javier found the number, Jonah retrieved the metal trash can full of dead leaves and newspapers from the trunk.

After three rings, someone answered. "Thank you for calling Joey's Pizza. Is this for pickup or delivery?"

"Pickup. I need a large pepperoni."

Fifteen minutes later, with the hot pizza in hand, Javier headed to the station. He could only hope Jonah was ready to execute their plan.

Taking a breath to settle his nerves, he reached for the door handle and pulled—it was locked.

Crap. Javier looked around the door and through its small window. If he couldn't get into the building, he'd have to count on the guards escaping with the prisoners without his help.

"Can I help you?" The male voice crackled from . . . somewhere.

Javier looked for the source of the voice, finding a speaker next to the buzzer he was apparently supposed to push. "Uh, yeah. I work at Joey's pizza across the street. I just got off my shift, and they told me to take this extra pie with me. I won't eat it, so I thought you guys might want it."

114

"I think we're good here. Thanks, though."

Crap. Javier pushed the button again. "Are you sure? It's a twenty-dollar pizza. I'll just throw it away otherwise." He silently begged for the cop to buy the story.

A few seconds later, as sigh came from the speaker. "All right. You convinced me." A buzzer sounded followed by a click from the door lock. Javier swung it open and strode inside, heading straight for the reception desk.

A uniformed young man sat behind it. Behind him was a row of monitors showing different parts of the building. On the edge of one screen, Javier could see Jonah using the lid of the garbage can to fan smoke.

Javier's pulse ramped up. It was only by some miracle Jonah hadn't been discovered yet. The guard must have become used to nothing happening at midnight on a Wednesday.

"So," Javier set the pizza on the desk. "Lucky for you guys the last caller messed up her order. Wanted pepperoncini, not pepperoni. Who does that?" He offered an exaggerated laugh— anything to keep the guard's attention on him and away from the monitors. He opened the pizza box while glancing at the interior door to the left—the glass was too dark to see through. The cells had to be on the other side of it.

The guard stood, peering at the greasy treat. "Oh, awesome. This is way better than my Cup 'O Noodles. Let me give you a couple bucks for bringing it by, at least." He started to twist around, towards the monitors, reaching for his jacket pocket.

"That's okay!"

The yell startled the guard, who faced Javier again.

Whew. "Sorry. I had too much Mountain Dew." With another exaggerated laugh, Javier put out his hand. "No tip necessary. You guys take care of us over there." He hoped that was true enough for the guard to believe it.

"Right." He nodded. "Armed robbery last weekend. How's the girl?"

"Oh, good." *Please don't let this be a test.* As Javier debated how much to elaborate, the unmistakable odor of burning papers reached him. "Hey, what's that smell?" He noisily inhaled through his nose, then wandered towards the interior door, sneaking a quick peek through the tinted glass. He couldn't see the cells, but another guard sat at a desk on the other side, startling Javier. Pretending not to be shocked by the other guard's presence, Javier grimaced. "Do you smell that?"

The desk guard hurried to the door. "Yeah, I do now." He pressed an intercom button. "Hey, check that out, Brian."

Brian pushed a button on the other side. "You see anything on the monitors?"

"I think it's in the ceiling!" Javier pretended to squint through the locked door. "The smoke is getting thicker."

"I, uh . . ." The guard stepped towards the desk as the fire alarm came on, echoing through the building. A second later, sprinklers sent water raining down on them.

****

"What the hell is going on?" Charlie yelled down the corridor, to the guard sitting by the door. "I smell smoke!"

The guard hustled to the cell door, reaching Charlie as the alarm blared. Two sprinklers came on, but neither were directed at the cell.

"Shit." The guard eyed Charlie, then the exit.

He's gonna leave us here! "You better not, son. If we burn, you're done. That's murder."

"You're traitors. All of you." He yelled over the noise while pointing. "No one would judge me if you burned."

"Man," Charlie stood straight, making himself taller. "I'm a federal agent. All you need is a judge who isn't completely sold out to the crooked government, and you'll be locked up with all the other guys you've busted." He leaned close to the plastic wall separating him from the corridor. "I'm sure they would love to show their appreciation. Is that a risk you want to take?" Charlie clenched his jaw, only half-believing what he said. The odds of getting a judge not on the cop's side were slim.

The guard looked up at Charlie, apparently weighing his options.

Liz appeared next to Charlie, leaning into the transparent wall. "Don't let us burn. You'll live with that the rest of your life."

****

"What are you still doing here?" the cop asked.

116

"What?" Javier squeezed his fist, digging his nails into his palm and yelling over the noise. Sprinkler water dripped from his hair and down his face. "I'm not gonna leave if I can help."

"You did come at a convenient time." The guard reached for the gun on his hip.

Javier yanked the taser from his jacket pocket, aimed, and fired.

The cop collapsed to the floor, twitching. Javier wrenched the gun from his hand and headed for the front door then returned to the desk. Jonah wasn't on the same monitor—he had moved next to a door, but it didn't look like the front entrance. That meant he was guarding a rear door, the mostly likely way for the other guard to bring prisoners.

Javier darted outside.

He ran halfway down the path and froze…what if the other guard brought Liz through the front? If the back was too smoky he might do exactly that. It didn't make sense for Javier to join Jonah.

Javier stationed himself by the front door.

****

Liz pulled her collar over her mouth, but the smoke still burned her eyes. They had to get out of here.

The guard tossed three sets of handcuffs through the small opening in plastic wall. They clanked on the cement. "Put these on each other. Behind your backs."

Charlie instructed Mattson to turn around, and he secured the bracelets on his nephew's wrists. He held a second pair out to Liz. "Put these on me, and then I'll get yours. I can do this without looking."

Dropping her collar, Liz grabbed the cuffs and tightened them around the cop's wrists.

"Okay." He wiggled his fingers. "Now put the last pair in my hands, as open as you can get them. And turn your back to me." He coughed.

Liz took shallow breaths and kept her eyes open a slit as she followed his directions. She showed him where her hands were by touching his fingers, resisting the urge to jump when he touched her butt.

The cold metal circled her wrists, and the cell door clicked open. The guard grabbed Charlie's arm, pulling him towards the back door. The smoke grew thicker as they reached it. Her throat tightened and burned, and the sensation reached her lungs. She was suffocating.

Eyes burning, Liz pushed her way past the guard and Charlie. She didn't care if the guard shot her. She had to get out.

"Hey!"

The yell didn't stop her. She pushed against the door with her shoulder and hip, and fresh air hit her in the face.

A hand grabbed her arm, pulling her off the path. She fell to the ground.

A second later, Charlie yelled. He fell, convulsing on the path.

The cop shook out his hand and grabbed his gun.

"Shit." Jonah jumped over Charlie and rushed the cop, punching him in the face. "Liz, run!"

Unable to use her hands, Liz struggled to her feet and stumbled away from the building, heading for the street.

****

As Javier kept an eye on the front door, movement in his peripheral vision caught his attention. Liz, with her hands secured behind her back, ran across the lot.

Javier followed. "Liz!"

She slowed, looking at him, then lost her footing. Her shoulder and face hit the pavement.

Javier winced and grabbed her arm, helping her up. A new scrape graced her cheek and the skin around her eye.

"Go. Over there." She tilted her chin up. "Jonah needs your help."

"You want me to leave you here?"

"Go!"

He left her sitting in the middle of the lot and ran for the back of the building.

Panting, he arrived to find Charlie twitching on the ground and Jonah reaching for him. The other cop lay unconscious, blood streaming from his nose. Mattson stood over them, helpless with his hands secured in cuffs behind him.

Javier rushed to them, grabbing Charlie's arm as the twitching stopped.

"I accidentally tased him." Jonah groaned as he took Charlie's other arm, helping him to his feet. "Can you walk?"

"Yeah." Charlie stumbled to the side. "God, my head."

"Do we have a key for these?" Javier pointed to the cuffs. Without waiting for an answer, he crouched and rummaged through the cop's pockets. Finding only a dollar, he moved to the shirt pocket and then checked for a chain around the man's neck. "There's nothing here."

Jonah, Charlie, and Mattson were already heading towards the lot.

Javier caught up. "I couldn't find a key."

"Forget it." Jonah caught Charlie before he fell over again. "We'll figure it out."

Liz ran from under a tree on the edge of the lot and joined them. Together, they hurried to the car.

Chapter Fifteen

As Jonah drove towards the sun peeking above the eastern horizon, Liz squinted at the bright sunlight and stretched her shoulders the best she could with her hands cuffed behind her. "When can we get these things off?" The only things in sight were trees and desert, broken only by the unbending road—no buildings or other obvious places to get lock picking tools. Her irritation grew. Why hadn't Jonah bought anything useful at the same time he bought pants to replace Charlie's blood-stained and ripped up pair?

"We might not be able to until we get back to Robert." Jonah changed lanes and accelerated. Since they'd left several hours earlier, he'd stopped only once, when the car needed gas. "I don't want to buy anything that might trigger a search. There are cameras everywhere. A picking kit or even bobby pins could do it." He put on his sunglasses.

"Where are we meeting Robert?"

"Missouri."

"And where are we now?"

"Middle of New Mexico."

After some quick math, Liz guessed she'd be stuck in the things for at least the next twelve hours. Her shoulders ached at the thought.

Charlie had lapsed in and out of consciousness through the night. He sat between Liz and Mattson in the back seat, and more than once he'd rested his head on her. She'd promptly shoved him over to his nephew. Now awake, he seemed more lucid than he had since they left.

She took the opportunity to ask the question that had nagged her since he'd spoken to her back at the station. "What can we do about that thing in your hand?"

Charlie shrugged.

"What thing?" Javier twisted around in the passenger seat.

"There's a tracker implanted in the back of his hand. It's how the cops found us."

"Are you kidding me?" Javier huffed. "Is it still active?"

Tilting his head to the side, Charlie moaned and stretched. "I don't know. Probably."

Javier's eyes widened as he looked around the car. "Does anyone else here see a problem with that?"

Charlie shook his head. "As long as we're moving they won't do anything."

"How can you be sure?"

"Procedure. They don't activate backup until the tracker is still for half an hour and the cop doesn't check in and can't be reached. Otherwise they're tracking thousands of moving officials at once, twenty-four seven."

"But you're a fugitive! No way they'll wait. They wouldn't if they *knew* a cop was kidnapped, would they?" Javier flopped back into the seat. "Jonah, stop the car."

Liz sat up straighter. "What are you doing?" Sure, the tracker was a problem, but she'd figured they'd leave Charlie in a hospital somewhere and not have to worry about it. He'd likely end up in custody again, but at least he had a chance at getting treatment for the gunshot wound that way.

"We can't keep him with us. The cops will be after him. They won't follow procedure."

"Javier," Liz leaned forward, "We can't leave him in the middle of nowhere."

"Why not? They'll come pick him up in an hour. He said so himself."

"But he knows where we're going." Liz sat back, crushing her numbing hands. "He'll lead them to us either way."

121

****

Charlie's stomach knotted. This kid was serious about dumping him, wounded, in the middle of the desert. "Leave me in the next city. I won't tell them where you're going." He kept the fact that the cameras covering almost every inch of a city would record the car and likely put out an APB for anywhere between there and Missouri.

But he'd told the truth when he said he wouldn't say where Jonah was taking them. Missouri was a big place, and that was all the information Charlie had. There was more to it than that, though—while he still felt a strong sense of duty, those bastards, his supposed colleagues, had shot him for protecting his own. What was he supposed to do? Let them kill Mattson?

If Jonah dropped him off, even here in the desert, he'd get picked up. And questioned. And likely jailed . . . maybe even tortured for information. He shifted in his seat. There were no good solutions.

Several minutes of silence followed, which Javier broke after facing Jonah. "You have a knife, right?"

"Yeah." Jonah glanced in the rearview mirror. "Why?"

"We can't trust him not to talk. And we can't take him with us with that thing in his hand. So . . ." Javier twisted around again. "You're gonna help me get it out."

"What?" Charlie scowled. "You think you're going to cut it out?"

"Yep."

"I don't know where it is exactly." He squeezed his fists, digging his nails into his palm.

"Look." Javier leaned between the seats. "You're the reason they found us. That thing in your *hand* is the reason. We can't trust you not to talk if we dump you somewhere. That means we take out the chip and keep you with us, or . . ."

"You kill him," Mattson stared out his window. "You wouldn't have a choice."

Charlie's stomach knotted tighter.

Mattson faced Charlie, connecting with his eyes. "Let him cut it out. Please, Uncle Chuck."

His nephew using that stupid nickname caught up to him. He forced himself to stay in control. He was the cop. Keeping his emotions buried was a job requirement, as he saw it, a requirement that had ultimately led to his wife leaving.

Mutilation or death. What a choice.

Of course, he could fight and escape. These people had a place to go. They wouldn't waste too much time following him.

But that would mean he would likely never see Mattson again, a thought that hadn't hit him so hard before. The only way he could prevent that was to agree.

"Okay." Charlie cleared his throat. "Cut it out."

****

Holding his breath, Javier steadied the knife over Charlie's hand, as if a lack of oxygen would keep him from shaking. The warm, steady wind wasn't helping his concentration. It carried a choking amount of dust at times.

Jonah had stopped at a remote rest stop, and Javier sat across from Charlie at an ancient-looking picnic table that was likely held together with dirt and old paint. Being in an isolated place would buy them more time, if they somehow broke the hour limit before the cops started heading their way. The chip had already been still for ten minutes.

"Just do it already." Charlie had managed to get his cuffed hands in front of him, an act that required lying on the ground, folding himself in half and nearly dislocating his shoulder. Mattson and Liz tried the same move after seeing him do it. Mattson succeeded; Liz didn't.

After more twisting, Charlie's palms faced each other, and with his hands pancaked on the table, he gave Javier the easiest possible access.

"Okay." Javier released his held breath. "Here goes."

Squeezing the handle, Javier pressed the blade between the bones leading to Charlie's middle and ring fingers.

Charlie smashed his eyes closed and screamed through his clenched teeth.

Javier forced himself to ignore the cries and pressed on. Blood ran down Charlie's skin, pooling on the table.

Liz groaned and stared at the ground. Jonah stood behind Charlie, in case he needed to grab the cop's arms and keep them still, but he focused on the sky.

Mattson had returned to the car.

After creating an inch-long incision, Javier dropped the knife and reached for the tweezers Jonah had retrieved from a first-aid kit, doing his best to steady them. "Describe what I'm looking for."

Sweat glistened on Charlie's bald head. Keeping his eyes closed, he took a long breath. "It's small, about the size of a corn kernel. And it's flat."

"Okay." Javier gently separated the skin, peering into the wound.

Charlie inhaled sharply.

After what felt like an hour of exploring, Javier spotted a thin fiber that resembled a grain of rice. He pinched it with the tweezers and pulled slowly, hoping it didn't belong to Charlie's hand.

The fiber resisted then snapped back into place.

"Ouch! Shit." Charlie squeezed his eyes tighter.

"Sorry." Javier winced. "That was attached."

Liz stole Javier's attention when she hurried back to the car, opening the door with her hands still restrained behind her back and making Mattson scoot over.

"Are you waiting for something?" Charlie had opened his eyes but kept his attention on Javier.

"No." Javier took a long breath and poked the wound again, looking for any corners or straight edges. Something shiny caught his eye.

Steadying himself, he pulled gently, and this time there wasn't resistance. The corn-sized, blood-covered chip emerged.

Javier's heart raced. "I got it."

Charlie opened his eyes, and upon seeing his hand, groaned. "I think I'm gonna be sick."

****

With everyone back in the car, Liz leaned towards the driver's seat. "Why Missouri? What's there?"

Jonah started the engine. "That's where the others headed yesterday. We didn't know how long it would take to get you out, so we told them to go on ahead."

"But why *there*? What's the goal?"

"We're not sure." Jonah offered a small shrug. "All we know is there's a facility that has much tighter security than anything we've seen and LifeFarm has something to do with it."

Liz sat back as a foul taste took hold in the back of her throat. "So we're just charging in with no plan."

"Not exactly." Jonah adjusted the AC vent. "We'll do surveillance first, to make sure it's something we need to pay attention to."

Next to Liz, Charlie ran his fingers over the bandage encircling his hand.

She stared at him until he looked up. "Do you know what it is?"

He shook his head.

"Why should we believe you?"

He held up his hand. "I think it's safe to say I'm on your side."

For a reason Liz couldn't identify, the urge to cry plowed into her. Maybe it was the images of Javier digging around in Charlie's hand, or of Brenda's lifeless body, or maybe it was the frustration of not being able to do something as simple as move her hands.

She squeezed her eyes closed, but tears escaped, and with nothing else available, she wiped her cheek and nose on her shoulder. Through the window, she watched the landscape race by.

"What's wrong?" Javier asked, bringing her attention back to him.

Shaking her head, she ignored the new tears his question invited. "I don't know. It's just . . . a lot." She cleared her throat. "I don't think I can keep running from place to place. I'm tired."

"The running is done, Marie. I mean, Liz." Jonah scratched next to a dreadlock. "Missouri is more than where the unknown facility is. It's the meeting place for all the Seeds. Robert has an underground location—"

"I don't care!" Liz pursed her lips. "I don't want to hear any more. When we get there, and I get these cuffs off, I'm leaving. I need to leave."

"Liz—"

"Don't, Javier. I've made up my mind." LifeFarm had already taken her husband and her son. Why should they have more time from her, more heartache? What was the purpose in giving that to them?

Javier faced forward. "You know, if it weren't for you, I would have died in Colorado."

His words made her want to cry again, but she kept the tears at bay.

Chapter Sixteen

Two hours after crossing into Missouri, Jonah parked in front of a decrepit building. It might have been a storefront a hundred years ago, but all Javier could identify was a shadow where a sign had blocked the sun from bleaching the bricks behind it. A decaying street ran through the ghost of a town that likely resembled Hayes at one time.

Javier leaned over and peered through the store's large, broken window. "Why are we here?"

"This is where we're meeting Robert and the others." Jonah set the brake. "These old towns aren't monitored like populated areas. I'm surprised we beat them here. They were taking a different route."

"You're sure we're in the right place?"

"Yeah."

Jonah opened his door. "Let's head inside and look for something to get those cuffs off while we're waiting."

"What was Robert gonna use?" Javier left the car and opened the rear door, allowing the others to pile out.

"Same thing we are. Whatever we can find."

After Jonah tried the door and discovered it locked, he led the way through the broken window. The interior reflected the exterior's neglect: dirt and garbage covered a counter that ran along the wall, scrap metal and other debris cluttered the floor, and a family of possums scattered from a corner upon seeing the new guests.

Mattson coughed into his shoulder. "This looks promising."

"Don't give up so easily." Jonah shoved what looked like a car bumper with his foot.

As he picked up a screwdriver, an SUV stopping outside drew Javier's attention. Robert, Trent, Damien, and Sam piled out. Sam tossed her hair over her shoulder and smiled upon seeing Javier, making his pulse race.

Javier unlocked the door and held it open for them. Sam was the last one inside, and she wrapped her arms around him. Leaning back, she stroked his cheek. "I'm glad you made it out."

"Were you worried?" A smile tugged at his mouth. Of course she'd been worried—a jailbreak wasn't exactly the same as running to the store for milk. But they hadn't discussed it beforehand. He imagined they both preferred not giving voice to the worst-case scenario.

Robert set a duffel bag on the counter, sending a cloud of dust into the air. "Let's see if we can get those cuffs off." He opened the bag and pulled out several items, including a small tool kit. Using Liz's cuffs, he tried three screwdrivers before finding one that worked, and in a minute all three were rubbing their wrists and stretching out their shoulders. He then retrieved granola bars and bananas from the bag, offering the former prisoners their first unassisted meal since Arizona.

As Robert repacked his bag, Charlie hobbled over to him. "You must be the guy in charge."

Robert stopped packing, holding the kit in mid-air. "And you must be the police officer."

"Federal agent. But yeah."

"I've known too many of your kind the past few years." Robert thrust the kit back into the bag and forced the zipper closed. "You're out of the cuffs. I suggest you pick a direction and start walking."

"What? Are you serious?"

"Hold on." Javier joined them—letting Charlie go on his own wasn't smart. If he was picked up, he'd likely turn the authorities on them again. Robert was letting his anger cloud his judgment. "He let us cut the tracker out of his hand."

"He agreed to that so we wouldn't leave him in the desert," Liz said from her spot against the wall.

Javier considered her point. Charlie would have been picked up by other cops. He'd be in jail now if that had happened, but still. Wasn't jail preferable to allowing anyone to dig around in his hand?

Robert looked down at Charlie's bandage. "Samantha told me he tried to shoot you, Javier. Is that not correct?"

Shifting on his feet, Javier cleared his throat. "He did. Mattson stopped him."

"And you're okay with letting him stay after that?" With a glance around the room, Robert focused on Mattson. "Young man. Come here, please."

Mattson hopped up from his seat on the floor and jogged to the group. "What's up?"

"This man is your uncle?" Robert gestured to Charlie.

Mattson nodded.

"What are his leanings?"

"His leanings?" Mattson raised an eyebrow. "Like, what does he think about stuff?"

"Precisely."

"All right." Mattson arched his back, and with one arm across his front supporting the other, he rubbed his chin. "What. Does. He. Think. Hmmm."

Charlie slugged Mattson on the shoulder. "Stop being a smartass. This guy wants to send me out."

"Okay, okay. Chill." Mattson sighed. "He was all LifeFarm until recently. Thought I was nuts for thinking different. But . . ." He shrugged. "He got shot trying to protect me. And he let Javier cut that thing out of his hand. I don't think he'd go through all that and still be on the level with them."

Robert tilted his head. "I'm sorry?"

"He's good. You can trust him, I think."

"You think."

"Look." Charlie ran his hand over his bald head. "Maybe nothing I say will convince you. But I didn't expect my own people to shoot me. I mean . . ." Wincing, he leaned against the counter. "They told us what would happen if we impeded an arrest, which is what I did. They followed the book. But it wasn't right."

Robert slung the bag on his shoulder. "How long have you been law enforcement?"

"Fifteen years."

"And you're so quick to turn after all that time."

"A lot has happened the past few days."

Mattson laughed.

"I'm serious." Charlie rubbed his neck. "They shot me. They jailed me. And if we hadn't escaped, I'd likely be tried and put to death for treason. Doesn't matter that I was protecting family."

As they spoke, Javier studied the former agent, the man who'd days ago had every intention to kill him. If Mattson hadn't been there, Charlie likely would have succeeded. Robert wanted to send him out, and for various reasons, everyone else wanted him to stay. Did Charlie want to stay here because of Mattson, or to avoid jail? Or both? In either case, what would keep him from trying to get back into the government's good graces by turning Javier and the others in?

"I have a question," Javier said.

"What is it?" Robert adjusted the bag.

"If you were to turn us all in, would you be able to get your old job back?"

Charlie shook his head. "No way. They'd make an example of me first. We'd all end up in prison together."

"How can you be sure?"

"I've seen it."

Javier weighed Charlie's answer, having no way to know what he'd do regardless of what Robert decided. Let him go or let him stay, he could ultimately turn them all in. Or because he had insider knowledge of federal law enforcement, he could help them take down LifeFarm.

After a measured stare, Robert stepped away and said to the others, "We need to leave. The compound is a few hours from here, and it would be best to observe it at dusk. However . . ." He glanced at the cars. "I haven't been able to reach one of the Seeds. The third one, in North Carolina."

"What does that mean?" Javier asked.

"I'm unsure. I hope it's nothing more serious than a degraded communication grid. But . . ." He cleared his throat. "It could be something worse. We have no way to know without going there."

"So you want to go to Missouri *and* to North Carolina?" Javier did the math in his head—whatever Robert had planned wouldn't happen quickly.

"No," Robert said. "I want us to split up. Trent, Damien and I will go to the Third Seed. Jonah will take the rest of you to the Missouri site to check it out. The meeting point for all of the Seeds is in Virginia. Jonah knows the way. We'll all come together there in a week, no matter what we find."

"Wait." Liz stood, tossing her banana peel aside. "I want to leave. I can't stay with you guys anymore."

Though she'd said as much in the car, Javier had hoped she'd change her mind once everyone was back together. But she hadn't, and the realization hit him in the gut—she'd saved his life and stuck with him, abandoning her own life to help him.

Javier's eyes connected with hers, and he met her where she stood. "Where will you go?"

Liz blinked and looked away. "I don't know."

"Stay with us." He squeezed her shoulder. "Please. We need you."

"With all those Seeds? I don't think so."

"Liz . . ." Javier rubbed his neck. How would he convince her? "I don't know what's going to happen, but I have a feeling we'll need as many people with us as possible."

"Yep, that's absolutely true," Damien said from the floor.

Javier shot him a dirty look for interrupting, but his comment might have helped. "What do you mean?"

Damien stood and brushed the dust from his pants. "No matter how many we have, it will be David versus Goliath, you know? It's us and the Seeds taking on LifeFarm, if for no other reason than to get the vaccine from them and stop the virus."

Javier scowled. Damien knew which buttons to push.

"But what are we going to do?" Liz crossed her arms. "Storm the castle?"

"Liz, please." Desperate to connect, Javier took her hand. "You've come this far. Don't quit now."

She looked around the room, as if assessing the likelihood their present company could defeat a multinational corporation and perhaps the government. "I'll see what's at this place in Missouri and how many Seeds have gathered in Virginia. If it's a lot, I want you guys to leave me in a city and let me be."

Javier nodded, keeping his disappointment hidden. Robert wouldn't move on his plan if he didn't think there were enough to stand a chance. That meant Javier would have to say goodbye to the closest person he'd had to a mother in years.

****

Liz stared at the orange horizon as the sun set, certain whatever they were about to find wouldn't yield a reason for her to stay. More than anything she wanted to run off, find a new place to live, and assume a new identity. She'd done it before. There was something invigorating about starting over.

But Javier was right—she'd come this far. They'd helped each other, saved each other, more than a few times. She owed it to him to at least make sure she wasn't leaving them all in the lurch.

On the other hand, seeing as the Seeds didn't stand much of a chance of defeating LifeFarm, leaving meant she wouldn't have to see people she cared about ripped away. Again.

"There it is." Jonah pointed through the windshield.

Liz peered between the front seats.

From a distance, the place looked like a prison. Tall, concrete walls marked the perimeter, and a watch tower stuck out above the rest of the buildings' roofs. The only thing missing was barbed wire.

"What is this place?" she asked.

"We're not sure." Jonah twisted around. "We only have enough information to know it's sketchy, something LifeFarm doesn't want anyone to know about. That means we need to know about it." He parked on the side of the dirt road far from the compound. "We're gonna watch from a distance. There's a hill over there that should keep us out of sight." He pointed as he walked towards it.

"How are we going to find out anything?" Liz jogged, catching up to Jonah. "That place will be monitored like crazy, and we can't see anything from here. And anyway, what are we trying to see?"

Jonah faced the group, walking backwards. "We need to know what we're up against. If we can't see anything or we're discovered, we'll pretend we're lost tourists. Once we get inside, we need to scatter—look for restrooms or snack machines. We'll cover as much ground as we can until they insist we leave. Hopefully that will give us enough information to plan what to do next."

"Won't that get us on their radar?" Javier asked.

"It might." Jonah walked forward again. "But we can use that to our advantage."

They settled on the hill on their stomachs. Mattson rested his head on his arms and pretended to snore, which prompted Charlie to slug him on the arm. Sam and Javier claimed a spot next to each other on the edge of the group.

Waiting in silence, Liz started to doze until a roaring engine woke her. A military vehicle drove to Jonah's SUV. A couple of men dressed in dark uniforms and holding large guns inspected it while speaking to each other.

"What are they doing?" Mattson asked.

Charlie shushed him.

The men searched the area. Liz kept their eyes on them, holding her breath as they faced the hill.

One of them pointed to her. "Over there!" The men hopped back into their truck.

"Shit." Standing, Liz directed the others, "Come on. They won't believe we're lost tourists hiding here." She led the way down the hill, meeting the vehicle at its base.

One of the men opened the driver's door and jumped to the ground. "May I ask what you're doing here? State your business."

"Uh . . ." Jonah approached him. "We're on our way to a family reunion in Tennessee, and we got lost."

"I'll say." The man tipped up his chin, glaring down at Jonah.

Three more soldiers jumped out of the vehicle, circling the group. They each grasped large, semi-automatic weapons.

Liz tried to appear unaffected by the display. This felt more like showing off than a real threat.

Javier stepped towards the guard. "Our car started acting up and we thought we could get help down this road. We didn't know what this place was. We just need help."

He nodded to another guard, who opened the tailgate of the vehicle. "Everybody, climb in."

"Please." Jonah held up a hand. "I don't know what we stumbled onto, and that won't change if you just let us go."

"We have to question you and find out what you're doing here."

Liz crossed her arms. "We already told you that."

"Procedure, ma'am. Now let's get moving."

The soldier near the truck shook his weapon, as if she needed the reminder that he had it.

Charlie limped to the truck bed and climbed in, followed by Sam and Javier. Jonah waited until it was apparent Liz had no intention of boarding.

Liz tilted her head up. "You don't intimidate me. My husband was military. I know how you guys operate."

"We aren't military."

"Coulda fooled me."

"Ma'am," he stepped close, towering over her with disdain, "I suggest you get on that vehicle. We have procedures to follow. If you're telling the truth, you'll be free to go, but we don't get many *accidental* visitors." He tilted his head to the truck. "I don't think you want to know what we do to those who refuse."

"Liz, come on." Javier leaned over the edge of the truck bed. "It'll be fine."

How can he say that? With no arguments left and not wanting to get shot tonight, Liz staggered over to the truck bed and climbed aboard.

Two of the guards joined them in the back, while the others returned to the cab. After they were inside the compound, the thick garage door slammed closed behind them.

Chapter Seventeen

Charlie shifted his weight on the metal chair the guard had told him to use, making it rock on its uneven legs. Dark, small, and nearly empty, this room likely served only one purpose: interrogation.

"I told you already." Charlie leaned onto the table to keep the chair from rocking. "We were lost. That's it. I don't know what you're trying to discover here."

"And I told you. Procedure." The pudgy guard tapped a clipboard with his pen. "Why were you behind that hill?"

Sitting back, Charlie crossed his arms. "My answer's not gonna change. And if everyone else is locked up in these little rooms, I'll save you the suspense—they have the same answer I do."

"I'm sure they do. What happened to your hand?"

Charlie withdrew his hand, hiding it under the table. "Cut it fixing a sink." If the guard figured out he'd had a chip, this would be much more complicated.

Pudgy chuckled. "Not too handy, huh?"

Shrugging, Charlie played along. "Just trying to keep the wife happy."

"I hear that." He stood. "We're done here. You're staying in a cell with one of the other men."

"A cell?" Charlie bolted to his feet. "Are we under arrest?"

"No. This isn't a prison. It's—"

"Procedure. I get it." Charlie clenched his jaw. The longer they were here, the less likely an easy escape became.

"If you all check out, you can go in the morning. And hey," Pudgy playfully slapped Charlie on the arm with the clipboard, "you'll get a free meal or two out of it."

"Great." Maybe he could take advantage of the guard's friendly demeanor. "What is this place, anyway?"

"Don't worry about it."

Charlie rolled his eyes as he followed Pudgy out the door, expecting to be led down a hallway and into a cell. Instead, they headed out of the building, allowing Charlie to get his first decent look at the compound—or as decent a look as possible at two in the morning.

The guards outside had said it wasn't a military base, but it could have passed for one. Buildings surrounded an open area with a flag pole in the middle, where Charlie assumed morning and evening formations would occur. A few people uniformed in black jump suits—soldiers?—walked across the space, heading from one building to another.

"Hey, this isn't a military installation, is it?" Charlie decided playing dumb might get more information out of the guy.

Pudgy shook his head.

They entered what looked like an apartment building, though a locked door separated the lobby from the hall. Pudgy used a badge to open the door and led Charlie to the end of the hall and up a flight of stairs.

"Ow." Charlie limped his way up as pain shot through his hip. Stairs were harder to negotiate with a gunshot wound.

"What's wrong?"

He winced. "Nothing." If needed, he'd use the injury as a way to get out of wherever Pudgy planned to put him.

They exited the stairwell on the second floor, and halfway down the hall, Pudgy opened another door. Inside, Javier rested on a top bunk.

"Where are the others?" Charlie took baby steps past the guard and into the room.

"In other rooms."

"When will we get out of here?"

"I told you. When you're cleared."

Pudgy locked the door, leaving Charlie and Javier alone to figure out what to do.

****

Liz paced by the door to their cell—or dorm room, as the guard had called it. Nice spin. Dorms offer the freedom to come and go.

"Why don't you get some sleep while you can?" Sam asked from the top bunk.

Keeping her eyes on the door, Liz trudged to the bottom bunk and sat. *Should have left when I had the chance.*

Sam's face appeared over the edge of her bed. "You're not gonna rest, are you?"

"How can I?" Liz crossed her arms. "We're being held like prisoners here. And they separated us from the others. How will we get out?"

"They said they'd let us out in the morning."

Liz huffed.

"Look . . ." With a jump off the top bunk that only someone young could perform, Sam landed on the floor next to Liz and sat with her. "If they don't let us out, we'll figure out a way to break out. We have escape plans ready to go."

"How is that possible?"

"Well . . ." Sam lowered her voice and leaned close. "I probably shouldn't have said that. But imprisonment is a risk that accompanies going against these huge powers, you know? The plan my dad used to break you guys out back in Phoenix was one we came up with in case only some of us are captured."

"But that only works if not everyone is captured."

"They probably can't capture us all at once."

Liz gestured to the room. "They did here. I need to move around." She stood and returned to the door, peering through the small window and into the hall.

A guard was a few doors down, facing away from them. Another uniformed officer joined him and started a conversation.

"Hey!" Liz banged on the door.

"What are you doing?"

"We won't get out of here if we don't make some noise." She banged again. "Is this not in the list of escape plans?"

****

Javier lay back on his mattress, resting his hand on his forehead. "Do you know where the others are?"

"No." The bed frame shook as Charlie settled on the bottom bunk.

Swallowing, Javier rolled onto his side. "I think you were the last one they questioned. Did they say anything about when we can leave?"

"I'm not sure they'll let us."

"Why would they keep us here?"

"Because they can. They might see a use for us."

Javier leaned over the edge of the bed. "What kind of use?"

Charlie shrugged. "Who knows. The world doesn't make a lot of sense."

"So we may have to break out." Javier rolled back onto his back and analyzed the patterns in the ceiling tile. "If we're together, we can assume the others are paired up. That's . . . three rooms."

"Any idea which rooms they're in?"

"Jonah and Mattson are a couple of doors down. They locked us up at the same time. I don't know where the women are." A lump formed in Javier's throat—he hated knowing Sam was here somewhere but not being able to get to her. "They may bring us together for meals. That could be our best chance."

A repetitive, banging sound came from down the hall, followed by silence. A few seconds later, it happened again.

Javier hopped down and peered through the window. The hall's guard was twisted around, watching another guard walking away.

"What's going on?" Charlie asked.

"Beats me. Someone's unhappy." Javier climbed back onto his mattress. "So, I say we wait until morning, when we're all together. We can scope out the grounds that way and maybe connect with the others. If we're lucky, they'll decide we aren't a risk and just let us go."

"What if they bring food to us instead of taking us to a mess hall? They do that with higher-risk prisoners in the system."

Javier leaned over the bed again. "We're not prisoners."

Charlie made eye contact. "You sure about that?"

****

Liz banged on the door again, and this time, the new guard approached her room.

His face was familiar—the dark eyebrows, strong jaw, even the scar on his cheek. His eyes met hers.

"Oh my God." Liz fell backwards and against the bunk.

"What?" Sam rushed over and looked out the window.

The intercom speaker crackled. "What's all the fuss about?"

His voice! Liz's chest tightened. She brought her hand to it. Her heart raced, and sweat beaded on her forehead. *This can't be.*

"What's wrong?" Sam crouched, staring into her eyes. "Liz!"

The door unlocked and opened. Liz leaned around Sam, trying to believe what she saw.

He stepped next to Sam, looking Liz over. "Ma'am, do you need medical assistance?"

Her mouth went dry. Her eyes fixated on his, those familiar hazel eyes. What if he didn't recognize her? Ten years, thirty fewer pounds, and shorter hair would be enough of a difference. He might recognize her voice, but it took a minute before she could utter his name. "Kyle?"

His head tilted, and he backed away. "Uh . . ." He ran a hand through his hair. "I think you have me mistaken for someone else." He left the room, locking the door behind him.

Liz leapt to her feet and stared out the window. He was almost running for the stairs.

"You know him?" Sam asked.

"Yeah." Her voice shook. "That was my husband."

Chapter Eighteen

Javier scanned the cafeteria as soon as he and Charlie stepped inside. Mattson and Jonah, with trays of food in front of them, sat at a round table. Where the dorm had felt like a prison, this felt more like an office lunch room. The three guards watching over them and a handful of other "guests" stood by the walls, appearing disinterested in anything going on. One flipped through a small stack of papers.

Sam and Liz were nowhere in sight. Javier's stomach knotted.

Charlie had headed for the line, and Javier rushed to catch up. "I wonder where the women are."

Shrugging, Charlie grabbed a sectioned plastic tray. "Maybe they haven't been let out yet."

Javier took a tray and as he held it up for a cook to plop oatmeal onto it, he kept his eyes on the door. "Why would the guards not let them out?"

He and Charlie were taking seats before Sam arrived by herself.

Javier hurried over and wrapped his arms around her.

She smiled despite the fatigue in her eyes. "I missed you too."

"Keep it moving," a guard near the door said.

Javier scowled. "Where's Liz?" He walked with her to the line.

"She said she had a headache and asked to go to the medical room." Her eyes drifted to the guards, and she leaned close to

Javier. "Something really weird happened last night. A guard came to our room. Liz said he was her husband."

"What?" Javier thought back to his earlier conversations with Liz. "She told me he died in the war."

"She thought he did. But apparently, he's here."

"That can't be right. Why wouldn't he come for her?"

Sam held up her tray for the cook. "Maybe he couldn't."

"Did he look like a prisoner to you?"

"No."

Javier drummed his fingers on his leg. "Could she have been mistaken?"

"I suppose, but she kinda freaked out when she saw him. She sounded certain to me."

What did this mean? If Liz's husband was not only alive but working for . . . wherever they were, why would he let her think he was dead? Javier couldn't imagine abandoning someone he loved like that. "I'll meet you back at the table. Maybe she'll show up before we're done eating."

As Javier returned to his seat, Charlie stood. "I'm gonna find a restroom. I'll be right back."

****

Liz waited for the door to the exam room to click shut and the nurse's clicking footsteps to move down the hall before she hopped off the exam table. She'd been expecting something resembling a nurse's office in a school when she asked for medical attention, but this was closer to a real doctor's office—or how a doctor's office looked thirty years ago.

She gingerly wrapped her fingers around the door handle and pulled it down. It wasn't locked. Holding her breath, she eased the door open an inch and peered into the hallway.

A doctor entered the neighboring room, shutting the door behind him.

Liz opened the door wider and stuck out her head. If she was caught, she would say she needed to find a bathroom.

The hall was empty.

Her mind raced as she walked through the winding corridors, unsure if she was heading farther into the medical offices or towards the exit. Wandering until she found Kyle seemed hopeless. Dozens, if not hundreds, of guards worked here—lived here, in the complex. No vehicles had left since Liz and the others had arrived, and the only vehicle that had arrived was a food delivery truck.

She didn't care how poor the odds were that she'd find her husband. She needed answers. He had to have recognized her, or he wouldn't have run off like that.

Aside from being thinner, he'd looked exactly how she remembered—he hadn't aged at all. Maybe the people here had access to the longevity drug.

Did that mean he was working for LifeFarm now?

A burst of adrenaline hit her as she recognized the path to the lobby. A man dressed like a janitor was heading the opposite direction. Liz stood straight and walked deliberately, as if she knew exactly where she was going.

The janitor looked her up and down and offered a slight nod in greeting.

She smiled and quickened her pace as soon as she was past him. She didn't have long before the staff realized she'd run off.

****

"You're the agent, aren't you?"

Charlie held his breath, preparing to lie to the woman who had crept up behind him. These people paid more attention than he predicted—he'd only been out of the cafeteria for five minutes before this guard tracked him down.

He turned around, facing an older lady with a scowl so thick she could have passed for his mother. "I'm sorry?"

"We track intel here, you know. We know about a federal agent matching your description who escaped from a county jail in Arizona after impeding an arrest."

Charlie clasped his hands together behind his back. She hadn't said anything about the bandage. "Sorry. I restock inventory at a grocery store in California. I don't know what you're talking about."

"May I see your hand?" She held out hers.

"What for?"

"Please."

"Catherine!" A male guard at the end of the hall headed for them. "All hands on deck. We have a runner."

Oh crap. Charlie covered the bandage on his hand for good measure.

"I know, sir. I found him." Catherine pointed.

"Not him. The older woman that came in last night. She was in the medical wing and took off." A layer of sweat glistened on his forehead. He pointed at Charlie. "She was with you."

"Uh . . ." Charlie clenched his fist behind his back. *Dammit, Liz.* "Maybe. What's she look like?"

"Don't play dumb. You're coming with me." The man grabbed Charlie's arm and pulled him down the hall.

"Captain, wait," Catherine yelled.

"Head towards the dorm," the captain hollered back as he hurried around a corner. "This guy and I will take the perimeter." He glanced behind them and slowed while putting a finger over his lips.

After a few seconds, he relaxed. "Okay, she's not following. Look . . ." He stepped forward, standing inches from Charlie's face. "The woman you came in with last night, what's her name?"

Charlie stepped away, bumping into the wall. "Seems like you know already."

"Just say it. Please."

"All right." *What the hell.* "Her name is Liz."

"God." He ran a hand through his hair. "And you haven't seen her at all today?"

"No. I haven't seen her since you guys split us up last night. Anyway, why does it matter? She's not gonna leave without someone noticing."

"We can't have people sneaking around. She was agitated when I was doing final checks last night. If she gets caught in the wrong area . . ." He cleared his throat. "Well, it wouldn't be good for her."

"Why do you care?"

He pulled Charlie's arm again, leading him towards an elevator. "You have to help me locate her before anyone else does."

****

Liz waited for a phone call to distract the woman at the desk before heading for the front door. No sign of Kyle in this building. Two down, at least a dozen to go.

She froze as soon as she was out the door. A large formation of marching soldiers was heading towards her.

"Not military, my ass," Liz muttered to herself as she snuck around the side of the building. She pressed herself against the wall, listening for the troops to pass at the command of a Sergeant barking orders.

Once they were heading away from her, she crept across the front of the building again, heading for the next in line. It looked like an office building or maybe another dorm. As she put her hand on the door handle, a familiar voice from far behind her made her stop.

"Liz!"

Keeping her hand on the door, she glanced back. Charlie and a guard—Kyle!—were running across the courtyard.

She ran a few steps towards them before Charlie yelled something else at her. "Go inside!"

The intensity of his order sent a burst of adrenaline through her. She hurried back, opened the door, and darted inside. The man behind the desk looked up then grabbed a phone.

"Wait!" Liz ran to him with her hand out. "It's okay."

"I'm under orders, Ma'am."

The door opened again, and Kyle and Charlie rushed over to her. Kyle lunged over the desk and grabbed the phone from the man's hand.

"I've got this." Kyle dropped the receiver into the cradle.

"But Sir . . ."

"I said I've got it, Private."

The man nodded. "Sir."

Kyle tilted his head towards the door. "I'll take you back."

"Back where?" She swallowed. Was she really talking to him?

"Come on."

Once out the door, Kyle placed himself between Liz and Charlie. "I'm taking you back to the dorm for now. No one will question it."

"Wait, hold on." Liz kept up with Kyle's hurried pace. "Have you been here since . . ." Her memory flashed back to the phone call with the cold army representative on the other end, who flatly stated her husband was dead. Then came images from his memorial service, with only pictures and his service medals to fill his would-be resting place, while their young son sat beside her, watching in stony silence.

She ran ahead, facing him. "They told me you died in an explosion. And this whole time you've been hiding?"

"You two know each other?" Charlie asked.

"I can explain, but not here. Let's go to my office." Kyle led them inside and to the top floor.

"Do you two need to catch up? I can go back to the cafeteria." Charlie hooked a thumb down the hall.

"No, you can't. You'll be scooped up for walking alone. They don't know where you are, and I'd like to keep it that way." Kyle unlocked the door, held it open for his visitors, and once inside, closed and locked it. He gestured to chairs facing a large desk. "Have a seat."

By now, Liz's cheeks were hot and tears burned her eyes. While Charlie took a seat, she stayed frozen in place by the door.

Though he'd taken his place in the leather desk chair, Kyle hopped up again, and upon reaching her, took her hands. "Liz, I can't tell you how sorry I am."

"How can you be alive?" Her voice shook. "Why didn't you come back to us?"

"I couldn't." He rubbed his neck then held a hand out to the empty chair. "Please. Let me explain."

Blinking through the tears filling her eyes, she lowered herself to the edge of the chair.

Kyle settled in his place and clasped his hands on the desk, focusing on Charlie. "Liz and I were married." He swallowed then moved his attention to Liz. "I've lived here the past ten years. I was injured in the explosion—severe burns covered most of my legs. They flew me back to the states and set us up here—me and the other injured soldiers. As we recovered, we learned this place wasn't what we thought."

Charlie ran his fingers over the bandage on his hand. "What does that mean?"

With his eyes on Liz, Kyle tilted his head towards Charlie. "Any idea what his position is on LifeFarm? I figured it's safe to assume you're against them."

Liz huffed and wiped her face with an open hand. "Yeah, you can say that. Well . . . he did try to kill us for fighting LifeFarm."

"Now hold on." Charlie held his hand up. "It's been a very educational few days."

"Who cut out your chip?" Kyle asked.

"Javier did. He was the one I was supposed to neutralize. Do you think I'd let him cut me up if I hadn't had a change of heart?"

"I think guys like you do whatever you can to save your own ass."

Charlie pressed his lips and fell back into his chair. "I offered to leave, and you told me to stay. If you don't trust me, fine. But walk me back to the cafeteria so I can eat."

"No. Stop." Liz faced Kyle again. "Tell us what you want to tell us. I don't see how whatever side he's on matters now. He's in the same position we are."

Kyle nodded. "All right. This isn't a military installation, though it is modeled after one. It's run by LifeFarm."

"What?" Liz sat up straighter. "You work for LifeFarm? That would have been good to know before you made sure we were *against* them."

"It's okay. I only work for them because I'm forced to. Before they treated my injuries, they told me I could either live here and train their own recruits, or . . ." He sighed. "They'd make sure what they told you came true."

Liz's jaw dropped, and as she sat back in her chair, her ability to speak returned. "Recruits for what? What are you training them for?"

"For an eventual takeover of world governments. First ours, then others."

"But they already control our government," Charlie said.

"The legislative branch, yes. But there are still rogue police forces, the judicial branch, and the executive branch, depending on who's in office. They don't yet have as much control as most people think. Aside from Congress, it's just agriculture, the FDA, and the pharmaceutical industry."

"Oh, is that all?" Liz laughed sarcastically. "If they control the FDA and pharma, why is the virus still a problem? Javier almost had a vaccine. A conglomeration like that should do better."

"The virus was a fluke, from what I understand. The carrier insects can't be killed because the bugs are resistant to all insecticides. LifeFarm has been working on a vaccine. But since they're the reason the virus can't be stopped, they have to play politics with it. Make it look like they're the saviors even as they're the culprits."

"Wait. Robert told us they had a vaccine," Charlie said.

Kyle shook his head. "Mixed reports have come out, but I know they don't have one. We're fortunate that this facility is removed enough for us to stay clear of the virus. That's why we're keeping you for now, to make sure you aren't sick and that you didn't bring in any stowaway mosquitoes."

Liz imagined the dead guinea pig tucked away in the cooler back in the car. It could wind up saving everyone after all.

"How long are you keeping us here?" Charlie asked.

Kyle pursed his lips. "I don't know. Could be a week. Or a month. Or longer."

Liz leaned forward. "We're not the first people to stumble onto this place, right?"

Kyle shook his head.

"How long did the others stay."

"Varying amounts of time. But some were recruited."

Charlie stood. "Recruited like you were, you mean?"

Kyle put out his hand. "Please, sit. There's more to explain."

Charlie crossed his arms and glared down his nose at Kyle.

"Okay." Kyle leaned back and clasped his hands in front of him. "I have been training their recruits, but not in the way they think. After I had them convinced I was one-hundred-percent behind LifeFarm, I volunteered to take the 'gray' recruits, as LifeFarm called them. Those who weren't entirely sold on the idea of global domination. It was pretty easy to convince them to form a secret resistance force."

Charlie lowered himself back into his seat. "You're shitting me."

"Not today."

"This place isn't that big. You can't have very many."

"This isn't the only place they are. Once the recruits are trained, they're stationed across the country and around the world in various capacities."

"What capacities?" Liz asked.

"Some cops, university personnel, even business folks. They blend. When the time comes to fight LifeFarm, I'll send an alert and everyone will come together here. It's tricky because my gray recruits are mixed in with the others."

"The real ones."

"Right."

Liz reclined in the chair. "Is it a good idea for them to come here, if LifeFarm owns the place?"

"Don't worry about that."

Remembering what Robert said about the Seeds, Liz smiled. "There are more than *you* think."

As she finished her sentence, the phone on his desk rang. He picked it up, and after a few silent seconds, he said, "I understand." He hung up. "Something happened in the cafeteria. I have to report there, but I need to take you back to your rooms first."

"What happened?" Charlie asked.

"Not sure. I'd let you come along, but I can't let you be seen with me. I have to make them think I'm on their side as long as possible. The private in the admin building saw us together, so it has to be this way."

Liz stood. "Are our people involved?"

"I don't know. Come on." Kyle pushed past them and opened the door, leading them down one floor to the dorm rooms. After locking Charlie in his room, he walked with Liz down the hall to hers. He held the door for her and lingered there.

He stared into her eyes, apparently frozen in place.

The lump returned to her throat. "Don't you have to go?"

"How's Travis?"

His voice saying their son's name sent her emotions rushing to the surface again. She choked them back. "He, uh . . ." She sniffed. "LifeFarm recruited him from his college campus."

Shaking his head, he stared at the floor. "Shit." He cleared his throat and connected with her eyes again. "Do you know where he is?"

"No."

"When did you last talk to him?"

"Years ago." She hurried to her bunk, assuming—hoping—he would leave.

He settled beside her.

"I thought you had to go to the cafeteria."

"I do. But I need to ask you something first."

She tilted her head.

"Did you . . . I mean, after you thought I died, was there anyone . . ." He coughed. "It's just, I always thought I'd be able to go back to you eventually. And the years started to tick away, but I—"

"There was no one else, Kyle."

A smile took over his face but disappeared just as quickly. "Sorry. I didn't, um . . ." His eyes reddened, and he stared at the wall, forcing her to focus on the chiseled profile she'd forgotten. "I didn't think I'd see you again. And having you pop up here, it's like . . ."

He reached for her hand but paused midway.

She waited a second, and when she decided he was paralyzed by indecision, reached for him.

Their fingers weaved together, as if nothing had changed in a decade.

Without another word, he sighed, gave her hand a gentle squeeze, and left her room.

The lock clicked behind him.

Chapter Nineteen

The guard pressed his elbow into Javier's back, pinning him to the table. "Boy, you better start making sense."

"I don't know anything else, okay? Get off me." Javier strained beneath the weight, wishing he hadn't been smashed into his food, but this asshole wouldn't budge. Flipping his head around, he could barely see the tall guard keeping Mattson, Jonah, and Sam at bay with a big gun. The third one, the one who'd been flipping through papers, hadn't returned since saying he had to make a call.

"Come on, man." Jonah took a step but backed off when the guard held up the gun. "You don't need to pin him like that. Where's he gonna go?"

"Beats me. A kid that can escape across the country and find us has a few tricks up his sleeve. Nobody's moving until the captain gets here."

Javier took a shallow breath, the only kind the pressure would allow.

"Okay, everyone just stop." Sam held up both hands, one for each guard. "He'll cooperate. Right, Javier?"

He nodded as well as he could with his head stuck against the table top.

"We've been here since last night," she said. "If he was gonna try something, he would have done it by now."

"We have a procedure, young lady."

Despite his precarious position, Javier almost laughed at her scowl.

The pressure increased. "Anyone under warrant goes to the feds."

"It's a bullshit warrant," Javier mumbled.

"Yeah, I heard you. And it's *warrants*. Plural. As soon as your cop friend and the woman get back, you'll have company."

Javier's shallow breaths weren't enough. To keep from thinking about the growing pain in his chest and head, he tried to deduce how the guards figured out who he was. All he could figure was something on those papers tipped them off.

After an eternity, a loud male voice burst through Javier's waning consciousness. "Get off him, soldier!"

The weight lifted, and through coughs, Javier took wheezing breaths as he rolled onto his back.

The captain shoved the guard's shoulder. "You should have taken him to an interrogation room."

"Sir." He stood straight, looking beyond the man. "I was following protocol. We're to hold suspected criminals until a superior determines what to do with them."

"Not literally, you moron." The captain rubbed the back of his neck then focused on Javier. "Come with me." He addressed the others. "All of you."

Sam helped Javier sit up and slide off on the table, wiping cold oatmeal off his shirt with a napkin. The groups left the cafeteria, forcing him and Sam to catch up.

The captain darted through the halls. Javier pulled more air into his aching chest. "Where are we going?" he asked between coughs.

No answer.

They ended up in the neighboring building, where they rushed past a woman sitting at a desk in a lobby, and into a stairwell.

As the men started the climb, Sam stopped on the landing. "Hold on. Tell us where you're taking us. You were the one who came to our room last night, right?"

He stopped, and the other men followed suit, forming a slanted line on the steps. "Yes. I can't explain here."

He resumed the climb. As Javier regained his breath, he pulled Sam's arm from around his shoulders and took her hand. "He's the one from last night?"

She nodded.

"Liz's husband?"

"Shhh."

The captain left the stairwell on the second floor and took them to a conference room. Once inside, he shut the door. "My name is Kyle. Please, take a seat." He held his arm out to the table.

"Are we having a meeting?" Jonah asked.

"Of sorts."

"Hold on," Jonah said, keeping his place by the door. "We've been patient enough. You guys need to let us go."

Kyle crossed his arms. "Liz said something about people in a resistance. What did she mean?"

Javier's stomach sank. *She told him?*

"What?" Jonah inched towards an empty chair next to Javier. "When did you talk to Liz?"

"Let's cut the crap, okay?" Kyle sat in the chair at the head of the table. "This is a clean room. No mics or wires of any kind. Liz is my wife. Or she was, before the Eurasian War, when the army declared me dead." He went on to tell them about training a resistance of his own. "Before I get you out, I want to know what she was talking about."

"Where is she? And Charlie?" Sam asked.

"Back in their rooms. Look." He stood. "I'm an authority figure here. My superiors trust me, but it won't stay that way if I keep having to drag you guys around the complex. I'll take you all back to the rooms when we're done here, and as soon as I can, I'll figure out how to get you back to your car."

"If you're an authority figure, can't you just let us go?" Javier asked.

Kyle shook his head. "Not if we want to coordinate an attack on LifeFarm. That's why I need to know what other resistance Liz was talking about."

"Just a second," Mattson said. "If you're Liz's husband, why do you look younger?"

"Good genes, I guess."

Jonah laughed. "That's my line."

"I'm sorry?" Kyle furrowed his brow.

"Let me guess." Jonah leaned into the table. "You're getting some kind of supplement here. Something . . . .white and powdery?"

Kyle sat, keeping his eyes on Jonah. "What do you know about that?"

"I'm almost fifty. I've been taking it since she was born." He pointed to Sam.

"Fifty." Kyle's eyes narrowed. "I wouldn't have guessed more than thirty."

"Exactly. The stuff slows aging."

"Really." Kyle sat back, apparently lost in thought.

"You didn't know?" Javier asked. "What did you think it was?"

"A vitamin. They said it's the same stuff the executives and Congressmen take. Keeps us energetic."

Jonah laughed. "Well, they aren't wrong." He sat back in his chair and explained the full effects of the drug.

Javier and the others looked at each other, waiting for Kyle to speak again. When he didn't, Javier stood. "I think this is a good time to get back to our car. I have something in there that we can use to fight the virus." He had a moment of déjà vu, remembering saying something similar about the bees back in Hayes. Hopefully, whatever virologist helped him next time wouldn't get killed.

Kyle shook his head. "Not yet. The easiest thing would be to wait for you all to be cleared. Then you'll be free to go."

"Not me, though," Javier said. "I have warrants, remember? Liz and Charlie do, too."

"Right." Kyle pursed his lips. "I'll figure something out. Back to the rooms for now."

As everyone filed out of the room, Javier pulled Kyle aside. "I have an idea. But I need your help."

Chapter Twenty

Javier shook his legs on the top bunk as the last minutes of daylight shone through their small window. He hadn't been this excited about anything since the supposed luncheon back in California, the one that ultimately led to him in a wrecked car in Colorado. Hopefully, this anticipation would have a more positive outcome.

All he had to do now was wait until Kyle showed up with a cooler containing a dead guinea pig.

A tap came from the cell door, followed by the click of it unlocking.

Javier jumped off his bed, meeting Kyle at the door.

Kyle held up the cooler. "I made up an excuse for the guards who saw me get it. They won't be checking on us." He handed off the cooler and Jonah's key fob.

"What did you tell them?" After pocketing the fob, Javier peeked inside the cooler—the dry ice was doing its job, but it was almost gone. If they didn't get out tonight, the animal would rot before Javier could do anything with it.

"That you're a diabetic and you sent me to get your insulin."

"Good one."

Charlie sat up. "Do Liz and the others know about this? We can't all exactly make a run for it if they're asleep. And you know the guards could shoot you."

"They won't do that. I'll order them not to," Kyle said.

"They'll just obey? With Javier threatening you?"

"Yeah, they will."

Charlie pursed his lips. "All right, then."

"Did you bring the syringe?" Javier asked.

"Yeah. But . . ." He fished something wrapped in a tissue out of his pocket. "I had to get it from the hazardous sharps container. Otherwise I'd have to make up a story about needing to go to the medical room, and I don't want anyone questioning my health or ability to make decisions."

"Would they?" Javier took the syringe and unrolled it from the tissue.

"I don't know. We'll only get one chance at this. If we blow it, we're all getting arrested."

"I can't threaten you with an empty syringe, though."

"Right." Kyle bit his lip. "Back in a minute." He left without closing the door.

Javier laughed and shut the door.

Before long, Kyle reappeared with a bottle of cranberry juice. "Will this work?"

"It'll have to." Javier handed the cooler over to Charlie, opened the bottle, stuck in the syringe, and drew some of the red liquid. "It's not like a viral serum exists for them to compare it to." After wiping the drips away with the tissue, he calmed himself with a long breath. "Ready when you are."

The corner of Kyle's mouth curled up, and with a head tilt towards the open door, yelled, "Hey! Put that away!"

That was Javier's cue. As loud as he could, he yelled for the benefit of the other guards. "Get those goddamn doors open! Now!" He grabbed Kyle's arm and poked his neck with the needle, dimpling the skin. A bit of juice leaked out, giving the appearance of blood. Good.

Charlie stationed himself on Kyle's other side. "You still have your sidearm."

"Good point." Kyle pulled his weapon from the holster and stuck it in the back of his pants, pulling his shirt over it. "We'll keep it out of play, all right? Javier, get behind me or they'll have an easy shot."

Ignoring his pounding heart, Javier sneaked behind Kyle, using him as a shield and keeping the needle against his skin.

Charlie hustled back to their room's doorway.

As they inched into the hall, an armed guard appeared from the stairwell. He pointed his weapon at Javier. "Put that down, son."

Kyle held up his hand, keeping his neck craned as if avoiding the needle. "Private, do not shoot me."

The guard peered down the gun barrel. "What is that? And how did you get it?"

"He told me it was insulin in the cooler!" Kyle made a show of attempting to pull away, giving up after a second. "I didn't want the kid to die."

"What is it?" The guard didn't lower his gun.

"It's the virus." Javier offered what felt like an evil grin. "I'm working on a vaccine of my own. If you guys don't let me out, my research will be ruined."

"We can't do that." The guard crept forward.

"Get back!" Javier tightened his grip on Kyle's arm. "I'll infect him!"

"Do what he says, Private!" Kyle barked.

"Okay!" The guard held up his hands but kept a grip on the weapon.

"Holster it."

The guard moved the weapon towards his side but snapped it into arming position again. A bang echoed through the hall the same moment a bullet breezed past Javier's leg.

Javier's pulse ramped up. *This isn't going to work.* His hand shook as he held the needle in place.

"Private, what the hell are you doing? Drop your weapon now! Are you trying to get me killed?"

"No, sir."

Javier stretched up, glaring at the guard. "Put the gun on the ground. Slowly." He hoped he sounded more authoritative than he felt.

The guard set the weapon on the floor against the wall.

"That's better. Now open the other doors. We're all leaving. Charlie, pick up the gun."

"Captain," the guard stared at Kyle, "you know we can't let them leave."

"We have to. I don't feel like catching the virus. Do you?"

Raising his eyebrows, Javier angled the syringe upward. "I'll get his carotid. He'll be infecting all of you by morning. Open the doors."

"Okay. Relax." The guard held his badge up to a reader next to one of the closed dorm doors. It clicked, and he stuck his head inside. "Get your stuff. You're leaving."

As he went to the next door, Jonah and Mattson emerged. Both of their jaws dropped.

"Come here." Javier pulled Kyle down the hall, meeting them halfway. "Just do what I say."

Jonah's eyes shifted, but he nodded.

Sam and Liz joined them from a room several doors down.

"Oh my God!" Liz jogged to Kyle and glared at Javier. "What the hell are you doing?"

Ignoring Liz, Javier addressed the guard. "Now, get on your knees and face the wall. Stay there for ten minutes."

The guard didn't move.

Kyle tilted his head as if exasperated. "Private, do *not* make me repeat everything he says."

Javier suppressed a laugh.

The guard faced the wall and fell to his knees. Keeping his grip on Kyle, Javier shuffled past them and into the stairwell.

****

Liz's mind raced as she followed Javier and Kyle down the stairs. Whatever they had planned, it appeared to be working. But who fired a gun?

"Head for the big garage door. It's a faster escape," Kyle said. "Then straight for the car. Did he shoot you?"

"No," Javier said. "Brushed by my pants."

"Aren't you coming with us, Kyle?" Liz asked.

"No. If he takes me as a hostage, they'll hunt you down. That's less likely if it's just you guys and the virus. They'll call local authorities for assistance. I'll say you're headed to Nevada so they'll look the wrong way. When I can get away, I'll meet up with you guys in Virginia with the Grays. Jonah told me where to go."

Liz's eyes connected with Jonah's. Was that smart? Kyle was helping them escape, but he could still be setting them up for a betrayal. He worked for LifeFarm, after all, and until yesterday he was dead to everyone outside these walls.

157

Jonah offered a subtle nod, as if that were helpful.

They reached the base of the stairs, and Kyle pushed open the door. Javier picked up his pace, nearly running with a syringe held near Kyle's neck.

Soldiers approached with weapons as they left the building and headed across the mostly-dark compound. In every case, Kyle called them off.

When they reached the garage door, a woman with a semi-automatic rifle slung over her shoulder emerged from a neighboring shack that was connected to a watchtower. "Captain, I can't let them leave."

"Yes, you can." Kyle pointed to the syringe. "Unless you want the virus infecting this whole place."

"Three of these people have warrants." She gripped the weapon in both hands.

"I understand that. Let the feds handle it. We can't invite a party here."

She drummed her fingers on the gun, studying the group.

"Open the door!" Javier pulled Kyle's arm, jerking him towards the needle.

"Ow!" Kyle brought his hand to his neck. "Watch it."

"Relax. That was a warning poke. Next time I push the plunger." Javier tilted his chin up. "Ma'am?"

Kyle looked at his fingers, smearing the blood. "Do it, Lieutenant. That's an order."

She stared at them. "I can't do that, Sir."

Liz's breath caught. *This isn't working.*

Noise came from behind her, and she stole a quick peek. Soldiers approached from three directions.

"Lieutenant!" Kyle straightened up. "If I'm infected, then—"

"Then you all are!" Javier lifted his chin. "One sick person can infect hundreds. You'll all have it within twenty-four hours."

"We can quarantine him." The lieutenant's eyes shifted.

"I *know* you're not considering letting him infect me," Kyle said. "The feds will get them. Now open the door."

After a moment of hesitation, she returned to the shack, and a snap came from the garage door as it lifted.

Liz's pulse ramped up. They were really getting out.

When the door was half-open, Javier twisted his head around. "You guys go first."

Liz and the others did as instructed, though she lingered just outside, watching. Javier released Kyle, holding up the syringe. "I can fix this virus problem if you guys leave me alone."

"We'll give you a day's head start. Get the hell out of here." Kyle went to the shack, and the door rattled again.

Javier ducked under it and joined the others.

As they jogged towards the car, a shot sounded from behind them. Mattson yelled and fell forward.

"No!" Charlie dropped the cooler and rushed to his nephew. He helped the teenager sit up. "It hit your shoulder."

Mattson squeezed his eyes closed.

"I can't see anything out here. Let's get to the car." Charlie picked Mattson up, and limping on his injured hip, led the group into the dark night.

Chapter Twenty-One

Charlie helped Mattson climb into the third row in the SUV. Once there, he snapped on the dome light and maneuvered the kid out of his T-shirt. Javier and Sam twisted around in the second row, watching. Liz plopped into the passenger seat, holding the cooler in her lap.

God, I dropped it! Charlie winced at the thought of what would have happened if no one had noticed. Maybe Javier wouldn't be able to create a vaccine from the guinea pig, but he definitely couldn't if he didn't have the thing.

Jonah wasted no time in pushing the ignition and performing a tight U-turn, heading back to the highway.

Steadying himself as the car bounced on the dirt road, Charlie pressed the skin around the dime-sized wound in Mattson's shoulder, just above his right armpit.

Between the car's motion and the fact that his nephew had been shot, Charlie's stomach rolled. He forced himself to concentrate on his task to avoid throwing up.

"Ow! Quit it!" Mattson arched away.

"I need to make sure you're not gonna bleed to death." Charlie leaned closer. The wound bled less than he expected. "Can you move your arm?"

"Kinda, but it hurts a lot."

Javier leaned over the back of his seat, straining to get a better look. "The bullet probably broke a bone."

"Yeah, I figured that." Charlie shoved Javier back into his seat. "We'll have to fashion a sling or something. Mattson, turn around."

He did, and Charlie checked the front of his shoulder. "No exit wound. So it looks like you'll be leaving with a souvenir."

"Goodie." Wincing, Mattson grabbed the shirt, balling it up to create a cushion for his injury. "Any idea who shot me?"

"The woman lieutenant is my guess," Sam said.

"A shot from her weapon would have been much worse." Charlie replayed the escape in his mind—the only guard with a pistol by the exit was Kyle. But would he shoot at them?

"You think it was Kyle," Liz said from the front seat. She kept her gaze out the windshield.

Unwilling to respond, Charlie had Mattson lean forward, examining the wound again. "Jonah, the first aid kit is in the back, right? Can I get to it from here?"

"No. We'll get it after we get some miles between us and the compound."

Liz twisted around. "Kyle wouldn't do that."

"How do you know?" Charlie asked. "You haven't been around him much the past ten years."

"Yeah, no thanks to your bosses!"

"Why would he let us escape and then shoot us?" Sam asked.

"Maybe he didn't have a choice," Javier said.

"Maybe, if he had to save face." Charlie recalled their position from the compound. "He would have known a shot with his gun from that distance wouldn't likely be fatal. He might have tried to miss and Mattson got in the way."

"He was on the edge of the group," Sam added. "Might have just been bad luck."

After setting the balled shirt behind Mattson again, Charlie rubbed the sore spot on his hand, where his chip used to be. Maybe it was bad luck. But why did Kyle—or whoever—only fire one shot? They would have seen Mattson collapse. "Or they might assume we'll take him to a hospital where the feds can intercept us."

"Okay." Sam put her arm on the back of her seat, leaning into it. "But that brings us back to the original question. Why would

Kyle help us escape and then shoot us? He'd want us to get away, right?"

Charlie pursed his lips.

****

Javier weaved his fingers between Sam's, moving his gaze from her smile to the rising sun. Jonah had said they would be on the road most of the day, arriving in Virginia early that evening. That gave Javier a whole day to just be. He hadn't done that in so long he'd forgotten what it was like.

He gave Sam's hand a gentle squeeze, and she stroked his thumb with hers. The only sound came from the steady hum of the car moving over the pavement, with everyone besides the two of them and Jonah having fallen asleep. Javier let his eyes linger on hers until she looked away, usually after blushing or a quiet giggle.

For the day, they were normal teenagers, something Javier hadn't experienced. He'd jumped from precocious nerd to college student before he'd had the chance to consider being normal. He always had a job to do or someone's expectation to meet, and while that was still technically the case—defeating LifeFarm was no small task—for now, he could pretend that his only job was enjoying his time with Sam.

A wave of euphoria coursed through him. He closed his eyes for a few seconds, opening them again when Sam rested her head on his shoulder and took a long breath. He wrapped his arm around her, allowing her to snuggle up against him.

What would happen to them after this big plan Robert and Jonah had? If they succeeded in taking LifeFarm out of power, they'd likely have to find somewhere off the grid to settle until anyone wanting revenge or to restore the status quo gave up on them. If they failed . . .

Javier's stomach knotted. If they failed, they would all be imprisoned or killed.

He brought his other arm up and wrapped Sam in a full embrace.

****

Liz stretched her back in the passenger seat. These long road trips were wearing on her. "How much longer is it, Jonah?" The only detail he'd revealed about their destination was it was in

Virginia, and the state line was less than ten miles away. He'd exited the highway hours ago.

"About an hour." He drummed his fingers on the steering wheel. "I just hope it's in good shape."

"You hope what's in good shape? The town we're going to?"

"It's not a town. Not exactly."

"So what is it?"

Jonah offered a quick glance in her direction. "It's a remote cabin. There's no road going to it. I haven't been there in twenty-five years."

"Wait a second." Liz twisted her body, leaning against the locked door. "*All* of the Seeds and Kyle's people are supposed to meet in *one* cabin?"

"Not in. At. Around. I told Kyle to take a few of his best soldiers and meet us at the cabin. The rest of his people will wait in surrounding towns. We can't all crowd one place or we'll sound all kinds of alarms. Robert, Kyle, and the Seed leaders will go over the plan and pass the information to their respective groups. We won't all come together until D.C. or New York."

Liz blinked rapidly. "But everyone in this car is going to the cabin?"

"Yes."

Sighing, she settled back into the seat. *Kyle will be there.* She squelched the anticipation, feeling she should still be angry with him for abandoning her and their son for a decade, even if it wasn't his fault. He could have fought for them. She forced herself to remember that and focused on something else. "What do you mean D.C. *or* New York? Where is LifeFarm's headquarters?"

"That's the thing. We have to go after more entities than just LifeFarm."

"What other entities?"

"Congress."

"Oh." How was that supposed to work? She stared out the windshield. "So we have to split up."

Jonah nodded.

Liz picked at her nail as she played scenarios out in her head—a challenge, since she had no idea how many fighters there would be with the Seeds and Kyle's people combined. It could be hundreds or several thousand. And at least two buildings in two cities—one being the Capitol Building—would have to be confronted simultaneously. Successfully confronted. If one operation failed, they all failed. They'd all be tried as traitors—or killed on the spot.

Sniffling, she stared out the side window at the forested landscape racing by.

She would ask to be on Kyle's side. If they couldn't grow old together, they could at least die together doing something noble.

****

Shortly after sunrise, Jonah pulled into a dirt parking lot adjacent to what looked like an abandoned café. Besides Trent's parked car, theirs was the only vehicle in sight. The café's windows were shattered and the door boarded shut. That seemed an unlikely place for the others to wait. "Where is everybody?"

A rumbling engine sounded from a distance before Jonah answered. A motorcycle approached from the forest and over the short grass, driven by Robert.

Javier laughed. Robert didn't seem like the motorcycle type.

They all climbed out of the car as Robert stopped the bike near them. "The cabin is inaccessible by car. I'll take you each back one at a time on this. Who would like to go first?"

Javier raised his hand. "I will."

Robert patted the seat behind him.

All right. Putting his hands on Robert's shoulders, Javier swung a leg over the seat and settled. He moved his hands. *Where do I hold on?*

The engine roared and Javier lurched back when Robert accelerated. He grabbed Robert's shirt, gripping tighter as the bike bounced over the grass-covered earth.

In a few minutes, a small, solitary cabin came into view. It sat on the edge of a clearing, across from a slow-moving river. The morning sun glinted off the windows. Trent stood on the porch with a few people Javier didn't recognize.

Robert stopped the bike in front of the cabin, and Javier climbed off. A second later, Robert was heading back to the car.

"Javier." Smiling, Trent shook his hand. Javier had never seen the man in such a good mood. "Glad you guys made it."

"How long have you been here?"

"We got here yesterday." He gestured to the woman and two men leaning on the rail. "This is Cassandra, David, and Lamar. They're from the Fifth."

"The Fifth?" Javier greeted the strangers.

"The Fifth Seed," Trent said. "It's outside Baton Rouge. Cassandra is the lead in that one. David and Lamar worked at her lab."

"Are you from Hayes?" Cassandra asked. She looked to be in her mid-twenties, with her dirty-blonde hair pulled into a tight ponytail and no discernible wrinkles on her face. Of course, if she took the drug, she could be much older.

Javier shook his head and explained how he came to work with Trent.

"You were working on a vaccine?"

"Yeah. Brenda, the virologist, and I were close to having one before the lab was destroyed."

"We heard about that." Lamar lifted off the rail, causing it to wobble.

Cassandra grabbed on, laughing. This cabin showed some obvious wear. How long had it been here?

"Sorry." Lamar headed for the front door, eyeing Javier on the way. "You want something to drink?"

Javier nodded and followed Lamar inside, pausing in shock two steps inside the door. The interior looked nothing like the outside—it was kept up. Modern. There was even a holographic display for video calls on a desk in the living room, a luxury few outside the government could afford. A middle-aged, Asian man sat at the desk, reading something from a laptop screen. Strangers, likely from the other Seeds, filled every available seat, with the exception of Damien in one of the recliners.

Javier made his way into the kitchen, where Lamar put a glass of ice water into his hand. "Pretty nice, huh?"

Nodding, Javier took a sip. "It's not at all what I was expecting." Though he hadn't thought to expect anything before he'd arrived.

Over the next hour, the other members of Javier's group arrived, introducing themselves to some of the strangers and expressing the same shock Javier had upon entering the cabin. When Robert arrived with Jonah, the last in his group, he brought everyone together in the living room. Javier found a spot on the floor next to the wood-burning stove.

Robert stood by the coffee table. His smile grew, even as he twisted around to see those behind him. "I must say part of me thought this day would never come, but now that we're all here, it feels quite surreal."

The Asian man at the desk laughed. He'd spun the chair around to face everyone.

Did these men have any idea what they were getting into? They were about to plan how to attack LifeFarm, and they acted as though they were planning a party.

Javier hugged his knees.

Robert held his arm out to the Asian man. "For those of you who haven't met him yet, this is Gao. He and I started the Seed project twenty-five years ago, just after the corporation that became LifeFarm stole Deinix and developed it. He's been living here and maintaining the property for us, preparing for this day."

Gao offered a modest wave, apparently embarrassed by the attention.

"Now," Robert clasped his hands in front of him, "another man who's been training his own resistance force will likely be joining us in the next few days. I hadn't counted on extra forces but that will only work to our advantage. I'm afraid our investigation of the Third Seed yielded unfortunate news." He frowned. "They've been eradicated."

"What does that mean?" Liz asked from her spot near the kitchen, behind Robert.

He twisted around, acknowledging her, then faced forward again. "It means someone took out the whole community. It was deserted. The buildings were burned not long ago." He cleared his throat.

Murmuring moved through the room.

"We believe LifeFarm discovered what they were doing, in creating Deinix," Robert said loudly, quieting the crowd. "If we hadn't mobilized when we did after the Seventh, the same would have likely happened there. They can't have rogue communities creating the currency they use to control Congress."

"Can't it still happen there?" Javier asked. Though he'd left with Trent and the others, a whole community of people still called Hayes their home.

"Most of the town, those healthy enough to confront LifeFarm, have headed to their assigned locations. Those remaining have moved to other cities. So no, for now there is no risk to Hayes."

"Where are the assigned locations?" Liz asked.

"We'll get to that. But first, allow me to explain our plan."

As Robert spoke, Javier imagined what the Seed in North Carolina must have looked like—a war zone comparison was probably accurate and also apropos, considering what he and the others crowding the room were about to do. He pictured what Hayes would look like after LifeFarm destroyed it, and then it hit him—if he hadn't gone to Hayes to develop the vaccine, Robert's Seventh Seed would not have been discovered. Javier's presence, and Charlie following him there, was the only reason Hayes' lab was destroyed and its drug discovered. That triggered everything leading up to now, with all the Seeds gathered in this room and discussing how to take out a major world power.

And if Javier hadn't discovered the virus in the bees while doing seemingly innocuous research, and if he hadn't stumbled across Liz's shelter in Colorado, he never would have made it as far as he did.

Robert was discussing two targets, one in New York and one in D.C., but Javier was only half listening. A crushing weight settled on his chest, and he stared at Liz, the selfless woman who'd saved him. Because of her, they were all here, and because of that, they could free their country from the grip of oppression. He would then create the vaccine without fear of someone killing him for doing the right thing. For saving people.

An immense sense of gratitude filled him, and he cleared his throat to keep it from bubbling to the surface. He had to thank Liz somehow, but anything he offered would be inadequate. She would say she simply offered him a ride to Iowa. But it was so much more than that.

Taking a long breath, he focused on Robert's words. He had to do whatever he could to make sure they succeeded.

Chapter Twenty-Two

On the bank of the river flowing a few dozen yards from the cabin, Liz held an itchy wool blanket tight around her body, watching the sun rise. Puffs of her breath appeared before her.

She'd lost track of the days. It had to be close to Thanksgiving by now. When Travis was a kid, Thanksgiving was his favorite holiday. He'd wake early to watch the parade and eat cinnamon rolls. Kyle prided himself on roasting a perfect turkey, and Travis sat by the oven, watching it turn a golden brown. At the feast, the boy would eat his weight in food.

She laughed to herself. The last Thanksgiving they'd had together was a distant memory, but she could still see the gravy dripping down Travis's small chin. How much of Kyle's feast would Travis have eaten as a teenager? Kyle had died— disappeared—before that happened, and Thanksgiving became a formality after that. More often than not, Liz bought ready-to-eat food from the grocery store, and she and her son ate it without discussing what used to be.

"Hey."

She twisted around. Javier stood over her, wrapped in his own thick blanket. He'd shaved his beard, reminding her of how he looked the night she found him. "Good morning. I bet your face is colder now."

Smiling, he plopped next to her and shivered. "I figured it doesn't matter if anyone recognizes me from the news now." He

168

pulled the blanket tighter around himself. "Why are you up so early? Couldn't sleep?"

"Strange place, you know? Plus, it's really crowded in there."

"Yeah. I stirred every time someone flushed the toilet."

She laughed. "Hopefully we won't be here much longer."

"Any idea when Kyle will get here?"

"Jonah seemed to think he'd be a few days behind us, depending on how soon he could get out of the compound and gather his people."

"I think he must have had a mobilization plan in place." Javier tossed a stick into the river. "So it might not take as long for him to get here."

She watched the stick bob with the current. "Have you decided which location you'll go to? When it starts?"

"Kinda. I want to strike at the heart."

"Where's that?"

Javier hugged his knees. "We have to think of LifeFarm like a human body. The heart would be what gives them life. That's Congress. The news outlets are their voice, so we have to hit those too."

"Right. In New York." Liz scowled. Robert had said that about the news agencies yesterday. Had Javier not been listening?

"Yeah." He cleared his throat. "Anyway, I want to hit D.C. The Department of Agriculture, the FDA. Health Department. And of course the Congressmen who are bought and paid for."

"But what will you do?"

"I have some ideas that I want to run by Robert and Damien. Why? Are you going to D.C. too?"

"I'm not sure." Though the blanket was already as tight around her body as she could make it, she pulled on it. "Honestly, I'd like to go wherever Kyle goes."

"Robert told me he wanted to steer Kyle's people towards New York."

"Then I'll go there."

"I guess that makes sense." Javier rested his head on his knees, facing her. "You know, we wouldn't be here if you hadn't helped me back in Colorado."

His playful posture reminded her of Travis again, bringing a niggling question to the front of her mind—would her son be in one of the places they planned to attack? Working for LifeFarm could put him in their headquarters in New York City. She played with the grass, wiping the dew onto her palm. "I don't know about that. You're smart. You would have figured out what to do on your own."

Javier shook his head. "I know how the world works. Anyone else would have stolen the case while I was passed out in the courtyard. You came for me."

Liz replayed the day she found him in her mind—maybe he was right. Others were working that night, but she was the only one who ran to help him. She couldn't have been the only one who saw him.

"Anyway." He turned, facing her. "I wanted to say thanks. Not just for saving my life repeatedly, but for getting us here. If we beat LifeFarm, it's because you set it up, whether you meant to or not."

The corners of his mouth lifted, showing his boyish charm. He was still so young. She was likely the closest he'd had to a mother in years, and he was a nearly constant reminder of her naïve son. They would go to different places to confront LifeFarm—but did he need her in D.C.? Not because she would make the difference between victory and defeat, but as an encourager. A support. Like a mother.

Before she could ask, Javier stood and headed back to the cabin, leaving her to decide the weight of his words.

She shook her head. Maybe she got the wheels moving, and those wheels brought them here, but it took all of them to get this far. And it would take all of them, and then some, to win.

****

"Uncle Chuck, can you help me?"

Reclined on the couch, Charlie looked up from the tablet screen—no news about a compound in Missouri or about escaped fugitives. Kyle was doing a good job of working behind the scenes. "What's up?"

"I need to shower and I can't get my shirt off." He tilted his head towards the sling supporting his injured shoulder. Liz had fashioned it from a long-sleeved shirt when they stopped for gas just outside Missouri.

"Sure." Charlie set the tablet on the coffee table and followed Mattson to the bathroom.

Mattson hadn't complained much about the gunshot wound, and Charlie hadn't asked about it. If his nephew had managed to push the pain from his mind, Charlie didn't want to be the reason it came back. On the other hand, Mattson could have been avoiding the subject because he was scared—he was shot and they couldn't get help for him. Doing so would mean going back to jail.

Inside the bathroom, Mattson turned his back to Charlie. "Liz tied it back there. Just loosen the knot and I can pull it over my head."

Charlie tugged at the knot, then froze. "This will hurt like hell, having your arm unsupported."

"Probably. But I can't get cleaned up with it on and I feel nasty."

"All right." As gently as possible, Charlie pulled the fabric, and when it was loose enough, he lifted it. "Look down."

Mattson did, and together they pulled the sling off. When the shirt stopped cradling Mattson's arm, he gasped.

"That was the easy part." Charlie analyzed Mattson's T-shirt. It had been a pain to get onto him in the first place. "Let's do this backwards from how we got it on you."

Keeping his eyes closed, Mattson held his good arm out to the side, allowing Charlie to hold the sleeve in place. Mattson pulled his arm inside, and Charlie pulled the collar over Mattson's head.

All that was left was getting it away from Mattson's injured shoulder, and he obviously didn't want to move his arm.

Stepping around to Mattson's front, Charlie slid the shirt over his nephew's arm without Mattson having to move it more than a centimeter, but even that slight movement resulted in a groan.

"What about the bandage?" Mattson asked.

Charlie examined the square of gauze and tape they'd used to dress the wound – no blood had seeped through. "It's been more than twenty-four hours. We should clean it."

"We?"

"You can't do this by yourself. Trust me." Charlie pulled the tape and removed the bandage, expecting to see a scabbing wound on the other side. Instead, puffy, hot skin surrounded the hole covered by a thin, yellow membrane. "Shit."

"What?"

"It's infected. Hurry out of your clothes. We need to get this taken care of."

Charlie got the shower going. When Mattson stepped into the tub and water hit the wound, he yelled.

With a soapy washcloth in hand, Charlie held his breath as he cleaned the area. Mattson sucked air through his teeth.

Annie would have treated it correctly and avoided the infection, if she were here. Then it hit Charlie—Annie didn't know Mattson was hurt or even where they were. He hadn't talked to his sister since before Javier took him hostage back in the lab in Iowa days ago. All she knew was that Charlie had found him.

Charlie laughed.

"What's so funny?"

"If LifeFarm doesn't kill me, your mother will."

Mattson found the humor, hopefully distracting him from the pain.

As Charlie finished, the wound bled again, but he figured that would help antibiotic ointment to get to it easier, so he didn't worry about it. He handed off the cloth and instructed Mattson to finish cleaning himself while he gathered what he needed to dress the wound and hopefully kill the infection, or at least delay it worsening before they could get help.

The motorcycle wasn't outside. Unwilling to wait for Robert to return, Charlie resigned himself to a long hike and headed to the car, where they kept the first aid kit. Whatever battles loomed before them, he had to keep Mattson where there wasn't risk of further injury. It wouldn't be too difficult to persuade Robert and the others—Mattson was only seventeen, after all.

The roar of a motorcycle engine reached him and he paused on the porch.

Robert drove over the grass towards the cabin with a new passenger—Kyle.

Chapter Twenty-Three

An hour into her walk, Liz stretched her arms and took a long breath. This air was almost as crisp as Colorado's. The river and occasional wildlife had provided the perfect respite from all the planning talk going on at the cabin—what was the point of doing all that now? They'd have to rehash everything when Kyle arrived, and most of what they discussed was likely speculation.

Kyle. She took another long breath. Her anticipation rivaled what she remembered from when they were a new couple. He occupied her every thought, and while pangs of anger still struck, she knew he would have come back for her—for them—if he could.

For now, she let herself imagine his face, his smile, and she let his voice echo in her memory. He'd worried she'd found someone else, and the thought made her smile. He'd kept her in his mind and heart all that time, planning to come home.

Her happy family had been closer than she'd thought.

After taking in the landscape one last time, she started back to the cabin. Hopefully, Kyle would arrive soon so they wouldn't have to live in such cramped quarters for long. Of course, his arrival meant the fight was closer. Facing—confronting— LifeFarm had felt like a distant dream, something they talked about but would never happen. But every day it was less of a dream and more of a certainty.

The dry grass crunched under her shoes, and as she neared the cabin, the increasing volume of a rumbling motor reached her ears.

The motorcycle.

She jogged the rest of the way, checking faces as she approached. A stranger rode with Robert—one of Kyle's soldiers? Only one way to find out.

"Liz!"

Her breath caught, and looked towards the porch, where his voice had come from.

Kyle was already down the steps and heading her direction. She met him halfway, and he wrapped her in his arms.

She inhaled his scent, his warmth. His embrace brought back an old comfort. Seeing him at the complex must have been too much of a shock for her to allow herself to be happy. And now here he was, where he didn't have to pretend he was imprisoning them.

As he pulled back, he framed her face in his hands and brought her close, pressing his lips against hers. Warmth filled her. For the first time in a decade, she was kissing her husband, an experience she'd thought would remain a memory.

His kiss hadn't changed one bit.

When he pulled away, he stroked her cheek with his thumb. "I was dying to do that back at the complex."

Before Liz could stop herself, she laughed. "I guess guards don't typically make out with the prisoners."

"Only the hot ones." He gave her another quick kiss.

She laughed again, allowing the levity to flow through her. *There's the sarcasm I remember.*

"Join us inside when you two are finished." Robert passed behind Kyle, heading to the cabin.

Heat rushed to her face—she hadn't been busted making out since she was a teenager.

Instead of acknowledging Robert, Kyle ran his fingers through Liz's hair, keeping his eyes on hers. "When did you cut your hair short?"

Liz pursed her lips. "It was after . . . well, after Travis and I moved. A few months after the funeral."

Kyle offered a subtle nod, and for a few seconds, sadness filled his eyes.

Time to bring him back to the present. "How did you get out of the complex so quickly?"

"I told them I was pissed that Javier had taken me hostage and I insisted on finding him. I fired a shot as you guys were leaving so it would be believable."

"Oh. It was you." She stepped back.

"I fired off center so it would miss you guys. Sorry if it scared you."

"It didn't miss. You hit Mattson in the shoulder."

"What? Is he okay?" He glanced at the cabin. "Where is he?"

"He's alive, if that's what you're wondering. We'll need to get him some real treatment after all this."

"All right." Kyle bit his thumbnail. "Damn. I feel terrible."

Liz took his hand. "Let's go inside. The sooner we finish this, the sooner we can start over."

Instead of the crowd that filled the cabin yesterday, only a handful occupied the family room, including Trent, Jonah, and Javier. The rest were the leaders of the other Seeds, Liz assumed. With drinks in hand, they sat on the couch and in chairs surrounding the coffee table that held sandwiches and fruit. The scene could have passed for a friendly lunch gathering instead of a planning session for an attack.

Gao pulled the desk chair over and offered it to Liz. After taking a sandwich, Kyle leaned on the edge of the desk behind her.

Robert had propped himself on the arm of the couch next to Cassandra, the leader of the Fifth Seed. When Liz spoke with her yesterday, she'd learned Cassandra was a little older than she and Kyle, though she looked mid-thirties. Maybe after all this was over, Liz should get her hands on that magic powder.

"I know your people have been discussing plans amongst themselves," Robert said. "I was happy to hear many have volunteered to go to one of the targets. That will save us from having to assign positions, and as long as the numbers are adequate in each place, I see no reason to move anyone. However," Robert's gaze went above Liz's head, "I would like you, Kyle, to be in the New York group, along with your people."

"Why? What's happening there?" Liz asked.

Robert set his drink on the table. "The plan is to hit the major media outlets there. Take them over, and once we do that, we can hijack the broadcasts. Kyle should appear and tell his story, the truth about what LifeFarm is and what they've done around the world. How they made you believe he was dead, forcing him to abandon your family."

"It will take more than that to convert the sellouts," Javier said.

"I agree. And because of that, I think you should also tell your story about the virus."

Javier rocked in his recliner. "I want to go with the D.C. group. Maybe Kyle can tell about the virus too?"

"Why do you want to go to D.C.?" Kyle asked.

Liz turned her chair so she could see them both. Now that Kyle was back in her life, it seemed silly to not look at him.

Javier described what he'd told her about hitting LifeFarm in the heart. She wasn't convinced that was in D.C.—their headquarters were in New York. But maybe he was right about Congress being the source of their power. LifeFarm was using the drug to control legislators, who in turn worked things in LifeFarm's favor. So who was controlling whom?

"All right." Robert stood. "Javier will go to D.C. with the Seeds. Kyle will head to New York with . . . what should we call your people?"

"I called them the Grays back in the compound," Kyle said.

"Why?" Liz finally grabbed the sandwich she'd been eyeballing from the tray.

"They didn't believe in the black-and-white reality that LifeFarm propagated. I could persuade the Grays to go against them, even though the odds were against us."

"How did you do that?" she asked.

His eyes fixed on hers. "I told them what LifeFarm did to me. To you. It didn't take much."

All words left her. She froze holding the sandwich halfway to her mouth.

Robert brought her attention back to the group. "Okay, so now that we know where everyone is going, let's talk it out. It starts by taking out the networks in New York and all electronics in D.C."

****

Javier took Sam's hand and they walked along the river. The setting sun gave everything around them an orange glow, and though the air was cold enough to give him goosebumps, Javier couldn't remember feeling as warm as he did with her.

Tomorrow they would all leave, heading into what might be a hopeless battle. How could a few handfuls of people take out something as huge as LifeFarm? He pushed the thought from his mind. Whatever happened tomorrow had no bearing on where he was now or that his fingers were neatly laced between Sam's.

They walked in silence as stars appeared. Looking up, Sam asked, "Are you scared?"

"A little." He followed her gaze. "How many people will there be?"

"We have a lot, but losing the North Carolina Seed hurt us. After we take out their networks, we'll be able to swarm them, I think."

"Like Napoleon and the rabbits."

She frowned. "Huh?"

Javier grinned. "It's an old story from history class. Napoleon wanted to hunt rabbits, but in his location, there weren't any. Someone brought a bunch in. But they were domesticated rabbits, not wild. They weren't afraid of people."

Sam laughed. "Uh oh."

"Yeah. They swarmed him. The conqueror of most of Europe was almost taken out by rabbits because there were so many of them."

"Maybe we'll have the same good fortune as the rabbits." Sam gazed at the sky, and the moonlight reflected in her eyes.

"Do you think we will?"

She smiled. "I hope so. How's that?"

He laughed. "It will have to do, I guess."

"The Seeds have been preparing for this. They're ready." She took his hand. "Your job is to stay safe so you can work on the vaccine later. Damien can help you with it."

"Yeah. No problem." He laughed.

"Just try, okay?" She sniffed, and her gaze went back to the sky.

Guilt struck him—she was scared and he'd teased her.
"Sam?"

Her attention stayed on the stars.

"I'm sorry. You're worried and I didn't get it." Choking on his words, he brought his hand to her cheek.

Her eyes came back to him. Tears pooled in them.

His heart ached. Though they hadn't had many private moments, she obviously felt more for him than he'd thought—of course, he wasn't great at reading anyone, especially girls. At a loss for what to say next, he simply kept his hand on her cheek and brought his lips to hers.

She welcomed his kiss, bringing her hand to the back of his neck. Her lips warmed his against the cold night, and though he worried his lack of experience would be distracting, she responded to his every move. As heat coursed through his body, he pulled back, playfully brushing her lips with his.

Giggling, she pulled him close again, and any worries he had melted away. All that mattered was her.

Chapter Twenty-Four

Charlie stepped onto the porch, interrupting Kyle's conversation with Mattson. He'd overheard enough to know Kyle's plan. "Why do you want him going with you?" Charlie was next in line for Robert to take back to the cars on the motorcycle, but he had to get this cleared up. "We're supposed to go to D.C. with Robert and Javier."

"He's good with computers," Kyle said. "He can help us take over the news networks' broadcasts."

"None of your 'Grays' can do that?" Charlie raised his eyebrows.

"They can, and they will. Mattson will assist, It's just . . ." Kyle cleared his throat. "The night you guys left the compound, I fired a shot into the darkness in your general direction—"

"It *was* you." Mattson brought his hand to his shoulder. "I haven't been able to move it. Javier thinks the bullet got stuck in a bone."

"I know. I feel terrible. My son is about your age, and if anything like this happened to him I don't know what I would do."

"Do you know it's infected?" Charlie asked. Sure, the guy felt bad, but he had to make Kyle understand the gravity of his choice. Shooting into the air wasn't without consequence. "Not to mention the bullet was inches away from his neck. You could have paralyzed him. Or worse."

"Shit. Really?"

"Yeah. I treated it best I could but I'm no doctor. We need to get him real care as soon as we can." Looking at Mattson, the weight of what could have happened settled on Charlie. The only reason Kyle hadn't killed Mattson was blind luck. Literally.

Charlie clenched his fist, trying to ignore the heat building within him.

Kyle rubbed the back of his neck. "Do you have a fever? Feel sick?"

Mattson shook his head.

"Okay. After this is over, we'll get him taken care of. I'll make sure of it." Kyle put a hand on Mattson's good shoulder. "And I still want you helping my people, if you're up for it."

A smile crept across Mattson's face. "You said something about computers?"

"I did. I don't suppose . . ." Kyle leaned close and whispered, "you know anything about hacking?"

"Pfff. Only since I was ten years old."

"I thought so."

"Hold up. You're a hacker?" Charlie asked. "You know LifeFarm could have had you arrested if you were caught, right?"

Mattson waved a hand. "Relax, Uncle Chuck. Your ride's here." He pointed to Robert driving up on the motorcycle.

Charlie glanced at Robert on the bike, then focused on Mattson. "I really think we should stay together. You're hurt. It's my responsibility to make sure it doesn't get worse." He couldn't stomach that possibility.

Mattson put his good hand on Charlie's shoulder. "Wouldn't it be safer for me to be hiding out somewhere with a computer instead of in the middle of a fight?"

"I guess, but—"

"Then this makes the most sense. Liz will be with us too. She can contact someone in your group if something happens, okay?"

Charlie pursed his lips. When did Mattson get to be so smart?

"I'll make sure he stays out of danger," Kyle said. "I know I have no right to ask for your trust, but I'm asking."

Robert honked the motorcycle's horn and revved the engine.

"God. Your mother is going to kill me." Charlie stepped off the porch, pointing at Mattson. "Okay. But you stay out of anything dangerous. Got it?"

Mattson saluted.
Smart ass.

****

Javier held Sam's hand in the back of Jonah's SUV as they headed to Washington. Damien twisted around in the passenger seat and reviewed the smaller details of the attack plan with them on the way—what to expect from an EMP, who would go where, what to do in case of gunfire from bodyguards. Miles and hours passed quickly, as if fate was in a hurry to get this confrontation over with.

For Javier, battling LifeFarm was only the first step—he still had to work with Damien to create a vaccine. He'd likely be starting from the beginning. And they had to get it completed before the weather warmed and mosquito populations took off.

"Are you okay?" Sam asked.

"Oh. Yeah." He squeezed her hand and offered a polite smile. "Just a lot on my mind."

She kissed him on the cheek. "Still have questions about what's going to happen?"

"Yeah. How did you guys get an EMP device?"

"We actually have three. A few of the Seeds with more technical know-how were put in charge of that."

"Three? Because we'll use all three or in case the first two don't work?"

"Both. Best case scenario, we use all three. They're kinda small so the range isn't as good as you might think. We need to disconnect Congress from LifeFarm while the Kyle and his Grays hijack the news networks and everyone from the Seeds moves in. But if one doesn't work, we have two backups."

"How do you know all this?" He smiled. *She's so smart.*

"I dated a guy who worked on one in the Seventh. He filled me in."

Oh. "How long ago was that?" He tried to keep from visually cringing, unable to keep his imagination from picturing Sam with another guy.

She leaned close, gazing into his eyes. "A while. You're not the first guy I ever kissed, you know."

"Hey, I don't need to know that," Jonah said from the driver's seat.

Heat rushed to Javier's face. He sat back, playing it cool.

"Wait a second." She placed her nose an inch from his and whispered, "Am I the first girl you've kissed?"

In response, he gave her a quick peck on the lips.

She giggled.

"This is the part where you say I'm a natural," he said.

After another quick laugh, she pressed her lips against his.

"Come on. Knock it off." Jonah honked the horn.

Damien chuckled under his breath.

"Anyway . . ." she sat back in her seat, "any electronics within range of the EMPs will be wiped out. If we can get the entire Capitol Building while Congress is in session and the Seeds move in, they'll have to pay attention."

An hour later, as Jonah turned onto the highway leading to D.C., his phone rang. He passed it off to Damien.

After a short conversation, Damien disconnected. "They're in New York City. We're on schedule."

Javier swallowed. That meant in about two hours, the question of whether LifeFarm stayed in control would be answered.

****

"There they are."

Kyle's words snapped Liz out of her dream—leaving the cabin well before dawn had worn on her. She didn't remember dozing off.

He leaned towards his window.

Liz leaned over him, eyeing a crowd that filled a field adjacent to a small playground. Crowds weren't uncommon in New York City. Maybe only some of these people were his. Around them, skyscrapers loomed and drivers voiced their displeasure with traffic with yelling and honking. For a secret mission, this location was anything but secretive. "Are all of these people yours?"

"Yep. Ben, stop over there, by that tree."

The driver parked, and Kyle hopped out. Those on the edge of the gathering smiled upon seeing him. Liz eased her way out and into the bright afternoon sun, but it did little to warm her.

Kyle hurried to the group while she and Mattson lingered behind. After he shook hands and received hugs, Kyle waved them over. His smile was as bright as the daylight.

This is what he's been preparing for. She took a calming breath. *This is why he didn't come back to me.*

She reminded herself that he didn't know during all those years he would have help from thousands of people living in the Seeds, and he likely didn't think he'd be engaging LifeFarm this soon. Would it have been another ten years or more? How long would it have taken for him to train enough people for it to not all be a waste?

After Kyle introduced them to a few people, a young woman with dirty-blonde hair pushed her way through the group. "You made it!" She focused on Liz.

"I'm sorry?" Liz racked her mind. Was she supposed to recognize this person?

"I was one of the agents who was supposed to take you and Mendez into custody back in Colorado. My partner forced you off the road and you landed in a river."

"Oh." Images from that day flooded her memory, along with the fear she'd had at losing control of the vehicle and the cold that reached her bones that night. "I thought you guys were gonna kill us."

"Those were our orders, and my partner was anxious to follow them. I stopped him. When I found out what Mendez had been doing, in finding the virus . . . I had to make sure he made it out. Is he here?"

"No, he's with the other group." Liz studied the woman— would she and Javier have died without her? Or could they not have been run off the road in the first place? "Why didn't you stop him from ramming us, if you were so concerned?"

"I tried. He didn't go for it." She held out her hand to shake Liz's. "I'm Kristen. I've been a mole inside Homeland Security for Kyle for the past six years. Most of us have worked undercover in one form or another. How do you know him?"

Liz offered Kristen a limp handshake. "He was . . . is . . . my husband. I thought he died in the war."

Kristen's jaw dropped. "Oh my God. You're her. Kyle talked about you a lot. You have a son, right?"

Liz shivered, though maybe not from the cold. "We did."

After a few seconds of contemplation, Kristen nodded. "Well, your husband is the reason we're all here." She offered a gentle smile. "I think we're ready."

Liz politely smiled back, and as Kristen made her way over to Kyle to say hello, Liz sneaked back to the car. Kyle's words directing his Grays into small groups followed her as he instructed them on the plan they would execute in two hours. He was their general again.

Her heart filled with a combination of pride and jealousy. These people had spent time with her husband, time that was supposed to be hers. It was silly to be jealous—Kyle could be the reason LifeFarm released its grip on everything. Wasn't that worth losing him for a decade?

As she fell into the car and closed the door behind her, silencing his words, she hoped his time training these people wasn't fruitless.

Chapter Twenty-Five

Javier watched the Capitol Building loom in the distance. He'd never visited D.C. before. He'd wanted to for years, to see the monuments and take in the history, appreciating a time when the government existed for the good of the people. It was created to gain freedom from oppression. Now, he and the others would get that freedom back.

Jonah parked behind an abandoned warehouse. At the back of the SUV, Damien distributed walkie-talkies as Javier, Sam, Charlie and Jonah gathered their supplies.

"Really?" Javier examined the device in his hand. "Kind of archaic, aren't they?"

"Archaic will keep us from getting caught. The EMP won't affect the simple batteries in these. It probably won't affect cell phone batteries either. That's why we're hitting the tower." Damien zipped up his backpack and slung it over his shoulder. He twisted a knob on the top of Javier's walkie. "Channel four. I'll say 'set' when I've triggered the EMP that will take out the nearest cell tower. That one should take out the perimeter cameras too. You do the same when yours has fired so Sam knows when to do hers. That will take out the wired electronics inside the building."

"Then we smoke them out. Just like the jail in Phoenix," Javier said.

Charlie clicked on his walkie talkie. "First, you have to trigger the second EMP, or the whole building will still be connected to New York and have operative internal cameras."

"I know that." Javier scowled. "I got you out of the jail, didn't I?"

"I think the smoke did that."

Javier buried his irritation.

Charlie strode ahead of the group, catching up with Jonah, who casually walked down the sidewalk. Javier and Sam headed down an adjacent side street for a block, where Sam branched off.

"Test, test." Damien's voice crackled through the walkie talkie.

Javier found the button and pressed it. "I hear you." Charlie and their others echoed their confirmation.

Go time. Javier took a long breath.

****

Liz joined Kristen and a handful of other Grays who waited in a grocery store across the street from one of the cable networks and a block away from LifeFarm. She stayed close to the window, keeping an eye out for the signal. Everyone else pushed carts in the aisles, careful not to draw attention to themselves.

Somewhere in a neighboring building, Mattson and Kyle worked with a few other tech-savvy folks on breaking into the news stations' networks. If the D.C. group was on schedule, they'd hit the Capitol Building in fifteen minutes. Then, it was New York's turn.

Hack the network, hijack the signal, and blast their own message over the airwaves. Easy.

Liz laughed to herself.

She meandered around the displays in front of the windows, occasionally picking something up and pretending to look at it. As each minute passed, the knot in her stomach grew. If they moved before the D.C. group knocked the Capitol Building off the grid, she and everyone here could be arrested. Or worse.

A young lady wearing an employee uniform approached. "Ma'am, can I help you find something?"

At the same moment, the window of the sedan across the street lowered and an arm waved. That's it.

Liz offered a friendly smile. "Oh, no. Thank you. I'm just browsing."

As soon as the girl walked away, Liz loudly coughed three times, telling the Grays that Kyle was on the air, and rushed out the door.

Liz's heart pounded. She didn't have a place to go yet, but as soon as the message was delivered, she would. Right now, she had to find a TV. She was supposed to wait in the store, but seeing Kyle deliver his message was something she couldn't miss.

****

Javier lingered on a corner down the street from the Capitol Building, waiting for his signal. He feigned an interest in a nearby statue but frequently glanced at the traffic light.

They went out without a sound. Damien's EMP worked.

The slamming brakes of a few cars and the swears of their drivers provided all the cover noise Javier needed. Or rather, all the cover Damien's voice coming through the walkie needed. "Set."

Breathless, Javier jogged towards the Capitol Building. Security personnel were unloading from SUVs parked in front of the steps. There wasn't a street there. They'd stopped amid tourists—and a few hundred Seed members—wandering around the area. While some officers ran into the building, others corralled the spectators towards the street. Could he engage the second EMP without being detected? Could Sam engage hers on the other side of the building?

He ducked in the shade of a tree a hundred yards from the building. It wasn't as close as he was supposed to get, but it would have to do. If he was caught and searched there would be no EMP. At least the security cameras were out. If they weren't, someone would already be heading his way, no doubt.

Holding his breath, he pulled the device from his backpack and armed it, just like Damien had showed him. With the flick of a few switches, everything electronic in a quarter-mile radius would be fried.

Here goes. He triggered the device. It didn't make any indication that anything happened, but a few tourists shaking their phones offered confirmation. *Thank God for modern electronics.* He held his walkie talkie to his mouth. "Set." A minute later, Sam repeated her own confirmation.

Somewhere around the building, Charlie and Jonah were lighting the smoke bombs. Instead of heading for a warehouse, where he was supposed to join Robert and the waiting Seed residents, Javier swallowed and ran for the Capitol's front steps. He had more to do to make sure their efforts had a lasting impact.

****

On the north side of the Capitol Building, Charlie lit the fuses of three smoke bombs and squeezed them into an exterior vent. They wouldn't produce enough smoke to force anyone out like the fire had done back in Phoenix, but all they needed was to set off alarms. Making the sprinklers go off would be a nice touch but was unlikely. After lighting and distributing his remaining bombs, he sealed the vent with plastic wrap. It was the only way to keep the smoke from escaping back outside.

He didn't know how much time they had before the security cameras came back online, but Damien had said it would take hours for everything to return to normal. A building less important than this one could take days to recover. Hours would be quick. He could only hope the government wasn't more efficient than they all thought.

Crouching on the edge of the building and hiding behind convenient trees, Charlie moved towards the side entrance. From the buildings across the street and neighboring blocks, thousands of people were coming his way.

"What the hell are you doing?"

Charlie turned towards the voice. A young cop—likely just out of the academy—pointed a gun at him.

Great. "Is standing by a tree illegal now?" Charlie made a point of obviously sizing up the cop. "A capital offense?"

"We're clearing the area. You need to move on."

"Like they are?" Charlie tilted his head toward the crowd, which he could no longer see but he assumed had grown. "Will you get all of them to move with that little pea shooter?"

While the cop gaped at the mass of people, Charlie karate-chopped his shoulder and pried the gun from his hand. *That was too easy.* "They don't train you guys so well anymore."

"Drop the weapon!"

This time the command came from a woman cop flanked by four other guards.

Sighing, Charlie let the gun hit the ground and put up his hands while pointing across the street. "Okay, but you have bigger fish to fry."

****

Liz rushed down the street, peering into every window. A café four doors down from the grocery store had a TV on and tuned to a sports channel.

She pushed her way inside and located the channel button on the side of the set. Holding her breath, she pressed it repeatedly. Sports. Sports. Sports. Crime show. Commercial. Commercial. News. There!

Kyle sat in front of a tiled wall, eyes boring into the camera. He had already started delivering his message. "... for our country in the Eurasian war, which was a cover for LifeFarm to take over food production on those continents. I was gravely injured. They told my family I had died. I was taken to a facility in Missouri, where LifeFarm is training a secret army that they plan to use to take total control . . ."

"The hell is this?" An old man at a nearby table stood, staring at the screen. "Who's this guy? And where did the game go?"

Muttering moved through the café. Patrons saying things like "Another conspiracy nut," "Is this real or a show?" and "I knew LifeFarm was dirty" reached Liz, but she didn't acknowledge any of it. Her eyes were glued to the screen, watching her husband start a revolution.

"The time to act is now," Kyle said while leaning forward. "Thousands in the resistance are swarming Congress and LifeFarm. Join us. Fight. The elite have had absolute control for too long. If you've lost a loved one in their underfunded hospitals, fight. If you were forced to defend a cause that oppressed foreign citizens, fight. If your children were plucked from you, coerced by corrupt promises, fight."

Every voice in the café had gone silent.

"Technological advances have been withheld from us. Healthcare has been made a privilege for the wealthy. Our time is now. They don't have as much control as they want us to think. We're in New York and D.C. rising up as I speak. Join us if you're in the area. If not, find recordings of this message and play it in your communities. We've all been lied to for decades. We The

People will take our country back, and we have to do it now. We may not—"

The screen flashed then went dark. A still shot appeared with a message about technical difficulties. Liz stared, her heart begging Kyle to come back.

"My son might be alive!" a woman yelled.

Liz looked behind her. The old woman had her elbows on the table and face in her hands, sobbing. "They told me he was dead. But that man wasn't!" She pointed to the TV.

Sirens wailed on the street. Time to leave.

Liz ran out and joined the Grays crowding the sidewalk. Cop cars had stopped in front of the network building, and officers were rushing inside.

Kyle was in a different building but she didn't know which one. Didn't matter right now. Their job was to meet at LifeFarm.

****

A fire alarm blared as Javier crept into the building. He found a dark corner and waited. Tourists and employees crowded the hall. Some were anxious to evacuate while others stood frozen in place, eyeing the front door and then down the hall. A faint smoky smell filled the air. It wasn't strong enough to cough, but it was plenty to force people out. Perfect.

Liz and the others in New York were supposed to be swarming LifeFarm right about now, but of course Javier had no way to verify if they were on schedule.

"We can't go out there. Did you see the mob?" A man in his thirties and wearing a suit pointed at the door, pleading with an officer who was directing people outside. Javier thought he recognized the man from TV interviews. A Congressman. What was his name . . . Willis? Warner?

The cop mirrored the Congressman's pointing. "You can't stay in here, sir. We have to find out where that smoke is coming from."

"It's an attack! Our electronics go and now this? And where did all those people come from?" The Congressman's skin turned beet red, showing even through his thinning, blond hair. A vein in his neck protruded.

This guy had something to hide.

190

"Sir, you need to evacuate. Right now. I don't think you want me forcing you out with all those people watching."

"You're threatening me?" The Congressman stretched up. "I can have your job!"

"Take it." The officer pushed his way past the angry man, directing more compliant lingerers to the door.

Javier moved into the crowd, hiding in plain sight, as he made his way to the opposite side of the door, where the representative still hadn't moved. He inched his way into earshot. "How old are you, Congressman?"

His attention snapped to Javier. "Excuse me?"

"I was just wondering how long LifeFarm has been buying you off with a mysterious white powder."

The color drained from his face, and he took off down the hall. "I don't know what you're talking about."

Javier smirked and caught up. "Willis, right?"

He scoffed. "Warner. Jeff Warner. If you're pretending to know everything, maybe learn the names of your representatives."

Javier ran in front of Warner, stopping him before he reached the stairs. "I thought you might like to know why you aren't able to contact your bosses at LifeFarm. Oh, and I know how to combat the virus you guys are hiding."

"Is that so?" Warner shoved Javier out of the way and stomped up the stairs. A guard passed them, but he seemed uninterested.

Javier followed. "Let's see. The powder was discovered twenty-five years ago, so that would make you . . . sixty? Am I close?"

Warner didn't look back. When he reached the third floor, he branched off.

Javier kept after him. "I'm curious. Have you passed any legislation you found immoral so LifeFarm would keep you young? Was it worth it?"

"Look, kid." Warner stopped outside an office door. "You've obviously been reading too many conspiracy sites." He pressed his thumb onto a glass plate next to the door, then slumped. "Right. No electronics." He knocked, and a few seconds later a well-dressed woman opened the door.

Warner pushed his way inside, and Javier stuck his arm in the opening, stopping him from slamming the door. "People are dying. You need to look outside. Those people know what I know, and we're about to tell the world. Which side do you want to be on when that happens?"

****

The crowd descended on the Capitol Building, and Charlie grinned. The cops who'd stopped him were no match for the Seeds. They gave up and ran around to the west side of the building again, where they would likely join their ilk and fight.

Let them.

Charlie joined the mass of people moving across the grounds, yelling the truths about LifeFarm. *They staged a phony war. They caused a virus. They control Congress with a drug.* Alone, they would have sounded crazy. In a group of thousands, they were a resistance.

Instead of shouting, Charlie listened, struggling to recall what he believed when he was on the other side, back when Mattson had tried to convince him of what these people had known for over two decades. If he hadn't been shot and jailed by his own, he could possibly still think that way.

Mattson. Had he succeeded in taking down the news networks? Whatever gains they made here largely depended on how many in the general public could be persuaded to go against LifeFarm, and that meant hijacking the media. The revolution started today, but if they didn't have enough support, it wouldn't stick.

As the crowd headed to the west side of the building, shots rang out, echoing across the courtyard. A scream followed.

Before Charlie could process what happened, the movement of the entire group accelerated from front to back, rushing the guards on the stairs. *Oh no.* Charlie squeezed his eyes closed as several more shots cracked.

****

Pain shot through Javier's jaw, followed by the door to the Congressman's office slamming shut.

Great.

Javier rubbed the spot. Thankfully, the old man didn't have much power to his punch. He walked to the window to see if the Seeds had arrived.

The sight made him freeze in place.

Two lay dead—or bleeding, at least—in the courtyard just shy of the steps. A few tended to them, but the others were rushing the door; a few were fighting the guards. Something had gone wrong.

Charlie, Sam, and Jonah were supposed to be in that crowd. Where were they?

Javier ran down the stairs.

People poured into the building, pinning guards to the wall. Others held professionally-dressed men and women by their arms, keeping them from going anywhere. The mass of humanity behind them made escape impossible.

This isn't how it was supposed to go.

"What are you doing?" Javier yelled over the crowd.

One of the suited men dropped, and a civilian punched him repeatedly.

"Stop!" Javier couldn't yell loudly enough. While a few looked up, most ignored him.

Javier grabbed the nearest thing he could find—fake flowers in a glass vase set on a thin table against the wall—and thrust it to the ground. It shattered, making several in the mob freeze. "I said stop! Now!"

The man beating the Congressman glared at Javier, incredulous. "They shot at us!"

"So?" Javier ran over. "We knew that might happen. This could ruin everything. You know that. Were you waiting in your Seed all this time to blow it?"

After staring at Javier for a second, the man released the Congressman. In the rest of the hall, chaos continued.

Javier climbed onto the table and cupped his hands around his mouth, yelling as loudly as he could. "Stop!"

With the exception of a few holdouts, the entire crowd looked at him. Those slow to respond followed suit shortly after.

"Let them go." Javier pointed to the officials the Seed members had captured. "This isn't why we're here. Is this what you've been preparing for?"

"We have to protect ourselves," a woman said.

"Yes, but this isn't how to do that. How will we stop LifeFarm if they see us as combatants? All they'll do is fight back. Then what? They would be stronger. Is that what you want?"

They stared at him. Those holding officials released them.

"People not affected by the EMPs have no doubt arrived, and they have cameras." Javier pointed outside. "We have to be seen as the nonviolent force. LifeFarm staged phony wars to get their way. Violence is what they know. We have to *be* different if we're going to *make* a difference. Now," he hopped off the table and approached a Congresswoman, "I'm going to find one of those cameras, and you and your colleagues are going to tell the truth about LifeFarm for the first time."

"What if we don't?" she asked, looking down her nose at him.

"Then don't. Between our message that aired in New York and your lies, people will know the truth either way. Your job depends on what you say in the next few minutes."

She laughed. "So naïve."

"Maybe." Javier ran to the door and yelled out to the mass of humanity, "Does anyone here have a working camera?"

A few hands went up, and others ran to him. A middle-aged woman reached him first, thrusting her phone into his hand. "I heard that soldier on the TV. LifeFarm took my daughter from me. I'll do whatever I can to take them down."

Javier couldn't help but smile. Kyle's message had gone out. If all was going well there, they had the powder in hand.

He pushed through the crowd and went back inside, switched on the video camera, and focused it on the Congresswoman. "Ma'am, tell us everything you know about LifeFarm."

****

"Liz!"

Nearly at the growing mass of Grays assembled across the street from LifeFarm, she stopped. *Kyle!* She ran to him, crashing against him and wrapping her arms around him. "You did it. Half the people from the café are here with us. They've all lost people."

"Café?" Kyle leaned back. "What were you doing there?"

"I had to see your broadcast. Come on." Taking his hand, she pulled him into the middle of the group, where any cops or unfriendly bystanders wouldn't see him. "Where's Mattson?"

"I told him to stay inside. He's not doing well. The infection is getting worse."

She stopped, surrounded by Kyle's soldiers. "What infection?"

"From the gunshot." He eyed the building and cleared his throat. "We need to finish this and get him treatment." He let her go and pushed his way to the front of the group, apparently unconcerned about being recognized. Facing everyone, he scanned the group. "This is it, everyone. You know what to do. Remember why we're here." With an arm wave, he led them across the street while pulling something from his pocket.

Four armed guards had stationed themselves outside LifeFarm's entrance. Without a word, Kyle, Kristen, and two others went straight for them and tased them to the ground, as if they'd trained for this exact scenario. The guards didn't have a chance to fire a shot.

Pride welled in Liz's chest. She hadn't known what to expect from Kyle's Grays, but it wasn't this. The focus these people displayed was unlike anything she'd seen.

Kyle broke the doors open, and the mob crowded inside, filling the lobby. They branched off into hallways, each knowing the target—the drug. Deinix. The only reason LifeFarm had control of the government. It could be locked away, but the people around her had trained to deal with that circumstance.

Liz followed the group following Kyle. He beelined for a stairwell, as if he'd worked here. Had he studied blueprints?

She was panting by the time they reached the fourth floor. Three employees met them at the stairwell. One had a gun.

Kyle tased the armed man without hesitation. Well-placed punches from other Grays took care of the other two.

They hustled down the hall, stopping at a door in the middle of it. After three kicks, Kyle had it open.

The space looked like a bank, with several rows of locked boxes. A pane of glass, likely bulletproof, separated the boxes from where Liz now stood. A young woman with her dyed-purple hair done up in a ponytail sat on the other side of the glass. A locked door big enough to pass small items appeared to be the only possible contact point between the attendant and the outside.

Purple Hair's eyes grew big. "What the hell are you doing here? None of you are authorized."

"Very observant. Good job." Kyle analyzed the seam between the glass and the wall. "I'll tell your boss to give you a raise."

She stood. "Seriously, you have to leave. This is a secure area. How did you get in here anyway?"

Kyle ignored her, opting instead to continue scouring the glass for weaknesses.

"I'm calling security." Purple Hair fell back into her chair.

"Hold on." Liz put her hand on the glass. "We're not here to start trouble. We just need to get something. A white powder called Deinix. Give it to us and we'll leave."

The girl scoffed. "Yeah, let me just go get it." She pushed a button on the counter. "I need security in the vault."

Shit.

Kyle drew his sidearm. "Give us the drug. Right now." Two other Grays followed his example. Liz backed away, allowing them to take position in front of the glass.

"This glass is bulletproof, soldier." Purple Hair crossed her arms.

Kyle fired, creating a perfect hole in the glass near the ceiling. "I guess my bullets are special. I wonder how many shots it will take to break through."

"Are you stupid?" Purple Hair stood. "We have a pretty extreme protocol to follow if the vault is compromised. You can't just come in here and start shooting."

Three guards stormed through the vault's door. One grabbed Liz and spun her around, shoving her against the wall.

"Come on!" Her words were directed at the corner, as her cheek was pressed against a framed picture of a cornfield. "I'm not armed."

In the same moment she relayed the information, the guard released her as four more gunshots filled the small space. The guards tackled Kyle and the other two Grays. A deafening siren echoed from the hallway.

The guards leapt to their feet, dragging Kyle and the other armed Grays out. Liz lingered behind. What the hell was going on? Should she follow Kyle or keep trying to get the drug, now that the guards were gone?

As Purple Hair shoved items into a backpack, a male employee appeared behind her and yelled something that could have been, "Is this a drill?"

Oh my God. Anxiety filled Liz's stomach as recognition flooded her mind. He'd lost weight and was taller, and his hair was shorter, but there was no mistake—her son was here. Travis was alive and standing feet from her.

Purple Hair shook her head and ran to the back of the vault.

Liz banged the glass with both hands. "Travis!"

The wailing sirens drowned her cries.

"Travis!" She kept banging and as he followed Purple Hair.

Staring through the window as if it would make Travis return, Liz took a shaking breath. She had to find him.

That siren likely meant they were evacuating the building. Heading for the door, Liz faced a new fear—she was alone. The Grays had left her.

She rushed to the stairs, looking down every hallway in the vain hope that Travis would be in one of them. She ran with the crowd through the door. As she reached the sidewalk, a deafening boom followed by heat and dust hit her.

Chapter Twenty-Six

"I don't have to answer to you." The Congresswoman eyed Javier as if he were one of his insects.

"Pretty sure you do." He kept his focus on her image in the phone screen. "Aren't you supposed to be a representative of the people?"

Those surrounding them shouted their agreement. They'd created an alcove with their bodies, a space large enough for Javier to get an unobscured shot but not large enough for the Congresswoman to escape. With the crowd at his back, Javier hoped any other cops wouldn't easily stop him.

"How about starting with your name and which state you represent?" Javier said.

The people quieted, all eyes on their Congresswoman. Even if she didn't represent their state, at this moment she represented either the American people as a whole or her own fellow legislators and lobbyists. Javier imagined their silence was to see which it would be.

She cleared her throat. "Charlotte Holleran. Idaho."

Crap. No Seeds there. "What can you tell us about LifeFarm? Or about the virus?"

"Virus?" Holleran kept a straight face.

"Yes, the virus. We know quite a bit, Ma'am. I hope anything you tell us will be supplemental."

A few in the crowd chuckled.

Holleran stood in silence.

"They killed my daughter," a woman behind Javier said.

He took a quick glance—it was the woman who'd given him the phone. Javier focused the camera on her. "Tell us about her."

The woman's eyes were already puffy. "Her name was Jade. Nine years ago, she was a student at Northwestern when LifeFarm's recruiters visited the campus, saying they were showing students the 'possibilities of a new world.'" She used air quotes for the last words. Tearing up, she pursed her lips before continuing. "Jade was so excited when she called me, saying all those starving kids in the third world would finally be saved, and she had the chance to be part of it."

Javier panned back to Holleran long enough to see her stony silence, then went back to Jade's mother.

"The last time I talked to her, she was getting ready to go on a LifeFarm-funded humanitarian trip to Kenya. War broke out there less than a month later. They told me her hostel was bombed in the middle of the night." She wiped her tears with her open hands. "I found out later LifeFarm was there to take over the country's agricultural industry, and when leaders resisted, they brought in *our own military* to bomb them. They killed my baby. My only child. Because they couldn't bully a third-world country into submission. And she wasn't the only one. I don't think it's unreasonable for us to know why."

Javier brought the camera back to Holleran. "Ma'am?"

Holleran blinked rapidly. "I'm sorry for your loss."

"Stop!" A Seed member yelled as two cops pushed their way through the crowd.

One reached Javier in seconds. "Step away from the Congresswoman, young man!" He grabbed Javier with a massive hand, pulling him away. Javier dropped the still-recording phone.

"No!" Javier kept his eyes glued to the phone as he was dragged away.

Congresswoman Holleran picked it up.

Javier was out of the building before he could see what she did with it.

****

Coughing, Liz got her arms under her. Dust fell around her like snow—no, it was thicker than snow. She couldn't see more

199

than one person beyond her, and they all looked like they'd endured Pompeii's eruption. The ringing in her ears wouldn't let any other sound through.

She rolled onto her butt. The blast had thrown her almost completely across the street. Through the dust, a jagged outline of what was LifeFarm's headquarters remained. At least ten floors reduced to three, give or take a floor. As the dust cleared, smoke rising from the ruins became apparent.

Sirens wailed in the distance. Help would be here soon. Liz found her feet and spit out the grit in her mouth. Stumbling through the crowd, she analyzed every face. Kyle and Travis had to be out here. She was one of the last out of the building.

After completing a round through the mass of people filling the street, she debated with herself. What if they *hadn't* made it out? Should she look for them in the damaged building? The thought that they might have survived nagged at her, but this level of destruction was crushing. There was no way they could have survived.

Still, she had to make sure. For a few minutes and for the first time in a decade, her family was in the same place. Giving up on that possibility again was unfathomable. She'd thought Kyle was dead once before. Until she laid eyes on them, she wouldn't believe they were gone.

She climbed up the rubble, which went from ground level to ten feet high in short order. The debris shifted under her feet, keeping her from moving as quickly as she wanted to. Step, steady. Step, steady. After several minutes and with her heart pounding, she was back in the building. Or on what was left of it.

"Kyle! Travis!" Her yells mixed with the din of the crowd and the sirens. "Kyle!"

So much debris lay before and beneath her. Where would she start digging?

She headed towards where she thought Travis had been, where he would be now had he stayed in the vault and fallen straight down with the building.

With six floors on top of him.

Shaking off the thought, she picked up pieces of drywall, handfuls of papers, and jagged chunks of metal, tossing them aside. For all she knew she was piling material on top of Travis. But she had to do something.

"Ma'am! Come out of there!" A uniformed firefighter was climbing the debris, heading for her. "This isn't a stable area."

"You're telling me." She grabbed more debris, tossing it away.

"Ma'am!" The firefighter reached her in seconds and grabbed her arms. "You have to leave. Paramedics are here to check you for injuries."

"My son is in here." The words hit her like a punch in the gut. He was. "He was *right here*."

"I understand." His voice had softened. "We'll get a search team here right away. Please."

Taking her wrist, he led her across the wreckage, stopped her from falling when she tripped, and offered a comforting presence.

She kept her eyes on the place she'd dug until it was out of sight.

Back on the street, a paramedic met her and after checking her vitals, gave her a bottle of water. She mindlessly took a drink, washing the remaining grit away from her mouth.

"Liz!" Kristen ran over, her own bottle of water in hand. "Have you seen Kyle?"

Taking another drink and with her eyes locked on the building, Liz shook her head. "We got separated."

"Oh." Kristen put her hand on Liz's shoulder. "I'll circle the perimeter and look for him, okay?"

Liz nodded, watching the search team take their positions.

****

With the cop's shove, Javier fell into the back of one of dozens of squad cars that peppered the side streets blocks from the Capitol Building. It took that far to get through the mass of Seed members crowding the Capitol grounds. They'd been arriving in a constant stream during the last hour, and like the woman who'd let Javier use her phone, several had to have arrived as a result of Kyle's broadcast. But how many? How effective was their attempt to destabilize LifeFarm?

Other people were being loaded into the surrounding cars. There wasn't likely enough space in a jail to house all of them. What was the plan?

And where were Sam, Charlie, and Jonah? The cop had taken Javier's backpack, but even if he still had it, he couldn't very well talk to them via the walkie talkie while being arrested.

As Javier watched the crowd move towards the Capitol, some shouting and some marching in silence, they all did something he never expected: they cheered in unison, as they might if their underdog sports team won a championship. They hugged each other, and a few cried. Through the thick glass of the cruiser, Javier could make out a few of their shouts. *Can you believe it? It's gone!*

What the hell was happening?

"Hey!" His yell didn't make it past the car, and he couldn't bang on the window with his hands cuffed behind him.

Finally, a young cop arrived, but instead of taking the driver's seat, he opened the back door. "Get out."

"What?" Javier cautiously inched his way towards his escape.

"Riots are breaking out in other parts of the city. That's more pressing than you making a Congresswoman talk."

Javier scooted out. "Riots? Why?"

The cop unlocked the cuffs. "The LifeFarm building in New York exploded. People are either out celebrating or freaking the hell out." He walked around his cruiser and left Javier standing alone on the curb.

LifeFarm is gone! Or at least their headquarters was. That had to make a dent in their operations.

He bolted into the crowd of protesters-turned-revelers. He had to get to Sam.

****

"It's gone?" Charlie grabbed the arm of the guy jumping around with his phone, yelling some nonsense about LifeFarm being wiped off the map. "What are you talking about?"

"The building exploded!" The guy almost shook his man bun out from jumping around. "Boom!" He laughed. "Take that, assholes!"

Man Bun hopped into the middle of the crowd, where he filled more people in on the news.

It was gone? That couldn't be right. It had to be more propaganda. But to what end?

What if it was true? Mattson was in New York hacking the broadcasts. What if he was close to the blast?

Charlie chased down Man Bun. "Can I see the report?" It would be pretty easy to tell if it was real—fake stories always came with extra doses of sensationalism.

"Sure, I guess." Man Bun calmed down and handed over the phone, staying inches from Charlie, apparently guarding his baby.

Charlie skimmed the story—it was more straightforward than propaganda suggested. Shit.

"Thanks." Charlie handed back the phone and hurried up the stairs. He had to find the others and get the hell out of here.

****

Javier shoved his way through the crowd and reached the Capitol Building in minutes. "Sam!" He scanned the hundreds—maybe thousands—of faces surrounding him. "Sam!"

He had to get above these people. Maybe Sam would find him.

Running up the front steps, Javier eyed the other people camped out there. A brown, bald head popped above the crowd on the other side of the entrance—Charlie was climbing the stairs too.

Javier reached the top and crossed to the other side. "Charlie!"

The former agent's eyes connected with Javier's for a second before he plowed his way through the group. "Did you hear what happened?"

Javier nodded. "Where are the others?"

"I don't know. Should we go back to the car?"

As Javier scanned the crowd, frustration grew in his gut. If he and Charlie met at the car and the others weren't there, then what? Of course, what were the odds of finding them here? "Yeah. Let's go back." He hustled back down the stairs.

The men had to cross the grounds and a street before emerging from the growing mob. Once clear, Javier ran. A twinge of pain radiated from where the bullet fragment had hit back in Colorado, a subtle reminder of what brought him here. Behind him, Charlie panted, and his limp became more prominent.

Javier had a passing moment of pity before speeding up. If Charlie needed to slow, he could catch up.

The SUV was on the street where Damien had parked it, only now the windshield was shattered and windows busted out. People were running through the streets and yelling. A group of young men armed with baseball bats targeted anything in their path while yelling about LifeFarm blowing up.

"Those assholes killed my mom!" One of the bat-wielders whacked a sidemirror off a pickup. "And now they're dead!" Laughing maniacally, he took off down the street with his buddies.

Slack-jawed, Javier watched them and the other rioters celebrating by reaping destruction. Those young men, like Javier, had never experienced a world that wasn't under LifeFarm's control. They were tasting freedom for the first time, even if right now it was only an idea. LifeFarm could recover. But the Seeds had been planted to be the first resistance force, and not only had they all made their presence known, countless others had joined them.

It was disorganized, but this was the birth of a movement. A revolution.

"I see Damien," Charlie said, snapping Javier out of his trance. "Come on."

Limping, Charlie walked to Damien as he headed towards them from the east side of the Capitol Building. While Charlie opted to wait at the car, Javier and Damien returned to the crowd in search of their missing counterparts. Damien used his flashlight, but all of the faces started to look the same, and the noise had grown louder.

"Sam!" Javier yelled. "Jonah!"

His cries were swallowed by the sea of humanity before him.

Chapter Twenty-Seven

Desperate but unable to get back onto the rubble, Liz paced on the street. She alternated between staring at the search crews work and analyzing the people in the crowd, which had thinned in the last half hour. Shouts from neighboring streets reached her. She didn't care enough to find out what those were about.

What if the crews found Kyle and Travis buried? Or what if they didn't? How would she find her family?

What if the debris was crushing them, and they were fighting for air?

She pushed the thought from her mind.

Needing to do *something*, she decided to search the surrounding buildings for Mattson. Kyle had said the kid wasn't doing well, and she guessed his injury had something to do with it. If he'd gotten sick, he wouldn't likely emerge into this mess on his own. He'd wait until Kyle came back for him.

Half a dozen buildings sat between LifeFarm and one of the news networks. She had no way to know if any of these were the right one. How much range would they have needed to hack the signal? It would make sense for them to get as close as possible, so she started with the building closest to the network's.

It was a small office building housing a dentist, a chiropractor, and some other businesses Liz didn't recognize. She checked all of the offices that didn't have a sign—would Mattson have locked himself inside one of them? About half of the unmarked spaces were unlocked. At the others, she peeked through windows. No sign of Mattson.

The next building over was an upscale gym. That seemed an unlikely place to commit cyber-crimes, so she skipped it.

The third building was a restaurant on the ground floor with lofts on the two floors above it. All of the patrons had crowded the sidewalk in front of the place and were watching crews work the scene. Liz located the hostess in the back of the crowd, asking if any lone teenagers had come through and if there was a way to access the lofts. The hostess said she didn't know in both cases.

How would she find this kid?

Liz recalled Kyle's video message—maybe there was something there that would help. Closing her eyes, she racked her memory for any leads. The lighting had been fluorescent and overhead. Kyle had sat in front of a dated tile wall, the kind that might be in a locker room.

She headed back to the gym and talked the front desk attendant into letting her inside to use the restroom. If Mattson was in the men's locker room, she'd have to sneak in and out quickly or ask another guy to help.

She walked past an area filled with mostly-unused cardio machines. The would-be athletes were camped out by the window, watching the chaos at LifeFarm unfold. As she walked past the small café, she saw Mattson resting his head on a closed laptop, taking a nap.

Sighing, she approached him. She placed her hand on his forehead, reminding her of the times she'd checked Travis for illness when he was a kid. Mattson's skin was hot, and he didn't stir at her touch.

She put her hands on his shoulders and gently shook. "Mattson."

He moaned but didn't open his eyes.

Oh no. "Hey. Come on, wake up."

Nothing.

How would she get him out of here and find medical attention? Was the hospital a safe bet? She didn't even know where the hospitals around here were.

The paramedic who'd checked her out seemed friendly enough. Maybe the big city hospitals were in better shape than the rural ones she was used to. In any case, it could be Mattson's only chance to get better.

But first, she had to get him out of the gym.

"Mattson, wake up. We need to get you outside." She shook his shoulder harder, and he fell to the side, landing on the floor in a heap.

****

Javier needed to get above the crowd, where Sam and Jonah could see him. There was no way he'd find them this way. He headed for the front steps of the Capitol Building again. Cops and building security had pushed everyone into the courtyard and were working on getting them to back off further. Other officers had stationed themselves on the surrounding sidewalks, keeping anyone from leaving the grounds. Across the street, news trucks had raised satellite dishes. A few mobile lighting units attached to trucks provided the illumination that the EMP-fried permanent fixtures couldn't.

One of the guards stood alone on the steps and used a megaphone to direct the mob. "Stay on the grass. You can't leave." Some in the crowd weeded themselves out and headed down the street. No one stopped them.

"That's it. I'll be right back. Wait here," Javier said to Damien before he casually approached the guard—if he appeared to be a threat, there would be no way the guard would let him borrow the megaphone. He crept up on the guard's side. "Sir?"

Keeping the megaphone by his lips, the guard stared at Javier.

"Can I borrow that for a minute? I've lost someone."

"What's the name?"

"Sam. But can I do it? She'll recognize my voice."

The guard looked Javier up and down then held the megaphone to Javier's mouth. "I'll hold it."

"Um. Okay." Javier's words blasted through the device, surprising him. He concentrated on projecting his voice. "Samantha Ward. If you're out there come to the front steps."

No movement came from the crowd, though they did quiet a bit.

"Sam." Prepared this time, Javier let his voice ring out. "Sam, we're looking for you."

Looking around the megaphone, Javier took in the thousands of faces. He held his breath, his wish that she would appear growing more desperate by the second. *Come on. Where are you?*

Instead of Sam stepping forward, another woman did—the one who'd let him use her phone. She had it in her hand.

A voice crackled through a speaker attached to the guard's shoulder. "Contain all civilians in the courtyard. I repeat, contain all civilians. Do you copy?"

What did that mean?

"Okay, I need you down there with the others." The guard pulled the megaphone back and spoke into it. "Everyone stay on the grass. You may not leave. If you try to go, you will be detained."

As Javier went down the stairs, cops, some of them armed, came from all sides and surrounded the crowd. They formed a human wall between the people and the street.

Javier examined the cop wall for any gaps while clenching his fist. How would they get out of here now?

The woman with the phone met him in the front of the crowd. Fresh tears appeared in her eyes. "She gave it back. Holleran. She let me keep the video." She held up the phone and smiled in spite of her crying. "I already put it on YouTube. You wouldn't believe the comments it has already." After wiping her cheeks with her wrist, she wrapped her arms around Javier, surprising him. "Thank you. You made Jade's life matter."

A lump formed in his throat. He hadn't given much thought to how their plan would affect individuals—it was more big-picture than that. Get LifeFarm to release their grip. Make legislators answer to the people. Create the vaccine. All for the good of humanity.

But it was also for individuals like Jade's mom, now embracing him in front of the Capitol Building.

She released him. "Can I ask you a question?"

Javier nodded while scrutinizing the faces in the crowd. Sam's continued absence weighed on him.

"Why did you come here? Why do this? You know LifeFarm is dangerous. No one else cared enough or had the courage to confront them. So why you? Why now?"

A man shouted at the edge of the crowd, something about not being animals and they can't keep anyone trapped. The cops stood their ground, as if no one had said anything.

Javier tried to focus on Jade's mom. She'd been through more than he could imagine and deserved an answer—just like Liz did. "I think . . . freedom isn't given up all at once. It happens piece by piece, in the name of safety or health or convenience, until one day there's nothing left to give up." He quickly glanced behind her— there! Sam was a few rows back, standing next to Damien. Javier released a long breath as an urge to run to her raced through him.

"Is that what happened? We had nothing left?" Jade's mom asked, bringing his attention back to her.

"We weren't there yet, but we were close." More yells came from the edges of the crowd—they currently had no freedom, a fitting picture of what LifeFarm had reduced average Americans to over the years. "Our livelihood largely depends on those in power. And how they decide we should live depends on their bottom line."

Jade's mom chuckled sarcastically. "Boy, I know about that." She took a shaking breath. "They used naïve people like my daughter to build their empire."

"Exactly." Javier nodded. "Our lives become bargaining chips, and eventually we can't fight because we've sacrificed our ability to do so based on false promises. And that's why we did it. We had enough freedom left that we still could."

He looked at Sam. Her gaze was full of admiration. Love.

"Do you know who all these people are?" Jade's mom raised her voice over the increasing noise in the crowd.

"Everyone have a seat!" The cop's words through the megaphone were loud enough to echo off the building across the street.

The crowd quieted but stood in place.

"Sit down or we'll have to force you to sit down."

"Or you could let us leave!" a man yelled.

Cheers followed.

The cop with the megaphone nodded to another officer, who tased the yelling man. A woman jumped on the cop. A guard tased her. Those surrounding the two gasped but sat on the grass. Judging from the noises in the back, similar actions were being taken by other cops.

Javier held his breath and checked for any possible escape. Seeing none, he settled on the grass next to Jade's mom but kept an eye on Sam and Damien. Jonah was still nowhere in sight. Javier hugged his knees, trying to appear calm. The cops and guards were greatly outnumbered. It was only a matter of time before those from the Seeds took control. He watched those around him—some were whispering to each other and eyeing the guards walking the perimeter.

Yells from the rioters on the surrounding streets reached him. Several cops left their posts and headed to the sidewalk, breaking into a run a second later. The riots must have been a bigger threat.

Javier eyed the remaining guards. They were watching their own run down the street.

Crouching, Javier slinked away, heading for the side of the building currently ignored by the guards. Sam, Damien, Jade's mom, and a few others followed him.

He peeked around the corner when they reached the far side of the building. The guards had returned to their posts but were searching the area around the group.

One looked his way. Javier fell back against the wall then ran for the back corner, whispering to the others. "Come on!"

****

As soon as Javier and Damien were out of sight, Charlie retrieved the extra key fob from the magnetic box Jonah had hidden under the door frame, in case he or Damien were arrested and the others needed to take the car and escape. After brushing the broken glass off the driver's seat, he settled behind the wheel.

He buried the nagging guilt in his gut. There was no way to know how long it would take them to find Sam and Jonah or if the cops would let them leave. Charlie was the only one in a position that guaranteed a quick exit, and he had to get to New York. To Mattson. With no phones, he had no way to know if his nephew was near the explosion.

Mattson could be dead. Charlie couldn't tolerate not knowing, and getting stuck here wasn't an option.

He pushed the ignition.

Charlie slammed the SUV into drive and pulled onto the street, narrowly missing a rioter swinging a golf club over his head. He crouched, peering through the section of windshield not completely shattered. It would be hell driving all the way to New York like this.

He headed down Constitution Avenue for several blocks before turning onto a residential street, but it was blocked by rioters. He turned around. A few rioters ran in front of him, but they were nowhere near as densely packed. He could get the car through.

Creeping down the street, he slipped the car into neutral and revved the engine to get the rioters to move. It worked the first few times. When he approached an intersection, rioters from surrounding streets, some holding burning pieces of wood, joined the group. They were now a mob—an angry one. They yelled and shook their weapons, apparently in response to one of them shouting orders. They blocked the street completely, though they hadn't seemed to notice his presence.

Charlie drummed his fingers on the steering wheel. He could go back to the main road. Or he could squeeze onto the sidewalk to get around them.

He went for the second choice. After hopping the curb, he drove with short, brick walls on one side and occasional trees on the other. The larger trees scraped the doors as he passed.

When he was near the end of the street, the mob moved in front of his car, then right for it.

Holding his breath, Charlie cranked the wheel to the right and gunned the accelerator, but the mob rushed him before he could clear the sidewalk.

He opened the door as the mob descended, keeping him trapped inside.

As most of the rioters took their anger out on the car, pounding the metal and breaking what remained of the windows, two opened the driver's door and pulled Charlie out, dragging him across the pavement by his arms.

"Shit! Let me go!" Charlie winced when the ground made contact with his hip wound.

A booted foot rushed for his face, and his vision flashed. Something—his nose?—crunched. The metallic taste of blood filled his mouth.

A kick to the ribs knocked his wind out. He pulled in a painful breath, wincing as his body took more blows. *They're going to kill me.*

Beyond his attackers, rioters cheered and whooped, sounding like a pack of wolves. The two beating Charlie left him, focusing on whatever made their faces glow orange in the darkness.

Breathing through the agony in his chest, Charlie rolled onto his side.

Jonah's SUV was engulfed in flames.

****

Liz ran around the backside of the ambulance. Paramedics were loading someone on a gurney into it—Kyle.

"Oh my God!" Liz pushed her way into the vehicle, ignoring the protests of a paramedic. "What happened?"

Kyle craned his neck up. "The security guards tried to take us out a rear entrance. We didn't get out before the blast."

She ran her shaking hands over his head and chest. There were no obvious injuries. "Where are you hurt?"

"My legs." He put his wrist on his forehead and closed his eyes. "They were crushed."

Her heart raced, but she remembered why she'd run out here. "Um . . ." She eyed the paramedic who'd yelled at her for climbing into the ambulance. "There's a young man in that gym over there. He has an infected wound and won't wake up."

Kyle lifted himself onto his elbows. "Mattson? He was groggy but awake when I left him."

"He isn't now."

Kyle focused on the paramedic. "Take me out of here. Get the kid. He needs help more than I do."

"Sir, we can't do that." The paramedic glared at Liz. "You need to get out. Now."

"No." Kyle started to sit up. "I'm not letting you take me before the kid."

"Sir!"

Kyle flopped off the gurney, landing on Liz's lap and pulling off the sheet the paramedics had used to cover him. He yelled in agony before directing Liz. "Get me out of this thing."

"I . . ." How could she do this?

"Okay, stop." The paramedic got behind Kyle. "Get his legs."

Liz lifted, and together they put him back on the gurney.

"We'll call another unit," the paramedic said.

"Not good enough! Get the kid! If you can't take us both, take him and I'll catch the next one." Kyle fell back on the thin mattress.

The paramedic scowled, then looked at Liz. "Where was the kid?"

Liz told them, and they left her and Kyle alone in the ambulance. A few minutes later, they returned carrying an unconscious Mattson. One had him by his armpits and the other by his legs. They told Liz to get out of the unit.

Laying Mattson on the ambulance floor, they closed the doors and with the siren wailing, drove off, leaving her alone on the street and watching them disappear.

Except she wasn't alone. The Grays were still there, mingling on the street or heading to the cars.

The LifeFarm people were gone. Maybe that meant Travis got out. If he didn't, the crews would find him eventually. If Kyle survived the blast, maybe Travis did too.

Liz peered down the road the ambulance had taken, then to the search crews digging in the building's rubble. Unable to decide where to go, she stayed frozen in place.

****

"Dammit, Charlie!" Jonah yelled as he stood on the spot where his SUV had been.

With clenched fists, Javier looked up and down the street. If he knew which way Charlie had gone, he'd chase him down and kick the crap out of him. How could he leave them all here?

"There are rioters everywhere," Damien said. "I don't think he'll get very far."

"But why leave us?" Javier stormed into the street. "What the hell was he thinking?"

"Maybe he decided to help his agent buddies. It doesn't matter." Jonah sat on the curb. "We'll have to figure out another way out of here."

Javier paced. Wailing sirens came from one direction while shouts from rioters came from another. Smoke billowed over rooftops on a few side streets. "What about Robert? Can't we ride back with him?"

"Nope." Jonah picked up a small rock and tossed it across the street. "We arrive in small groups and leave in small groups. That way, if the cops catch some of us they won't likely catch all of us."

Crap. A knot formed in Javier's stomach. "Damien, if you think Charlie wouldn't get very far, how were we going to get out of the city?"

"He probably doesn't know the layout of the city. We do. We can figure out how to get around the rioters. It was a possibility we planned for."

"Okay." Javier jogged back to the curb. "So when you planned the alternate routes, you weighed options that you decided wouldn't work, right?"

Damien nodded. "So?"

"So, we can find Charlie if we take the obvious routes you ruled out and hope he was blocked by rioters." *And not attacked.* "If he was rushing to get away he wouldn't have thought of the complications you did."

"All right." Damien pointed to a residential area. "Most of the rioting will start—started—on those streets and in the heart of downtown, where many people already are. Our plan was to use residential side streets, until we figured that out. We decided to take main roads that are farther away from larger buildings."

"Aren't they worried about cops?" Javier asked.

"No. The authorities are completely overwhelmed. They're arresting the ones that look violent and maybe using gas grenades, but their only real option is to let the riots burn out."

"And that's our only option now, unless we find a car," Jonah added from his spot on the curb.

"Well, I'm not going to sit here waiting around." Javier headed for the neighborhood.

Sam caught up and took his hand. A minute later, Jonah and Damien followed.

Walking down Constitution Avenue, Javier peered down every side street, hustling by the ones that looked especially dangerous. While some rioters were likely still celebrating the collapse of LifeFarm's headquarters, Javier suspected that many were caught up in the chaos.

He picked up speed as they checked street after street, dragging Sam along after a few blocks. They got closer to one where something was burning—where were the firetrucks? When they reached that street, Javier froze. Rioters celebrated around a burning SUV—Jonah's SUV—like college students around a bonfire on homecoming night.

"Dammit!" Jonah pushed his way to the front of the group and threw his hands up.

Javier climbed a half-wall edging a property, getting as much of a bird's-eye view as he could. "I can't see Charlie."

"He's probably surrounded or lying on the street," Sam said.

"Or," Damien added, "he's still in the car."

Javier's stomach lurched. *I hope they knocked him out first.* "We should figure out how to get closer. If he's in there he might need our help."

"Not while that mob is there." Jonah crossed his arms. "Let's find a place to hide out before those assholes see us."

Chapter Twenty-Eight

Charlie crawled away from the bush he'd hidden behind while the rioters finished off Jonah's SUV. They'd moved on, leaving a shell of the vehicle behind.

Grabbing a retaining wall and struggling to his feet, he assessed his injuries: his nose was likely broken, maybe a few ribs were too. He spat a blood clot onto the ground.

He needed to get to a hospital.

Alone in the darkness, he limped to the smoldering wreck. Where were Javier and the others? They wouldn't likely want to help him after he ditched them.

Of course, they were all stranded now. They'd do better if they worked together in figuring out how to leave. Maybe they'd take pity on him and Mattson and help anyway.

After a long, painful breath, he limped back to Constitution Avenue.

****

Javier's feet dragged as they reached the bus station. Walking on streets free of rioters required more than a few detours, but having a destination made the trek more bearable. Their ride to Roanoke with a stop in Richmond wouldn't leave until the next morning—they had seven hours to evade rioters and the authorities.

The station was a run-down reminder of how Javier got around when he was in college. The only places to sit were plastic chairs connected by a black bar, as if anyone would want to steal such fine pieces of furniture. Two vending machines sat against the wall—a paper with the words OUT OF ORDER was taped on one of them. Javier's stomach growled. An overhead fluorescent light flickered enough to give anyone a headache. Maybe the smartest thing to do while they waited was sleep.

Javier and Sam settled on the chairs and leaned against each other, trying to doze. He gave up after a few minutes—how could he sleep? They might have toppled a global power, and here they were, sitting at a bus station. He didn't know how Liz fared with the Grays or how Mattson was doing with his injury.

After offering to stay awake so Damien could sleep, Javier watched the news broadcast, muted but closed captioned, on the TV mounted in the corner.

****

Liz and Kristen made their way back to the parking garage where the Grays had left their cars. If Kyle were here, he and Liz would use his car and figure out where to go together. Jonah had told her everyone would rendezvous back at the cabin in Virginia, but she didn't see much point in doing that. She had her husband back, and she'd become skilled at flying under the radar. They didn't need the cabin to be safe from any fallout LifeFarm might bring.

That was before he'd been hauled off in an ambulance, though. She cursed at herself for forgetting to get his key fob from him before he left the scene. Not only was his car stuck here, her purse was safely ensconced within it.

She fell into the passenger seat of Kristen's car. "Where are you guys going after this?"

"Back to our lives." Kristen started the engine. "No one back home knows why we left."

"But you were a mole, right? You'll just go back to being a cop—or whatever you were?"

Kristen laughed. "I worked for Homeland Security. And I still do. Most of what I did was legit." She backed out of the space. "Where should I take you? I'm heading to the airport. I'm guessing you don't have a ticket anywhere."

Liz pursed her lips. "Any idea which hospital they would have taken Kyle to?"

"Let's see." Kristen pushed buttons on the dash GPS. "Want to go to the closest one? I don't have time to drive around to a bunch of them, I'm afraid. I hate to leave you alone when he's hurt."

"The closest one is fine. I'll figure it out." Liz kept her anticipation of not competing for Kyle's attention to herself. The Grays had completed their mission, at least for now.

Ten minutes later, Kristen dropped Liz off on the steps of a hospital, half of which was closed off for construction—or covered by huge tarps, at least. Maybe that part had deteriorated beyond repair.

Liz wandered into the emergency department, which was surprisingly empty given the hospital's proximity to the scene of an explosion. She approached a grumpy-looking man sitting behind bullet-proof glass. He looked up, his face asking what on Earth she could possibly want that was so important he had to lift his head.

"I'm looking for someone who was in the LifeFarm explosion. He would have arrived in an ambulance."

"Name?"

Would Kyle have given his real name? She gave it a shot.

Grumpy checked a monitor in front of him. "No one here by that name. Might have gone to another hospital."

Liz slumped. "Okay. Thanks anyway." She considered giving Mattson's name, but not knowing his last name would be suspicious. As she stepped away, she had another thought and returned to the window. "How about Travis Carson? Can you see if he's here? Or Travis James?"

With an eye-roll, Grumpy checked the monitor. "Travis James is a patient here." He hit a buzzer, swinging a door next to his station wide open. She walked through it and under a metal detector.

Grumpy watched her over a counter, unprotected by bullet-proof glass on this side. He pointed. "Sit in one of those chairs against the wall down there. Someone will come get you."

Hope filled Liz's chest as she headed down the hall. Kyle had used their son's first and middle name to get in—he must have known she'd think of it.

Or maybe Travis was here himself, and he was using that as his last name.

Sitting in the chair with the least-stained cushion, she shook off the possibility. Travis didn't speak to her anymore, but it wasn't so bad that he'd get rid of the name they shared.

Would he?

What if he had? She'd be brought to see him, not Kyle.

She buried the anxiety. If she ended up facing Travis, she would handle it. Somehow.

As she settled into the chair, she rested her head against the wall. Images from the day flashed in her mind, and she focused on the few seconds she'd seen Travis. If only he'd seen her—would he have realized what he'd missed?

The minutes became an hour, then two, then more. As Liz fought her eyes' begging for sleep, a heavyset woman wearing scrubs approached. "Ma'am? You're here for Travis James?"

Instantly awake, Liz nodded.

"Come this way." The woman didn't wait for Liz to move before walking away.

"How is he?"

No answer.

The woman led Liz to the third floor and down a long hall, to a room with an exhausted-looking security guard stationed outside it. She addressed the guard. "This is the visitor."

Looking down his nose at Liz, the guard cleared his throat. "What is your business with Mr. James?"

"He's family."

"You have ID?"

"No. My purse was in the building when it blew."

The guard scowled. "Come here." He headed into the room.

The only light came from a small fixture mounted to the wall over the bed. Kyle lay there, both legs casted. He appeared to be asleep. An empty chair was next to the bed.

While relieved to see Kyle, a small part of her lost hope—she wouldn't see her son.

"The local police are coming for him as soon as the docs clear him. Leave the door open. You have fifteen minutes." The guard stepped towards the door.

"But he's asleep."

"Fifteen minutes." He returned to the hall.

A lump formed in Liz's throat. Kyle had said he'd suffered injuries to his legs in the war, injuries she hadn't known about, before LifeFarm shipped him to the facility in Missouri. Now here he was, in that condition, only this time she knew he was alive.

She would have let him sleep, but fifteen minutes would pass too quickly. "Kyle?" Her voice shook. She reached out and squeezed his hand then leaned over, kissing him gently on his forehead.

He stirred.

"Kyle. It's Liz."

His eyes fluttered open. "Hey." He offered a weak smile.

Wanting to be strong, she fought back her tears and glanced at his legs. "What did they say?"

"They're broken but I'll live. How's the kid?"

"I don't know."

"They were more worried about him than me."

A pang of guilt hit her—she hadn't given Mattson much thought after the ambulance left. She'd been more concerned with her own family. But not Kyle. He'd always worried more about others than himself—it's why she fell in love with him all those years ago. It was also why he stayed hidden away so long.

She settled on the edge of his bed, keeping his hand in hers as her love for him, a familiar yet somehow distant feeling, awakened. "I'll find out where he is, but the guard only gave me fifteen minutes with you."

"Yeah." Kyle brushed her finger with his thumb. "He said I'm going to be arrested."

"Do you know the charge?"

"I'm guessing it has something to do with shooting inside LifeFarm's building before they blew it up. Or threatening them. Who knows."

"You think they blew it up?"

"Pretty sure that's why the alarm went off just before."

He said the words so casually she almost laughed. "Why would they do that, though? Destroy a whole building?"

"They have a lot to hide."

The image of Travis running through the vault hit her again. "I have to tell you something." She debated with herself—would this news cause him unnecessary stress? It's not like they'd be able to find their son.

"What?"

"I . . . I saw Travis in the LifeFarm building."

"What?" He stared, as if weighing her words against what was possible. "Are you serious?" He lifted himself onto his elbows and winced before lying back down.

She nodded. "It was only for a few seconds."

"Are you sure it was him?"

Another nod. Admitting she was so close was too difficult to say aloud.

"We have to find him."

"How?"

"There has to be a way. Can we call them?"

As tears pooled in her eyes, she laughed at the absurdity. "Call LifeFarm and ask for our son."

"Yeah. Why not?"

"Kyle . . ." She sighed. "He hasn't talked to me in years."

"So? Can you really let this go without doing anything? What if he saw me on the news? He could be looking for *us*."

She moved to the chair, staring at Kyle's bandaged legs. Could he be right?

A sob caught in her throat. "No. I can't." She rested her elbows on her knees and her face in her hands. "I can't hope like that anymore."

"Liz?"

She looked up.

"I can."

****

Fighting his heavy eyelids, Javier read the crawl on the bottom of the screen. Hundreds of rioters had been arrested. Dozens of cars and a few buildings burned. And a mob—*a mob*—that had stormed the Capitol Building had dissipated after authorities were called to deal with the riots.

No mention of the LifeFarm explosion or of anything happening in New York, including Kyle's message. At least, not yet. He'd watched the same five stories cycle through for the past several hours. Of course, LifeFarm wouldn't want coverage of Kyle hijacking the networks to get out. Letting everyone know their headquarters was gone would be even worse. For their own image, they had to bury the story.

As the sunrise brightened the eastern sky, an announcement came over the intercom, waking up anyone who'd managed to sleep. Three buses, including the one heading to Richmond, were now boarding.

Twenty minutes later, Javier sat next to Sam on the half-full bus pulling onto the street. On to Richmond then back to the cabin.

A passenger behind him coughed.

And back to finishing the vaccine.

Javier put his arm against the window and rested his head on it, closing his eyes. He let his mind wander, alternating between what they'd done the night before and what still needed to be done.

"Is that Charlie?" Sam's voice pulled Javier out of his doze.

He squinted out the window. "Where?"

She pointed at the battered man sitting on the sidewalk against a stone wall outside the Capitol Building. His eyes were closed.

In the seats in front of them, Jonah pulled himself over Damien and into the aisle, where he rushed to the front of the bus and leaned over the driver's shoulder. "Stop. We need to get that man."

"No can do." The driver glanced in the mirror. "There was rioting last night. Didn't you hear?"

"No kidding. That man is hurt and he's with us. Can you just give me one minute to get him?"

The driver's eyes shifted, and he pulled the bus to the side of the road. "One minute."

Jonah hopped out.

****

Squeaking brakes pulled Charlie out of his shallow sleep, reminding him of his throbbing head. A Greyhound bus was parked in the bike lane a dozen yards up—that's not the kind of bus that would stop anywhere. The doors opened, and Charlie held his breath when Jonah emerged and rushed towards him. *Shit.* He gasped, wincing at the pain in his ribs. Sitting here until someone noticed he needed medical attention had been a bust.

"What the hell, man?" Jonah held his arms out, as if gesturing to his surroundings. "You stole my car!" His face reddened.

"Hey." Keeping his place on the sidewalk, Charlie held his hands up in surrender. "The LifeFarm building blew up. I didn't know how long you'd be and I needed to get to my nephew to make sure he's okay."

"You were gonna take it to *New York*? Without us?" Putting his hands on his hips, Jonah turned away, glaring across the street.

Anxiety knotted Charlie's stomach, but he couldn't tell if it was from guilt after taking Jonah's car or from not being able to get to Mattson.

"Come on." Jonah grabbed Charlie's arm and pulled him up.

"Ow! Watch it." Pain radiated from the wound in his hip and ribs as Jonah forced him to the bus's door. His nose felt at least three times bigger than normal. He could only imagine how it looked.

"Liz and Kyle are watching after Mattson. You're coming back to Virginia with us. If you want to figure out how to get to New York then, fine. But you're sure as hell not staying here." Jonah boarded first, pointing to the driver. "Pay the man." He headed down the aisle, not looking back to make sure Charlie obeyed.

Charlie collapsed into the seat behind the driver after handing him the few bills he had on him, promising to pay the rest when they reached Richmond. The driver scowled but complied.

Richmond. That was the opposite direction he needed to go, but what choice did he have? His wallet and phone were back in the jail in Phoenix. Once he reached Richmond, he could convince Javier or someone to give him a loan. Or he could call Annie and have her wire him some money.

Shit. Annie. How could he tell her what happened to Mattson? Gritting his teeth, Charlie stared out the windshield.

****

The guard returned to Kyle's room, stopping just inside the doorway and focusing on Liz. "Time's up."

"Already?" She checked the clock. "I still have three minutes."

"Let's go."

Liz considered arguing, but if she wanted any prayer of visiting again, she had to stay on these guys' good side. She stood and squeezed Kyle's hand. "I'll check back when I can. Do you have your car key?"

He nodded then looked up. "It was in my pants pocket. I don't know what the paramedics did with them."

"The nurses are holding your personal items. They'll give them to the police when you're arrested," the guard said.

Liz slumped. "Even if he gives me permission to take them?"

He nodded.

Great. She buried her aggravation and headed for the door.

The guard followed her into the hall, where he pointed to a stairwell. "Go down that way. Check out with the emergency department receptionist on your way out."

"Wait." She put her hand on his arm. "There's another young man here I know. Can I see him too?"

"No. Visitors are supposed to be announced."

"Kyle—I mean, Travis didn't announce that I was here ahead of time. I had to find him."

The guard tilted his head. "What's his name?"

"Travis. I got him confused with someone else." *Crap.* She kept her focus on him. Better to not look nervous, right? "You know how it is with big families."

"Sure." The guard glanced into the room. "He wouldn't have a reason to hide his identity, would he?"

Her exhaustion and irritation came to a head. "You said he's being arrested." She headed towards the stairwell. "Have the cops figure it out."

She winced as the door slammed behind her. That last bit of snark probably cost her any chance of getting back here, and there was no way she'd be able to get to Mattson now.

Upon returning to the emergency department, with nowhere else to go, she reclaimed her chair.

Chapter Twenty-Nine

With an hour left in the bus ride to Richmond, Charlie leaned against the window while pressing Damien's phone against his ear, listening to the rings and imagining his sister digging through her purse. If he wasn't dreading the conversation, he would have smiled at the thought.

It had taken some digging to find Annie's number, but not as much as it took to locate Mattson. Charlie had figured that if Mattson had been close to the blast, he would have needed medical care. So he Googled New York hospitals and urgent care clinics and worked down the list until one said Mattson was there. The receptionist couldn't release any information about his condition, however.

The call went to voicemail. Annie was likely screening her calls. The bus was leaving Fredericksburg, and the phone was already down a bar on its reception. Charlie pressed "Send" again.

His imagination wandered as he waited for her to answer. What could have happened to his nephew? Broken bones? Burns? Something related to his gunshot wound? Or worse?

"Hello?"

"Hey. It's me."

"Charlie? What number is this?"

"I'm borrowing a phone. And I may lose reception soon so I have to be quick." He cleared his throat. "Um . . . have you been watching the news at all?"

"A little. Why?"

"See anything about riots in D.C.? Or about a building blowing up in New York?"

"No, nothing like that. Is Mattson there? I want to talk to him."

"He's not here." Charlie watched trees race by. "I'm on my way to Richmond. He's in New York. The LifeFarm building exploded and he was near it." A lump in his throat threatened to steal his words. He cleared it again. "He's in a hospital there."

"What! He's in a hospital in *New York*?"

Grimacing, Charlie pulled the phone away. He could hear her yells just fine from a distance.

"And why the hell aren't you there? What's wrong with him?"

"We got separated." The details of how that happened could wait until everyone was back in the same state. "And I don't know his condition. I'm not his guardian so I couldn't get his medical info. You'll have to do that. I'll text the number to you. But right now, I need you to send me some money so I can get to him. I can probably do that by the end of the day or early tomorrow."

"What for? Why don't you have money?"

"My wallet is in a jail in Phoenix."

"Jesus." She sounded exasperated. "Okay. Tell me what to do. And call me the second you get to him."

****

"Ma'am?"

Liz's eyes opened. The grumpy emergency room receptionist was shaking her shoulder. Sunlight spilled through the dirty windows—she squinted in the brightness. "What time is it?"

"Little after nine. And you have to leave." Grumpy stood tall and crossed his arms, waiting for her to comply.

"Why? I'm not bothering anyone. I want to see K—Travis again."

"The guard upstairs said not to let you. We can't just let people squat here. Should I call you a cab?"

"No." She stood. "I'll walk."

Trudging to the door, she wished she had money for a cab. A ride would have been a welcome relief.

She had to get her purse, then a phone. And a way to get the number to Kyle.

As she walked, she picked up rocks, trading small ones for bigger ones. She needed one that would break a window on the first try.

Her feet dragged across the last mile to the parking garage, but she eventually made it to Kyle's car. A parking ticket rested under the wiper. She laughed. Good luck getting that paid.

Holding a softball-sized rock she'd plucked from an office building's landscaping, she braced herself next to the passenger side window. She had no idea how easily the glass would break, so she assumed it would take a lot of effort. Better to overdo it than to strike repeatedly and draw attention to herself.

She heaved the rock at the window as hard as she could. With a bang that echoed through the space, the rock bounced onto the pavement, leaving a cracked window behind.

Grumbling, she picked up the rock. This time, she kept it in hand, hitting in against the window like a hammer. The glass shattered into hundreds of tiny bits, leaving no shards behind.

Liz examined the debris, impressed with the efficiency of the damage.

She reached through the window, unlocked and opened the door, and grabbed her purse from under the seat.

"Hey!" A male voice from across the garage echoed.

Without thinking, Liz spun around—an older man was rushing towards her.

Shit. Slinging her purse onto her shoulder, she raced for the garage exit.

"Someone call the police!" The old man called out behind her.

Without looking back, she desperately scanned the street for a busy place to hide. So much for being inconspicuous. She ducked down an alleyway that led her back to a familiar street—the LifeFarm building had been here yesterday.

Today, a dirt lot with a faded real estate sign occupied the space. There was no sign of the building. Even the busted sidewalk had been repaired—yellow caution tape surrounded the wet cement.

"What the hell?" Frozen in place, Liz forced herself to believe her eyes. Was she on the right street? She looked the other way. The gym and the restaurant that had teemed with curious onlookers were there. How had all that debris been cleared so quickly?

She peeked down the alley—the old man hadn't followed, but that didn't mean he hadn't pointed a cop in her direction. Heading for the restaurant, she pulled her wallet from her purse. Best to look casual. If the police did show up, she could show who she was with her ID and suggest the old man had been seeing things.

After the hostess seated her, Liz pointed out the window. "What happened to that building that blew up yesterday?"

The hostess tilted her head. "I'm sorry?"

"You know, down the street." She pointed at the dirt lot. "The LifeFarm building. There was twenty feet of debris there yesterday."

"Um . . ." The girl peered out the window. "I think you must have the wrong street. That lot has been there for months." She handed Liz a menu and headed for the kitchen, maybe a little quicker than was necessary.

What? Liz stood and leaned over the table as she scrutinized the buildings out the window—the store she and the other Grays had waited in was there. The café with the TV in it was down a few spots.

Lowering back into her chair, Liz studied the other patrons. All looked normal, as if nothing had happened yesterday besides some chilly weather.

What the hell is going on?

****

Once they reached Richmond, Javier left the bus with Charlie and waited in the terminal. They would both be heading to New York in about an hour. The swelling in Charlie's nose had decreased, and though he still seemed uncomfortable from the broken ribs, he'd said getting treated wouldn't be worth the time. So they waited, Javier with this man who had obviously had the crap beat out of him.

"Are you sure you want to do this? I can find Liz, too, while I'm there," Charlie said.

"I'm sure. I need to make sure she's okay." Javier figured it was the least he could do. Liz could have been injured in the blast right along with Mattson, and what if no one was looking for her? How would she get back to the cabin? Jonah had given him more than enough money to get there and spend a couple of days.

The men were silent for most of the journey. Charlie shifted in his seat periodically, and Javier tried to sleep as much as possible. Once they arrived, he'd search for Liz and not stop until he found her.

****

Desperate for answers, Liz headed across the street to the grocery store she'd waited in yesterday. The best she could figure was LifeFarm paid off everyone on the block to pass the story that they never existed. But why? And more importantly, if the LifeFarm headquarters no longer existed, could they still have Kyle arrested for shooting inside it?

She examined the store's interior. Someone with a lower level position would have likely been ordered by a paid-off manager to pretend the building never existed. Maybe a direct payoff would convince such an employee to tell her the truth. Was that a cashier? Or someone stocking shelves?

A teenage boy wearing a green apron was mopping in the produce section. He looked like he could use a little extra cash.

Approaching him, Liz pulled forty bucks from her purse, hoping it was enough to get the job done. "Excuse me?"

He stopped mopping and looked up.

After it was apparent he wasn't planning to speak, she stepped closer. "I was wondering if you could tell me something that happened around here yesterday." Palming the money, she held out her hand. "About a building that used to be across the street."

He tensed and looked around. He snatched the cash and put it in his apron pocket. "They told us not to say anything."

"Who's they? And why?"

"You know." He tiled his head towards the door. "Them. My boss threatened to fire anyone who talked."

"Did they say why?"

"No." He dropped the mop into the bucket hard enough that water splashed her shoes. "I have to get back to work." He hustled to the back of the store.

She headed to the front window, glancing at the street outside. It had been an hour since the old man chased her this way, and there had been no sign of a cop. Confident she'd eluded the authorities, she walked towards the busy street leading back to the hospital.

****

Charlie arched his back in the seat. Sitting this long was murder on his hip wound. Though they'd been riding all day and were now approaching the bus terminal, he hadn't been able to sleep. Javier had, though. Charlie may have to depend on the kid to get them where they needed to go. His mind was foggy enough they could accidentally end up back in D.C.

The bus pulled into the terminal, and with a hiss, the door opened. Charlie hobbled outside, and once out of the station, accessed a map on Damien's phone.

"Okay." Keeping his eyes on the screen, he pointed. "The hospital is about four miles that way."

"Let's take a cab." Javier went to the street and held up his arm until one of the iconic yellow cabs pulled over.

Charlie input the address into the GPS, which sent a map to the monitor on the dash. Without speaking, the driver pulled back onto the road.

Javier bounced his legs while he looked out the window.

"Nervous?" Charlie asked.

"Oh." Javier looked out the windshield. "I guess a little. I just hope Liz is easy to find."

Charlie clenched his jaw. "Yeah. Me too." In truth, he had given Liz little thought, other than she could lead him to Mattson, if they found her first. What if she was also injured? And what about the other Grays?

The cab stopped in front of the emergency room's doors, and Javier paid the driver. Charlie and Javier walked around the building to the main entrance. Once the receptionist verified Charlie's identity and gave them both badges, she directed them to Mattson's room.

As they headed upstairs, Charlie held his breath. What condition was his nephew in? What would he have to tell his sister?

Once they reached the correct floor, he followed the room numbers. He glanced towards the nurse's station and stopped in his tracks. "Liz?"

Javier ran to the woman asleep in the chair. She clutched her purse like a running back holding a football.

Shaking her shoulder, Javier woke Liz. Her eyes widened, and she stood, giving Javier a hug.

"What are you doing here?" she asked.

"Mattson's here. Come on." Charlie took the lead, heading for the back corner of the wing. "Why are you here?"

"Kyle was hurt in the blast. He's in that room." She pointed to a guard standing outside one of the rooms. "That bastard won't let me in to see him. Told me I could wait and see if I would be cleared. So I've been in that chair all day."

"What happened to him?" Charlie checked the room numbers—there was Mattson's. The door was closed.

"His legs were crushed in the explosion. They say he'll be arrested. But here's the crazy part. The LifeFarm building site was wiped clean. Anyone around there has been paid off to say it was never there."

"What? Why would they do that?" Javier asked. "And what about people putting it online?"

"They'll say videos were fabricated. I guess they think blowing up their building makes them look weak."

"It doesn't make sense." Javier shook his head.

While Liz and Javier debated LifeFarm's motivations, Charlie crept to Mattson's room and tapped on the door. When no response came, he eased it open and peeked inside.

Mattson was asleep on the bed. Aside from a bandage circling his shoulder and upper arm, there was no indication he was injured. The contents of an IV bag dripped into his arm.

"Do you know what happened to him?" Charlie asked Liz as he rushed to Mattson's bedside.

A knot formed in Charlie's stomach. He shouldn't have neglected to treat his nephew when he first realized what was wrong. "Mattson?"

He stirred but didn't wake.

"Mattson. It's Uncle Chuck."

The boy's eyes flitted open, and he grinned. "Hey. I get to call you that now?"

"No." Charlie swallowed to keep his emotions in check.

Javier and Liz joined them as Mattson closed his eyes. "How did you find me?"

"Same way anyone would. The yellow pages."

"Huh?" Mattson's eyes narrowed.

Liz laughed.

They told Mattson what had happened with the building and about Kyle being in the same hospital. With a little prodding, Mattson was able to convince the nurse to let Javier and Liz see Kyle, leaving uncle and nephew alone.

"Mattson . . ." Charlie cleared his throat. "I'm sorry you ended up here. I should have taken better care of you."

"Nah." Mattson waved a hand. "I wanted to do this, remember?"

Charlie put a hand on the kid's forehead. It was warm, but not burning up. "Yeah, I remember. When did you get to be so grown up?"

"While you were protecting LifeFarm." Mattson shoved Charlie's shoulder.

Smiling, Charlie pulled the phone from his pocket. "Before we do anything else, we have to call your mother." As he found the recent contact and handed Mattson the phone, he buried the lingering guilt. He'd ruined his marriage and missed out on Mattson growing up because of his devotion to a company that had killed thousands and manipulated millions to stay in control.

Mattson talked into the phone, and Annie's voice rang out so clearly Charlie could hear it without the speaker on. She was crying and asking Mattson how he was, when he would get out, and complaining about the exorbitant airfare keeping her from rushing to him.

Charlie lowered himself into a nearby chair, listening to the conversation. When Mattson was able to get a word in, he cryptically told his mother about his role in the plan to cripple LifeFarm, his excitement growing as he did so. Annie might have been upset that Charlie had let Mattson get involved, but she wouldn't be able to deny that her son's gifts had been invaluable.

What would happen after this? Mattson was an activist, and he had the skills to work with Kyle or Robert long-term. Though Charlie wanted to make up for lost time with his nephew before finding another job, he'd likely missed his chance.

Then it occurred to him: his relationship with Mattson wasn't the only one that had suffered. His ex-wife had been right all those years ago. She'd deserved much more than Charlie was willing to give.

Maybe she'd like to hear him say so.

Chapter Thirty

Liz placed the last ornament and stepped back, analyzing her handiwork. The tree set in the corner of the living room was the skinniest she'd ever decorated, but the modest apartment she'd found for her, Kyle and Mattson didn't have space for anything larger. That was okay with her. She decorated more out of tradition than for personal enjoyment.

A key clicked in the lock, and Mattson opened the door, pushing a wheelchair-bound Kyle inside.

"Hey!" Kyle took control of his chair and reached Liz. "Looks great."

She kissed him. "Thanks. How did it go?"

"We didn't do it." Mattson went to the kitchen and grabbed a soda from the fridge. "The hearing and vote for Holleran's bill was today. We didn't want to interrupt coverage of that."

"Oh, I didn't know it would happen so soon." Liz switched off the lamp, allowing only the colorful tree lights to illuminate the room.

"Holleran was pretty fired up about her bill." Mattson plopped onto the couch and sipped his drink. "Plus, our little broadcast interruptions didn't hurt."

Mattson and Kyle had hijacked the signal of various news networks during the month since the LifeFarm explosion, never hacking from the same location and once allowing Kyle to send a message almost five minutes long before it was shut down. In that one, he'd told how he was nearly arrested for shooting inside a LifeFarm building that supposedly never existed. Turns out charges don't stick when the victim makes the evidence disappear.

Liz figured LifeFarm would be searching like hell for Kyle and Mattson. Tonight's broadcast was supposed to be the last one for a while—long enough for LifeFarm to relax again.

"Any word from Javier?" Kyle asked.

"Not for a few days." Liz moved one of the ornaments to a different branch. "He said Damien was almost ready to test the vaccine."

"Wow, that was quick."

"I guess." Liz smiled, admiring the lights reflecting off the glass bulbs. The only thing that would make the moment better was if Travis were here. They'd decided to settle close to the city, partly because it would be easier for Mattson to hijack the news signals, but also because if Travis was nearby, he would be more likely to find them here. The hope felt hollow at times, but Kyle's was contagious. They'd spent more than a few long nights reminiscing about their son, and having Mattson staying with them was like a balm.

"You guys want to find out if the bill passed?" Mattson asked.

Keeping her eyes on the tree, Liz shook her head. "We'll find out soon enough."

****

After finishing for the day, Javier and Damien straightened up the lab Robert had built in the cabin in Virginia. The frozen guinea pig had provided enough genetic information about the virus and the vaccine Brenda had created that Damien could copy it, eliminating the need to start from scratch.

Damien injected two guinea pigs with two variations of the vaccine—one stronger than the other. He'd said they could more quickly determine an effective dose that way.

"You know," Damien said as they left the lab and headed to the living room. "If you hadn't saved that animal, this would have taken much longer."

"Yeah." Images of Brenda's body flashed in his mind. "Good thing I thought of it, huh?"

Smiling, Damien squeezed Javier's shoulder.

Sam was on the couch, watching a cable news show. A correspondent was discussing the latest bill going up for a vote in Congress.

While Damien went to the kitchen, Javier plopped next to Sam. "Did we win?"

"Too soon to tell." Weaving her fingers between his, she kissed his cheek. "Holleran had the floor for a while. She argued for all attempts to influence Congress from the pharmaceutical and healthcare industry to stop. She said any sign of it should get the representatives removed, even if it's technically legal. A few of her colleagues didn't like that."

"I bet." Javier remembered Congressman Warner punching him in the face. "A lot of them were depending on LifeFarm to keep them young."

"Right. It's part of the bigger healthcare bill. If it passes, the hospitals will be in much better shape. Doctors too. The insurance companies and government won't be able to hoard money meant to benefit patients anymore."

They watched for a few minutes. Holleran had put up a hell of a fight, sharing specific stories of families harmed by LifeFarm, including those of Jade's mom and Kyle. She'd argued that no company should be able to wield power via the legislative branch.

Even if her bill failed—and that was likely—enough information was out that LifeFarm's image was permanently damaged. Of course, the extra "shows" featuring Kyle on Mattson's hijacked broadcasts didn't hurt either.

Javier believed these little actions would bring down LifeFarm. They were chipping away at the empire, one piece at a time. Families fought against their children going overseas in any capacity that would benefit the company. Kyle shared all of Javier's information about the virus and vaccine on one of the broadcasts. The more truth the public had, the more reason they had to resist. And they were getting more all the time.

Sam rested her head on Javier's shoulder, watching the news of Holleran's bill unfold.

The front door opened, and Charlie breezed inside. He hung his coat on one of the wall hooks. "Did we win?"

Javier laughed. "Not yet."

Charlie sat in the desk chair, focusing on the screen. "I thought we might know by now. I promised Annie I'd make Mattson go home if Holleran got this through."

"Does she really think he'll leave? He loves working with Kyle," Javier said.

Charlie shook his head. "I can at least say I tried."

Javier laughed again. With any luck, Mattson's need to hack the networks' signals would soon be over. Then he'd have to find a new outlet for his gifts. "What about you? Will you go back to California with him?"

"Maybe." Charlie shrugged. "I was kind of thinking of Seattle."

"Seattle? That's random."

"Not really. My wife moved there after she divorced me. I called her and told her what happened."

"Really." Sam sat up straighter. "And what did she say?"

Charlie put his elbows on his knees and clasped his hands. "She said I could visit and we'll see." He smiled. "What about you guys? Are you staying here once you figure out the vaccine?"

Javier gazed into Sam's eyes. "I don't know. Have you decided what you want to do?"

"Yeah. Let's go back to Hayes."

"Back to Iowa? On purpose?" Charlie sat back, shaking his head.

Javier kissed Sam's head. "Yep. That's where her family is."

Sitting back, Javier wrapped Sam in his arms, and they watched the correspondent wrap up his report. The hearing went too late for a vote on Holleran's bill to happen tonight.

Oh well. Even if it didn't pass, Javier, the Seeds, and the Grays had proven that LifeFarm couldn't operate unopposed anymore. Citizens would soon have their healthcare, their technology, their media, and their freedom to live without fear. They would insist on nothing less, because for the first time in at least three decades, they realized they could.

And it had all started with a case full of bees.

THE END

Did you enjoy the story? Head to the book's Amazon page and post a review! Readers like you make a big difference to writers like me. Thanks in advance!

Acknowledgements

This book took over two years to complete, and it would not have happened if not for some key people.

First, I must offer my most sincere gratitude to my editor, writing partner, and friend, Dan Alatorre. My writing career wouldn't have had the strong start it did without you, and I am humbled that you continue to devote so much time and energy to my work.

To my writing partners on Critique Circle, including Al Macy, Dana Griffin, Drstarne, Harpalycus, and Vkkerji, your feedback made the book so much better in so many ways. I can't thank you enough for your attention.

And finally, to those who read and loved The Fourth Descendant, inspiring the creation of this story, thank you for the simple act of reading. Without you, I wouldn't be able to do this.

About the Author

Allison Maruska started her writing adventure in 2012 as a humor blogger. Her first published book, a historical mystery novel called The Fourth Descendant, was released in February, 2015. Drake and the Fliers followed in November, 2015. Project Renovatio was released in April, 2016, followed by Project Liberatio in August and Project Ancora in March, 2017.

In addition to writing, Allison is a teacher, a wife, a mom, a coffee and wine consumer, and an owl enthusiast.

Connect with Allison on the interwebs!

Blog: http://www.allisonmaruska.com

Facebook: http://www.facebook.com/allisonmaruskaauthor

Twitter: https://twitter.com/allisonmaruska

Amazon Author Page: http://amazon.com/author/allisonmaruska

Made in the USA
Middletown, DE
24 September 2020